TO
MY Friend
Jen. AV

Merry

My Grace is Sufficient For Thee

My Grace is Sufficient For Thee

Jack M. Waister

Copyright © 2020 by Jack M. Waister.

Library of Congress Control Number:		2020907365
ISBN:	Hardcover	978-1-7960-9926-3
	Softcover	978-1-7960-9925-6
	eBook	978-1-7960-9924-9

All rights reserved. No part of this book may be reproduced or transmitted in any form or by any means, electronic or mechanical, including photocopying, recording, or by any information storage and retrieval system, without permission in writing from the copyright owner.

The views expressed in this work are solely those of the author and do not necessarily reflect the views of the publisher, and the publisher hereby disclaims any responsibility for them.

Scripture quotations marked KJV are from the Holy Bible, King James Version (Authorized Version). First published in 1611. Quoted from the KJV Classic Reference Bible, Copyright © 1983 by The Zondervan Corporation.

Any people depicted in stock imagery provided by Getty Images are models, and such images are being used for illustrative purposes only.
Certain stock imagery © Getty Images.

Print information available on the last page.

Rev. date: 04/22/2020

To order additional copies of this book, contact:
Xlibris
1-888-795-4274
www.Xlibris.com
Orders@Xlibris.com
806709

CONTENTS

Blizzard 1
The Event...18
Dont Call God A Liar 50
Forever is a long time 93

11/19/06-02/13/20

Title taken From 2 Corinthians 12:9
(83,459 words)

I don't know where it originated but I like the quote. It proves that God always has our best interests in mind. Always! WE just need to learn the lessons and look at things from His perspective. for instance, "When God takes something away from you He isn't being mean, He's just opening your hand to give you something better." That not just a nice, little euphemistic thought. It is also as true as it gets. The hard part is us fighting the "letting go" thing. We might really, really, like the person or thing we aught to let go of. Do we listen, or follow our hearts which scripture calls deceitful and desperately wicked. (Jer 17:9) Only a heart committed to praying and listening will give you the peace to do the right thing that would be best for us.

It seems that round about every ten years or so "SOMETHING" happens to alter my course.

00-10 was bus collision.

10-20 was the back brace.

20-30 was the motorcycle vs. car (car won)

30-40 was the heart attack.

40-50 was the brain stem stroke and severe obstructive sleep apnea.

50— Have since endured round 2. Meaning a second open heart procedure, 3 more bypasses and the same valve was replaced yet again. They have about a ten year life span I've been told, so the timing was about right.

60? I haven't arrived there yet but maybe I'll meet it head on and go sky diving with a bed sheet? But likely not, although I do want to give sky diving a try; only not with a bed sheet. Unfortunately; I looked into it, was honest about my history and for some strange reason, none of the instructors would jump with me. So, here I sit, revisiting this story yet again, and at 51 now I have had a second round of open heart procedure to replace the valve again and also do 3 more bypasses, including 2 of the original bypasses. Not being allowed to skydive was a real let down;

but I scared off all the instructor's. Not one would perform a tandem jump with me and they wouldn't even let me use an old WWII static line you see in movies. I asked, so I guess I can hang that one up for good. Unless of course there is a jump instructor reading this and will take me up. Give me a call.

Anyhow, when I finally sat down to start this book I figured the best place to start was the beginning. Well, not exactly the beginning, beginning, as I was born a month early in the end of January 1968. My impatience streak had an early beginning as well, it seems. If you want to get super-technical my original beginning was sometime in the late spring of 1967 but still, the process started someplace. No Matter what the unbelieving heathen say or claim, life begins at conception. Traits of mom and dad are passed on, interests and skills of both are given to the life in the womb. Mom's artistic abilities, none of dad's math, were in part, and in some way, passed on. Each minute and each step we all take leads to the next, hopefully learning as we go so that our wisdom is not always retrospection, and our vision, not 20/20 hindsight. Unfortunately, without the assistance we all so desperately need; which I shall delve into deeper and progressively as this tale progresses, none of us will be successful. At least not successful in the right direction.

Loss is irritating and quite usually, painful, like ripping away pieces of living flesh. Learning things the hard way is never fun, but most times that is what it takes. The thicker the skull the bigger the drill must be, with more RPM's to spin it. I've already worn out many a bit throughout the years. Whilst procrastinating too long in penning this treatise I was attacked by a rare brain stem stroke which further slowed the process and added to the barrel of fun I was already having. It seems that round about every decade or so something happens, In decade one, I was not yet 10 when the bus VS. bike collision occurred. The back brace was not an accident but it effected the full compliment of my teen years. Boy, That was fun! It's a good thing that teenagers, especially the girls, are so kind and not vindictive or mean in any way or it mighta been kinda rough. That's a broad brush and I don't intend to include ALL girls in that brief inditement. Generally speaking though, that seems to be the case. The motorcycle accident attacked me in the early

20's, putting my left leg in a full length cast from hip to toe, eventually to have the "tib-fib" portion of that leg to be rodded. This of course meant less movement on my part. Always having been active this was frustrating to me. This combined with poor diet and downright laziness on my part, added weight gain to the scenario. Way too much, 40 to 50 pounds. I did work to shed a good portion of such, but it was too late. The damage inside was already done unbeknownst to me. Then the heart attack happened in the early 30's. By my late thirties I finally seemed close to fully recovered except for the memory glitches caused by the anoxia "lack of oxygen" during the heart attack. Then BANG, a rare brain stem stroke sneaks up and bites me in the keester in my early 40's. That was fun. Getting strength and balance back was lot's of fun. I can hardly wait for the 50's, Maybe I'll go sky diving! Fifty. That number can take it's sweet time getting here, I ain't ready for it yet.

Now at 51 I am still lumbering on. Once again, at my computer typing. It is not an easy thing to keep a good attitude. There's a part of me that want's to throw in the towel and quit, but I can't. There are others watching. In this story I jump back and forth between 1rst and second person a bit; perhaps even third. But, try and follow along and enjoy the ride. I sure have, well, not really, but it has been interesting. If I was a cat I'd be dead by now. The motorcycle and the heart attack where probably the two that brought me closest to death. As is usually the case, both events occurred faster then a lightning strike. Although I did put a will of sorts together after this latest incident; which was the stroke. However miniscule this WILL is; it exist's, somewhere. All this with what has recently been discovered and called by different doctors as severe sleep apnea. In part, stroke related I'm sure. Testing revealed that I stopped breathing 82 times per hour, whatever that means. That's more than once a minute so I guess it's a lot. I use one of those CPAP, (constant positive air pressure) machines to sleep. It just takes getting used to, and now I cant sleep without the thing. I started this tale with the heart attack because that was the biggie, and go on from there, and bounce around. There are certain redundancies but for good reason. You'll see why as you we progress.

I took the title I chose from Paul's letter the Church at Corinth. 2 Corinthians 12:9 And He said unto me. "My grace Is Sufficient For Thee...for My grace is made perfect in weakness." Paul never says what his infirmity was. Was he disfigured from; or did he have a limp or severe headaches from all the beatings and stoning's he endured? Maybe all three, and then some? He never tells us, he just by Gods grace determines to keep on going, and that is that. It's not relevant to what he was called to do, so he put it out of his focus and moved forward. That's our task as well, just keep going. Put the past behind you where it belongs, and keep going. Learn from past errors, of course. But don't dwell on them. leave the past where it belongs and press forward. The next portion begins in 3rd person:

He had a massive heart attack at age 32, requiring a quadruple bypass as well as a mitral valve replacement. The stroke would come ten years later and bring even more fun to an already ruptured household. But for now, the amount of time he had been out cold, down for the count, not breathing and without oxygen, thus quickly dying, was unknown. For certain an anoxic brain injury was riding the wake of this tumultuous wave, and he didn't even know what an anoxic brain injury was. Yet. But boy howdy, would he find out. His future was uncertain, hopeless and bleak by some accounts, new and unknown by others. It was touch and go for quite a while. The entire family was in uncharted waters with no compass, no sextant, no logbook, and no rudder. The storm clouds on the near horizon didn't look too comforting. It was going to be an interesting journey for sure. Would he even wake up? Would he be the same person...? Would he be able to function at all...? The unknowns were all anyone knew, and just like the dimwitted, fictitious Sgt. Shultz from that old TV show, Hogans Hero's, they knew Nu-thing!.. Nu-thing...! The only one who knew was Almighty God Himself, and He was working things out in His own good timing. Whatever His plan was, it was not any of our need to know at the moment. Our bit was like that of the Psalmist, and to simply "be still and know that He is God." To "be still" or to simply "wait on God" Is not always an easy task for us impatient, cantankerous humans. In fact, it is most often near impossible. Regardless, that was the way the cards fell, and in this game you gotta play the hand you are dealt. Keep bluffing, but keep playing. Make the other guy blink or fold first. Never quit. As you shall see, life is not blind chance like a card game.

In 50 short years that is more than half of the three score and ten that scripture tells us we have; (psalm 90:10, the days of our years (lives) are three score and ten; if by reason of strength they be four score,...) so we are clearly told that on average, we have been so graciously given about 70 years. POOF... WHOOSH... GONE...! More than half that was gone in a blink, in a heartbeat it was gone. It's been 10 already since I started this tale. What of any lasting value had been accomplished in that extremely short time frame? I can't help but to be reminded of this statement. "... Only things done for Christ will last..." the statement comes from a well known poem. I researched it and believe I found the correct origin, it was originally penned by Charles Thomas Studd, a missionary to China, India, and Africa. This is what I found concerning it:

Two little lines I heard one day, Traveling along life's busy way; Bringing conviction to my heart, And from my mind would not depart; Only one life, 'twill soon be past, Only what's done for Christ will last. Only one life, yes only one, Soon will its fleeting hours be done; Then, in 'that day' my Lord to meet, And stand before His Judgment seat; Only one life,' twill soon be past, Only what's done for Christ will last. Only one life, the still small voice, Gently pleads for a better choice Bidding me selfish aims to leave, And to God's holy will to cleave; Only one life, 'twill soon be past, Only what's done for Christ will last. Only one life, a few brief years, Each with its burdens, hopes, and fears; Each with its clays I must fulfill, living for self or in His will; Only one life, 'twill soon be past, Only what's done for Christ will last. When this bright world would tempt me sore, When Satan would a victory score; When self would seek to have its way, Then help me Lord with joy to say; Only one life, 'twill soon be past, Only what's done for Christ will last. Give me Father, a purpose deep, In joy or sorrow Thy Word to keep; Faithful and true what e'er the strife, Pleasing Thee in my daily life; Only one life, 'twill soon be past, Only what's done for Christ will last. Oh let my love with fervor burn, And from the world now let me turn; Living for Thee, and Thee alone, Bringing Thee pleasure on Thy throne; Only one life, "twill soon be past, Only what's done for Christ will last. Only one life, yes only one, Now let me say, "Thy will be done"; And when at last I'll hear the call, I know I'll say 'twas worth it all"; Only one life,' twill soon be past, Only what's done for Christ will last...

(In the finality of the final finish, that is all that will matter.)

That's what scripture refers to as gold, jewels and precious stones, wether its giving large sum to help a missionary build a school or giving a cup of cold water in His name, or even giving your time to help one in need. Not sure how God works that out in His economy, but He does. The Christian who does stuff for selfish reasons or perhaps with alterior motives is called wood, hay and stubble. It'll burn up and be gone. While the Christian still enters a heavenly eternity, yet with little or no reward. that seemed to be his point in that short poem, that his life would be spent in such a way as to have something to show for it in the end. Life is short so make the most of it.

The following is a poem written by my mom. After collecting her thoughts.

Once I said, Once I knew,
My biggest fear in life would be one of my children dying...
Once I said. Once I knew,
How would I ever survive?
We are taught, or we know...
The power is with us...
We're never alone, love is always here.
The snow was falling, A sparrow came to her...
Unknowingly we went to a scene of confusion...
My heart wanted to stop... My prayers began...
Help me to focus, Send me a plan!
It isn't real!
YES... IT IS!
My son went down... HIS HEART DID STOP.
Our reality changed... My legs did hold me...
Love was sent... It came all around...
our loved ones, our friends...

God did provide…
LIFE STAR arrived…
Many white coats…
Faces with love…
Eye's with concern…
Prayers in circles…
O.R's are readied…
Russell sleeps on…
Craziness and decisions…
Wonderful hands…
and knowledge…
MIRACLES DO HAPPEN!
Long weeks of recovery…
LIFE WILL NEVER BE THE SAME.!!
Different now…
Blessings now…
New ways of doing things now.!!
WE HAVE SURVIVED. C.Turner 10/02

Blizzard

The two of them sat in the living room. It was Sunday afternoon, January 21, 2000, The snow was falling quite heavily outside. The girl sat quietly in the warm house with her grandmother watching the wintry scene taking shape on the deck outside. Suddenly, with a distinct, attention gathering "thud" A bird flew right into the sliding glass door before their eyes. It fell to the snow covered deck surface outside and they went out to check on it. It was a sparrow, frail and small. It was still breathing. "It's alive, Nana…" the girl exclaimed excitedly. Gently she scooped her hands beneath the frail creature and held it up for a closer look. It's little chest heaved up and down with each breath. It appeared to be just knocked unconscious. As they studied it, its eyes suddenly burst open and it fluttered away like a flash of quicksilver. They were startled and they thought it was kind of neat, AND odd.

They went back inside and nana started the tea kettle for some tea and hot chocolate. Then nana made a phone call and was only on it a few minutes when the operator broke into the conversation with an emergency call from her sons mother-in-law. I don't know how many people reading this have ever received a call like that, but I have to speculate that the fear that rips through ones chest at that moment must be unimaginable. Pale-faced and stolid, the girls nana handed the phone to her husband, a flash of fear danced in her eyes. She said, "here, I can't take this..." He took the phone with a puzzled look and listened to the voice on the other end. Imagining that scene in my mind I can almost hear the throaty off-key notes of the piano, the kind played in old black and white monster movies just before someone's about to get pounced on or eaten. Sorry, just the way my mind works. C'mon now a storyteller's gotta paint the picture with words. Now it's stuck in your mind isn't it?

The peaceful afternoon had abruptly turned violently stormy. They had no clue what the incident with the sparrow meant until later on. Luke 12:7 tells the story of five sparrows being sold and not one of them being forgotten of God. The very next verse tells us that even the hairs on our heads are numbered. (for some of us, that wouldn't take more than a few fingers, but for most folks such a feat is an impossibility, and for us in and of ourselves it IS impossible. But not with God. Nothing is impossible for Almighty God. That is a brief paraphrase of Math 19:26. With men it is impossible, but not with God, for with God, ALL things are possible. That refers to ALL things that are within His will. People are far, far more important to God than birds, for man is made in God's image. Had God sent one of His sparrows to tell them all would be well? Looking back, it would certainly seem to be a connection of some type. If God cares so much for a tiny bird to feed and care and protect them on a daily basis. He would most certainly be looking out for one of His children; (a Christian), in a time of desperate need. For us, humanly speaking, the problem doesn't compute. The math only adds up when God gives the end sum.

A few towns to the North he lay in the snow. His unseeing eyes wide and glassy, his body motionless and straining for breath. The heart was twitching and quivering in the chest cavity. It was not beating. His lungs would not fill with air. His brain was being deprived of oxygen. Dying! This state continued for an uncertain amount of time, certainly not a long time, but what is long? Five seconds? Five minutes? More? Less? Dying! Nobody knew for certain but it was at the very least a few minutes. Dying! Without blood and oxygen being supplied to the brain Via the bodies pumping mechanism, the Heart; cells in the brain start dying close to immediately, and quite rapidly, if not sooner. With a busted pump, the blood obviously will not flow. The body needs a continuous supply of "flowing" blood to all the organs and extremities in order for us to live. Human beings need "flowing" blood to give them life, period. Genesis 9:4 But flesh with the life thereof, which is the blood thereof... Yes, I understand that this verse is speaking of sacrifices and foods and such required at that point in God's time table. But the point is that our life is clearly tied to our blood. Without blood, we die! Period! I believe it was George Washington who died because his doctors "bled" him a number of times thinking that his flu-like symptoms meant that he had "bad blood." To their angst, he got weaker and weaker after each "bleeding" and then he up and died on them! How ungrateful! I guess that's why they call it "practicing medicine." Wether or not there's any truth to that tale is beside the point. The issue here is blood. We cannot live without it.

Thankfully, today's physicians have a much broader knowledge of the human body and how to fix things. It's pretty cool the things they can do to repair a damaged body; much of it learned on the worlds battlefields. The rod that was put in my left leg after the motorcycle wreck came out the Viet Nam war era I've been told. Well; not the rod itself, but the knowledge and the surgery. The tools are getting more and more sophisticated each week it seems. For instance, heart / lung machines can breathe for us and even pump the blood if we need it to, but without the blood itself we will die. Lev 17:11. "The life of the flesh is in the blood." Too bad George Washington's doctors didn't see that particular verse before the leech treatment, if that is indeed what happened. The point I'm obviously trying to make is, we need blood to live, no synthetic alternative will work. Animal blood will not work, it must be human blood, and to narrow it down even further, it must be the same blood "type" to work, if not, from my understanding the body sees it as an attacking organism and fights it, and we'd be in just as bad a pickle; or worse, as not having enough of the proper type.

Of course, none of this happened by happenstance or accident. We were specifically designed and created. Man did not "evolve." C'mon now, use your head and THINK, man. The average dishwasher is planned and designed and then built. We people are far more complicated than a dishwasher. The individual cells that make up our blood are more complicated than that selfsame dishwasher. Even the most lackadaisical observer can see this clearly when they really look at the science and the evidence with eyes bent on truth, and not eyes bent on defending an outright lie. Even something as a simple as a screwdriver is planned and blueprinted; and some foolish folks want us to believe that our entire perfectly ordered universe is the result of some tremendous explosion? Explosions don't make beauty, they destroy! Nothing beautiful resulted from the atomic bombs dropped in WW2. The only good result was an end to a long and blood costly war. No... No... NO... Our universe is not the result of some random cosmic burp billions of years ago. Therefore neither are we; or our blood. Evolution is the lie of the ages, quite likely one of humanities biggest, ugliest, and juiciest lies of all time. Man did not "evolve." Man was specifically created, so was our blood. End of story. Evolutions false notions have it's beginnings not with such shadily vile characters as Charles Darwin and the like but with Satan's lies meant to cause doubt in Gods Word in the Garden of Eden.

Just like a toothache, man does not get better with time. On the contrary, we get worse, more debauched and more depraved each passing day. 2 Timothy 3:13... "But evil men and seducers (impostors) shall wax (grow) worse and worse, deceiving and being deceived." The most lacsidazicle of observers shouldn't need for God to tell us this. We can all see or hear the proof of it on the daily newscasts from all over the globe. From the halls of government to the local newsstand, deception is all around us. All through His Word, God warns us and tells us what's a'coming. But, in our stubbornness; it seems we have to learn things the hard way. Over and over and over again.

Since mankind liked to shed his own blood, God used that bloodthirstiness to drive home a point. Blood is essential to our life in both a physical way and more importantly, in a spiritual way. People don't like the word "sin" these days, but it is something that every single person born into this world will have to deal with at some point in their life. There is no getting around it. In Old Testament times; by His indescribable Grace, God allowed an animal blood sacrifice to be made in order for the sins of a person to be "temporarily covered," and thus overlooked by a Holy and Righteous God. Exodus 12:13 there is no remission without the shedding of blood... In both a spiritual and physical sense, blood is essential to our well being and our lives.

nd without the shed blood of Jesus Christ;
 of God, put to our accounts personally and
 live eternally. Living eternally is exactly what
 every man, woman and child ever conceived and/
 d was created to do, in one of two very real places
 individual has personally done with the Blood paid
 of the world, The Lord Jesus Christ. Like it or not,
 s. There is NO OTHER way to heaven but by Jesus
 sive as that may sound, it is altogether true. In John
 us this truth as it does is numerous other places. Acts
4:12 , rly tells any who will see or hear that "Neither is there salvation in ANY other, for there is NO OTHER name under heaven given among men whereby we must be saved. That one verse aught to end all arguments but it doesn't.

One can either reject that Grace offered Blood and trample it underfoot like so many today do. Or, one can humble themselves and admit to God they need His Saving Blood, and thus need a Savior. Then accept this FREE GIFT. Eternal life and/or eternal death is a personal choice. It is not "your way" or "my way" or some "religious leaders" way, but Gods way. It is the way The Lord Jesus Christ, who's name Emanuel literally means GOD WITH US provided for all of humanity. Jesus Christ IS God. Scripture is quite clear on this. The salvation He offers cannot be earned. You cannot buy it. And you certainly don't deserve it. It's FREE. That being said, it proves that Jesus Christ IS God. No one else could have fulfilled Gods promises or prophecies as Jesus Christ has done. Certainly no mere man could have done so.

Though it is free, it is still a choice. God (Jesus Christ) created us with a free will and dignity and does not force Salvation upon us, but willingly offers it to us again and again and again and by one means or another "draws" us to Himself. John 12:32 And I, if I be lifted up from the earth; will draw all men unto me. He was referring to The Cross of course. The Almighty, Everlasting True God of Love would never force a convert into submission by the edge of the sword; or muzzle of an AK 47 in some cases. Some false "religions" do this type of thing, not true Biblical Christianity. Christ willingly shed His perfect blood for the creations that spurn Him. His blood made that temporary covering of the old testament daily blood sacrifices into a permanent, once for all, covering for them that ask Him for it. He did this willingly, knowing full well that He would be rejected, despised and hated. As creator, He certainly didn't have to do this, but He did it anyway. That's true Love!

Oxygen is just as essential as blood is to our bodies and specifically, the brain. It even hitches a ride in that ever important flowing blood stream to get there. The brain needs this oxygen, without it, it dies, and when that happens, so do we. The process is quick. As it was explained to me; when oxygen is cut off to the brain, the effected areas begin with those that control the most recent memories; such as what you had for breakfast that morning or what color shirt you wore last night. Such memories are really nonessential and we can quite easily live without them. Yet the memory loss goes deeper the longer that blood and the precious oxygen it carries are kept from the brain. For example, things such as how to breath and how to walk and talk, and eat and swallow, are deeper rooted and take longer to be effected, while instances such as where you set your key ring down just seconds ago is gone off into hyperspace, to unknown whereabouts, and you drive yourself nuts looking for the next hour or two searching for a key ring that has just simply "vanished" into thin air. Quite literally, it could be sitting beneath your very nose, and you won't see it. It can be maddening. To this day they reside on a large key ring attached to my belt from wake up to bed. There are twenty some odd keys on it and I know what each one opens. If they were in different locations I'd be utterly lost. I always know here they are and don't have to think on them, or look for them. Repetition and patience is vital and absolutely "fundamental" in overcoming, or at the very least, dealing adequately with this type of "brain injury." Much like sniffing paint cans and glue bottles kills brain cells, not giving it oxygen does essentially the same thing. Cells die and the brain is damaged. Whether baking a cake or healing the brain, time is the key element. How much time elapsed from not breathing to resuscitation? Unknown! Often times the damaged or destroyed cells can grow back or "rewire" themselves via a different route to revive normal, or close to normal brain function again. We truly are wonderfully and masterfully created, just as scripture tells us. Psalm 139:14. Even so, this route is slow and more often than not, extremely frustrating for EVERYONE involved in the healing process. Especially immediate and extended family as well as employers and fellow employees. Often times it is more frustrating for others than the actual effected party, because it is normal for them now. First hand experience tells this author that a good deal of the time some memories are simply "Gone" so, leave it behind and keep on moving forward. Be thankful for the lessons learned and look ahead, not behind. Sure, events must be acknowledged, but you certainly can't dwelt on such. Saying, "I wish I had", or "I should have done…" or anything like that is pointless and counterproductive. All the hand wringing and "oh me, oh my" has no value or place in recovery. Don't do it! It's easy to fall onto such a pit, but dig and claw your way out of it if need be. You have to remind yourself that things are never so bad that they can't get worse in very short order. There is no going back in time and there are no do-overs. Whatever fanciful time travel entertainments Hollywood cooks up, it is just that. Entertainment. If you made a mess, deal with it and clean it up, move forward, LEARN from it, and most importantly DON'T DO IT again.

Youth needs to be wary and take warning. You will have to live with the consequences of your choices; whether they be good or bad, for the rest of your days. So heed wisdom and choose wisely. Philippians 3:13 reminds us "forgetting those things which are behind, and reaching forth to those things which are before." You cannot change the mistakes and failures of the past, so press on. Mistakes WILL be made. Be sure of that, but keep going and do not quit as hard as it gets. Glean vital nuggets from the lessons of your past experiences certainly, and accept the lessons they teach us. But don't dwell on failures. Dwelling on such things is counterproductive and serves no useful purpose. If your goal is discouragement, self-pity and misery, then by all means dwell on the unchangeable and stop reading here. Take this book back for a refund and wallow in the pitiful misery of your own making at your very own personal pity party. Boo Hoo. Go waste money on a "therapist" or "shrink" or whatever fancy label you want to call those types of folks by. That's the "worlds" method, and while it might seem to "help" for a certain period of time, it's eventual end is worthlessness, waste, and fruitless emptiness. If The Lord Jesus Christ is not the foundation of the counseling method, it is emptiness, nothing more. God ultimately has to be involved for any hope of success to be realized. Sorry, but that's an accurate assumption. King Solomon did and experienced all that a man could see, hear and do. He tried and had all the toys and pleasures that the "world of his day" had to offer and found it to be empty; or "vanity" as he called it in his waning years. Save for Jesus himself, Solomon was perhaps the wisest man that ever set a foot on the face of the ground, he was certainly the wealthiest. His bankroll would bankrupt some nations even by todays standards. Solomon came to find out in his waning years that anything done outside of Gods will, will leave you in discouragement, and drive you to all the empty and vain methods the world has to offer. But, if you are truly in need of some "encouragement" please, read on and Lord willing, you will be encouraged, and perhaps more. It is true that there is wisdom in a multitude of counselors, but one must seek biblical council above all else, and be very cautious of heeding advice that is grounded elsewhere. Not all unbiblical advice is unwise or worthless, just be cautious and weigh carefully the potential outcomes is all one might advice. If it's good advice however, it's basis can be found somewhere in scripture. That's the point, apart from God, man can do nothing good or righteous. John 15:5 tells us such, (in part) we can nothing without Him.

* * *

Good, you're still reading. A normal ambulance ride to Hartford Hospital was out of the question, for during the short trip from my house to a little community hospital not much more than two short miles, if that, from my home at the time; the ambulance had to pause twice for the crew to use the cardiac paddles on me. I would not have made it had Connecticut's Life-Star Helicopter not been available; it is that simple. It didn't look real promising from the human perspective. It was BAAAAD. Many were expecting, but nobody knew the extent of the damage to the brain. After being without oxygen for who-knew-how-long; But, that was the least of their worries at the moment. Keeping me alive was number one. If the heart was not repairable then being concerned about brain damage was a moot point, so as far as any type of brain damage was concerned, time would be the bean-spiller. Fix the pump first. All there was to do was to wait and see, and above all else, pray. Pray that the greatest of all physicians would guide the surgeon's hands. The first order of business was to repair the heart. The E.R. crew had been alerted and already put in a call for Life-Star. Helicopter was the fastest way of getting there in this lousy weather. Hartford Hospital was the place for cardiac emergencies such as mine. I don't know how long the flight was, but as I am sitting here and typing it obviously was a successful flight.

Family and friends prayed with the surgeon who admitted he could use all the help he could get. That just shows he was a smart man, and knew where his REAL help came from.

They did an angiogram first. The interventional radiologist gave his unsolicited opinion not to bother with surgery because (he assumed) I would only be a vegetable. Three weeks after surgery, during the lengthy recovery, this dude came to my room and apologized and said I was a miracle. I don't remember that but it happened. The angiogram showed the mitral valve completely obliterated. It also showed four completely blocked arteries. Apparently he had his works cut out for him, no pun intended. How many hours was I on the chopping block? 7-8 hours? More? Less? Most of the night from what I've been told. It was as they say touch and go for quite a spell. I had a femoral pump to pump the blood and keep the patched up heart functioning.

The Mitral valve was completely destroyed, obliterated, burst and shredded, and could not be repaired. The surgeon installed a bovine valve. Not an actual valve from a cow's heart, but one made from the sac around a cows heart. First things first, if the heart was a lost cause, then any brain damage was inconsequential. I'd be on a ventilator until a donor heart could be found. Which meant that someone else would have to die in order for me to live, how very interesting! The surgical team got to work and for many hours I lay on the operating room table. Gory details might be interesting and kinda cool to some but are merely gratuitous filler and completely unnecessary, so I'll exclude them. Sorry, no pictures either. It'd be cool if I had some but I don't. It was probably pretty cool to see, the surgeon even called it a salvage operation. It worked. I went from recovery to cardiac ICU for many days, under the expert care of numerous wonderful nurses. I'm walking and talking today, grateful for surgeons skills and Gods patience and unsearchable Grace.

The recovery time is pretty much eradicated from my memory, which is fine in my book. I have no real desire to recall any of that stuff anyhow, especially the pain. Sometimes memories can be retrieved via a trigger mechanism of some type; a color, a sound, an odor, a face… Other times, no. Even with all the right triggers, many memories are simply "GONE." Maybe to resurface one day, maybe, but likely not. Each day can be a challenge without some type of routine to follow. Repetition is a good, and often essential thing. A Palm Pilot or PDA as they are sometimes called, (Personal Daily Assistant) can be a lifesaver. I fought getting one for a long time and then one was given to me by a friend I worked with. Where once I never needed one, now I feel lost without one. I am on my sixth one as of this writing. This latest one is the nicest so far and I purchased an insurance policy for it. It is both a phone and a PDA with internet and e-mail so now when I "lose" my phone I also lose my PDA as well and vise versa. Smart phones they're called now. I jokingly call the thing "my brain" because I rely on it so much. It's either on my belt or on the charger. Anyplace else it will "get lost." I have my keys and wallet physically attached to my belt via a chain for the wallet and a retractable key holder for the keys.

I tried many things to help out my memory shortcomings. I tried electronic locators that had separate ID codes for each item. I kept the master locator on the kitchen window sill and if I lost something I could go to that unit and push the coded number for the item I had lost and listen for the beep so I could locate it. It sounds like a good idea, but it wasn't very practical and didn't work very well. The beep wasn't loud enough and if the sought after item was under a pillow or under the couch cushions; where lost keys usual ended up, I wouldn't hear it. I finally ended up with my current system of attempting to keep stuff in the same place all the time so I know where to at least start looking, or at least where to start retracing my steps. Sure, it's frustrating, but you get used to it. Your only other options are frustration or despair, neither one are very comforting. I still "misplace" and "lose" items. But that's just the way it is now, there's no getting around it, so I just keep plodding ahead. You can't let it bother you, it is a part of life now. Forgetting those things which are behind we must move forward. In other words, dont dwell on the loss, just move forward. You often have to force yourself to have to remember things. If you don't, it will drive you crazy. It just makes things simpler and cuts down on the headaches. No matter what frustration occurs you need to establish a routine of some type that you can pretty much stick too, without much deviation. Doing such is vital. Always remembering that things are never so bad that they can't get worse; in a real hurry too.

Some say, "When all else fails, Pray." Personally, I prefer saying "Before all else fails, Pray!" Because man's method's will surely, certainly, ultimately and absolutely without question, indeed fail and fail miserably, every single time. It is only a matter of time. If not today or tomorrow, then someday your carefully laid plans "aside from God", will ultimately fail. God's way will not fail, Ever!

Jesus is a personal God. Psalm 46:1 puts it like this… GOD is our refuge and strength, a very present help in trouble, and Psalm 59:16 for thou hast been my defense and refuge in the day of my trouble… That simply means that you don't only go to God AFTER you've already gotten yourself into deep trouble, like some do, and then have the gumption to get mad at Him when He doesn't fix everything right away just like you want Him to, and just the way you want Him to fix it, then turn your back on Him. No, You go to God "IN" the day of trouble, with foresight, even before the trouble begins, and then during and throughout the trouble. That's why the Christian has what's called "a daily prayer closet.", alone between you and God. That's when you see Him work the greatest. Psalm 27:5 For in the time of trouble He shall hide me in his pavilion; in the secret of His tabernacle shall He hide me, He shall set me upon a rock 138:7, Job 38:23, Psalm 32:6, 41:1. Besides that, God does not respond to the prayer of the unregenerate man (non-Christian) except for their prayer of crying out in response to His saving Grace. God will always answer the genuine cry for salvation of the unsaved individual. No matter the offense, God will answer. If you don't know Him, why wait? No matter the offense, God will forgive. But, you must humble yourself and ask Him. God has no rhyme or reason to help the unrepentant or stiff-necked but to cause them to turn to Him. Look at all the things He does to get our attention. God wants to help. He's holding His hand out, why not take it and let Him help. Man's own sinful pride is what searches for that god that is the fictitious genie in a bottle god that is there to fix all your ills and unwise decision that you have ever made. Idolatry loves this idea. We uncork the bottle and "we" are the master and ruler of our will and destiny. "we," not God Almighty who's very breath brought us into existence. Genesis 2:7- "And the LORD GOD formed man from the dust of the ground, and breathed into his nostrils the breath of life; and man became a living soul." We ignore this fact however and instead of giving thanks to the one true God, man makes his own god. We decide the size and shape and material of the statue we carve, we decide on and create the ritual we use to determine how to gain favor with Almighty God. All statues aside, God is there waiting for man to turn and look to Him. He is there to respond to us if we allow such.

God has been in the past, is now, and will be again in the future; a help. Psalm 46:1 tells us... "God is our refuge and strength, a very present help in trouble." Because of our fallen nature everyone is going to have trouble and pain and problems in life. Everyone. Especially the Christian. There is no getting around it. Satan absolutely hates and despises the faithful Christian because you remind him of The lord Jesus Christ. Still, It is far better to walk through trials victoriously with Jesus, The Savior at your side, or even carrying you when your steps are so heavy that you cannot go on, than to try and go it alone. If you try and do life as a solo act, you will fail, we all will. All need help along the way. If you are familiar with the "Footprints" poem, it is reminiscent of this thought. The one where the guy is talking with The Lord at the end of his life and looking back sees the sets of footprints in the sand and every now and again theres only one set. He asks The lord and was informed that he didn't leave him in those hard times as the man had thought, but he only saw one set of foot prints because The Lord carried him at those times. Yet, only the Christian has the security to know for certain and without any doubt that Jesus is indeed with them during such trials. That is not ignorant arrogance talking. Neither is it just a warm fuzzy feeling we work ourselves into, it is Bible fact. He has promised not to leave us nor forsake us. Difficult times require us to have the faith to cling to such promises.

Jesus Christ is one who will never leave or forsake us. Both Old Testament; Dueteronomy 4:31, and New Testament reveal this truth to us. Hebrews 13:5. He is the only way to God the Father, and His Glorious Heavenly home. John 10:30, I and My father are one. Clearly, just by that one verse alone, Jesus Christ is God Almighty. If He be not God, then we all are rightfully due an extremely bleak future. It is only because of The Lord Jesus Christ that we have any hope at all. It is because of Him that Salvation is offered to us. Without The Lord Jesus Christ, there can be nothing else. Without Him, Christianity would be just another empty, vain and impotent "religion" like is seen all over the globe. That fact alone, that man seeks and has a need for something higher than himself, is proof of our desire to be conected with our creator, even though it is unrecognized as such. Without the Lord Jesus Christ, Christianity is nothing more than just another soft and fuzzy "feeling" we convince ourselves of and that is all. "Religion" has no foundation whatsoever without The Lord Jesus Christ. He is the Rock and Chief Corner Stone. 1 peter 2:6 tells us the Christ is that stone and believing on Him will not confound you. Sorry, but there is no "re-incarnation." You cannot come back over and over again as a flower or bear or bird or bug or raindrop or anything else for that matter, and try again and again until you "get it right!" whatever that's supposed to mean. That would get pretty tiresome, seeing as how it is "Impossible" for mankind to "get it right." So, with that absolute fact firmly in place you must resolve yourself to pick yourself up and move forward. Life ain't a movie, there's no pause or rewind button, or better yet, a fast forward button. There are no do-overs. There is only one go'round on this ride we call life and that is that. So, make the best of it. Learn from the past! Learn from your mistakes! Seek forgiveness from God and any other party effected by any foolish "indiscretions" on your part, make peace with them and move forward. You might not be able to "forget" your past, but you can "choose" to not recall it. Certainly do not dwell on it. Most and more importantly than anything else is to Trust in The Lord Jesus Christ for Salvation. You are only given so many opportunities to do so. 2 Thesselonians 2:11, "and for this cause (REASON) God shall send he "strong" delusion, that they should believe the lie." You MUST be saved now, doing so will bring Glory to God. Ecclesiastes 12:13, tells us that such is the whole duty of man. Obedience is what brings God glory. It really isn't that hard, we tend to make it that way. Accepting Christ's free offer of Salvation is the greatest act of obedience one can show to God. It is not tricky, deceptive or cultish in any way. Certainly satan has used cults and false religions tremendously through the centuries to trash the Name of The Lord Jesus Christ. Jesus Christ offers Salvation free to any who will accept it. Wether you receive Christ at five years old or ninety-five years old, the offer stands. Both are equally saved.

As I was not ninety-five when this event occurred but merely in my early thirties, I at least had the strength of youth on my side.

If I were to make a not so giant leap and attempt to put this type of "brain injury" into an analogy for today's world, it might be to equate it with bombing an enemy out of a system of mountainous caves. When the bombs only hit the surface, the caves occupants are deep rooted and relatively safe, so, not much happens, but have one of those bombs drop down an air shaft, and you have potential for some serious damage, perhaps irreparable. Hypothetically speaking, the longer the brain is without that precious oxygen the bigger that air vent is and the larger the bomb is. With an anoxic brain injury you must disarm that bomb "after" it has already gone off. Things are never the same as they were before... Never! Remember the end of Star Wars? The entire, seemingly indestructible Death Star was destroyed with Luke's single proton torpedo shot that got sucked down the exhaust vent? Not the greatest comparison; I realize, but it will have to do.

The haunting question goes something like this… Is there a God? I suppose that "question" is as old as the human race. There is a painfully obvious answer even older than that question itself. Yes! Of course there is! I've already answered that. There has to be! Absolutely, positively, beyond any shadow of any possible doubt there most assuredly IS a Righteous and Holy God in Heaven. He has existed in three persons since eternity past. Father, Son (Jesus), Holy Spirit. He is Creator and King and Lord of all that there is or ever was and ever will be. This world is not billions or even millions of years old. Nobody in their right mind can get around the absolute fact that proof of an all knowing, everlasting, eternal and ever always wise creator, is apparent in every facet of our lives. To a truth, only pity can be felt for the one who says that there is no God. David gives us God's view. Psalm 14:1 and 53:1 start out the same - The fool has said in his heart, there is no God. Ignorance can be fixed, stupid cannot. Evolution is the lie of the ages thought up by humanistic thinkers that hate God. That is about as simply and nicely as it can be put. Look at it another way. The creationist believes everything was and is created by an all knowing all seeing ever wise always good creator. The evolution believes everything happened by accident in some monstrous cosmic burb millons or billions of years ago and we're all roaming around on thus lump of rock by mistake. The same God that could speak the world into existence can easily make starlight already visible to our world from a distance that has been calculated by mans wisdom to be in the millions of years or older range. Such a feat is cake to an all wise creator. This is a young earth! Question is, who do you wanna believe? Man or God?

Doubting your creator is extremely dangerous ground to tread on. God is evident in every nook, cranny, crevice and drop of water in the extremely ordered creation around us. From the invisible oxygen molecules that sustain our lives to the uncountable stars in the sky. Even those who dwell in the darkest jungles of our world, inherently understand there is a God. Acts 17:23… For as I passed by and beheld your devotions, I found an alter with and inscription, TO THE UNKNOWN GOD. Whom therefore ye ignorantly worship, Him I declare unto you… Man was created to worship God and therefor has a natural desire to worship "something", it certainly explains a lot about our human natures. The quick definition of Idolatry is the worshipping of anything, person, place, or statue other than the True and Living God, or having any thing or person take a higher place than God in our lives. From possessions to money to people to trees. Such is an insult to a Most Holy and Almighty God. Such as it was in Jesus day that those who hated and despised and spat upon their creator do so again with the pagan worship and idolatry of this world He has created for us to use. Not abuse, mind you, but use. Cut down trees and build houses and plant new trees for your kids to use in like fashion. Burn coal, oil and wood and stay warm and alive.

The 1980's Mount ST. Helens eruption in Washington State should have taught the government a lesson in both forestry and history. But, it appears to have done neither. They are as foolish and ignorant as ever. Private land was cleared and replanted and flourished while land owned by the federal government was hijacked by environmentalists who convinced them to let "nature" take it's course. Let the poor dead trees decay and rot just like the "theory" of evolution has done for society. Today both forests are indeed growing but the privately owned land is flourishing much more so. Kind of gives credence to God's Word when He tells man to subdue and care for this world. In the very beginning of Genesis, God tells Adam (man) GENESIS 1:28-31 to replenish the earth and subdue the earth. I by no means think man has always cared well for his surroundings as intended. When a monstrous government entity is in control of things, it unquestionably will fail. Same goes for monstrous corporations driven by greed that only look at the bottom line. Even a blind man could see such. Let the principles of Scripture dictate your steps and you will succeed. It's that simple. You may not see results tomorrow, next year or even in your lifetime. But there will be success as an offshoot.

Another question might be "Does God care about us and what happens to us? and why?"

Yes, affirmatively and absolutely He most assuredly does indeed care about seemingly insignificant man, and the eternal (everlasting) soul He has given to each and every single man and woman on Earth. How do I know you ask? Besides simply believing Him by faith because He says so, read and find out. Genesis 2:7 He breathed into man the breath of life. No other creature did He do this with. That is where the soul of man originates because that is what the text indicates. Genesis 2:7 and The LORD GOD formed man from the dust of the ground and breathed into his nostrils the breath of life; and man became a living soul. The rest is history. Man is the only creation He did this with. By that we can only concur that animals have only body and spirit, lacking the eternal soul. Sorry PETA, but it's okay to enjoy a steak! Acts 10:10-16 and Acts 11:5-7 are included in scripture to show us just that. The author (Luke?) was a Jews Jew and was no doubt a strict follower of the dietary code spelled out in The Law of Moses. He was horrified to have to eat anything that was considered "unclean". God gave him, and the rest of us a new view of dietary do's and don'ts. As this author found out the hard way, you might not live as long by eating pork products all the time but it can still be eaten. I heard it put another way. If God didn't want us to eat animals he wouldn't have made em out of meat. One can take that two ways. Enjoy a burger if you want or enjoy that salad. Folks eating the steak do the humane thing and kill the beast and grill it before it's eaten, the salad is eaten while still alive to a certain extent.

The Event

Snow in New England ranges from light, fluffy and pretty; to heavy, slushy and downright miserable, and anywhere in-between. This was Sunday, January 21, 2001. Today's snowfall consisted of primarily the heavy, slushy and downright miserable variant. As many people may already know, snow blowers don't like this type of snow very much and to be sure, shovels and backbones like it even less.

Thankfully, I used to own and operate a small landscaping business and had hung onto much of the smaller equipment for my own personal use. My snow blower was a nice, bright orange, 8 horse power machine, and "ate up" the snow like nobody's business. Even so it took some doing to struggle and muscle the machine around in the deep stuff, and I worked up a powerful sweat in my thick jumpsuit. Being able to go all winter in just a t-shirt and thin jacket while sweating like a swine should have been a tip off of things to come. But no. Once again, that hind sight thing.

The snow must have begun coming down sometime late Saturday evening and on into Sunday morning because it was snowing when we woke up. It was snowing as we went to church, it was snowing during the service, and it was snowing as we drove home from church. Needless to say, there were several inches to contend with on the driveway when we arrived home.

When we did reach our tiny homestead, my wife was not feeling well and went in and lay down. I took the kids inside for lunch and naps. I skipped lunch, donned my insulated brown one piece jumpsuit and went outside immediately to get the snow blower started. Yes, it was still snowing!

My snow blower had begun getting a bit temperamental recently, but she had always started eventually. It needed a good preventive maintenance (PM) most likely. Shamefully, to my neglect and laziness I hadn't done one in a couple years and she had been starting harder and harder lately, and now it was cold and wet out. But, now the snow had flown and I had to make do. I made a mental note to do a thorough (PM) on the machine in the Spring.

I recall that I would get mad at myself for being winded after only five or six pulls. After all, I was only 32 years old and considered myself to be in good shape. I had gained a goodly sum of excess poundage after my motorcycle accident, which I'll delve into later on a ways. But I had got rid of most of that, and at present I had no large midsection that might give indication of other lurking health issues. Thus I never even thought that there was anything wrong with my ticker. That was the farthest thing from my mind. Sure, cardiac issues were in my family history in a big time way, but I was still "young" and thus I had never spent the money to get the electric starter for the snow blower for I had no need for it. Hey, I was taking high blood pressure meds, what else was there. Anyway I was young, after all. Besides, at that time, these starters were in the neighborhood of a hundred and thirty dollars. I had never gotten around to visiting that particular neighborhood so I would just suck it up and pull start the thing. Besides I would normally leave the machine idling in the bed of my pickup truck while I plowed. If I had a helper with me that day, he would run it, or better yet, heh heh, he would start the thing. Thus, I saw, and had, no need for such bells and whistles as costly electric starters.

I'll assume that everybody reading this knows what they say about hindsight? You know, that 20/20 thing? Would I change the past if possible, Yes undoubtedly and unhesitatingly without question I would change it in the blink of and eye; even faster, but that isn't humanly possible. There are only forward gears on this ride, so sit back and buckle-up. Part of the reason in this penning is to pass on whatever meager wisdom there may be in this collection of words so others can possibly avoid the same or similar fates.

Anyhow, I opened the garage and got the snow blower filled with gas and checked the oil. It wasn't all that cold outside but it still took quite a bit of tugging to get it started, and I worked up a considerable sweat. I cleared my elderly neighbors driveway first. Then, I started on my own driveway. It was still snowing by the way.

I don't have a clue how far I got before "IT" happened, a couple of passes perhaps. I recall no lightheadedness, no dizziness, no tightness in the chest, nor a lick of pain of any kind. There very well may have been a great deal of pain; but thankfully, this event and my entire first month in the hospital is a complete wash. I consider it a tremendous blessing that I have no recollection of any of those events. I have pieced together this portion of the story from other family members recollections and notes that were taken by them while I was in that life sustaining sanatorium. Some of the tales of things I did while there in the hospital I'll get to later in the text, but for now, the "Event."

The space betwixt my house and the neighbor's house holds a portion of my driveway that continues on into the back yard and into my detached garage. Right next to the driveway there are a couple of bushes and a small space between them to walk through and another ten feet or so to my neighbors house. Today my work van was parked way back there on the side of my garage. This way, the entire length of my driveway was wide open, giving me nice; though long, easy passes from garage to street. Whenever I did snow removal I started at my garage and made a pathway between the bushes to my neighbors and then did her walks and driveway first. When that was completed I would then go out her driveway and start at the base of my own driveway. I usually did the first three or four feet directly in front of the house first and then started on the longer passes along the side of my house and right out to the back and up to the garage and around my work van which; as I stated above, was parked beside the garage. It sounds like a lot of snow removal, and with a shovel, I'm sure it would have been. But with my snow blower it didn't take very long at all. The system I had worked out had gotten the timing down to the barest minimum with very little or no wasted passes. One thing I didn't like to do was waste time, especially when lunch was waiting.

We had been getting more snow than usual this season, and today it was just over the top of the snow blowers front auger maw; but it was still eating it up no problem. Even so I had the thing in a low speed range. As many people may already know, most snow blowers have a safety feature consisting of two levers. One on either handle that must be clamped down under your palm when you grasp the handles. They are squeezed up like bicycle brakes. One starts the auger spinning and one controls the drive wheels. If you let go of these handles while the snow blower is in use, the auger and the forward motion stops, though the engine stays running. All this detail on something as mundane as blowing snow and the operation of a snow blower is included here for good reason.

I have no clue how many passes I made before "IT" happened, but I find it interesting that it happened in the portion of driveway closest to the road. This is virtually the only spot that I was sure to be seen from the street by any passing car, and also from the front windows of two or three different neighbors, as well as my own.. Twenty seconds sooner or later and I would have been out in the back and not visible from the street or any of the houses at all. I suppose one could say that a more perfect spot or time could not have been selected for it to happen! But happen it did; and in plain sight of both my next door neighbors view from her door and also from the street. I personally do not believe in coincidences or luck, blind, pot, or any other type. Everything happens for a reason.

Here is where two new characters enter the picture. Just like the old television show "dragnet" I changed their names. I'll call them Ben and Janet. They lived around the corner from us. I had never met them. In fact. It is somewhat odd to me that they would even drive by our house to get home at all. There are two other directions from the main road that were far quicker. Whatever their reason for going the way they did; the only explanation that is feasible to me is that they were "led" there by The Lord's gentile prodding. This fact will become even more apparent in a moment.

Ben was driving, his eyes where on the snowy road before him and he did not notice the brown jump-suited figure lying motionless on his back in the snow. However, his wife Janet did. She said something to the effect of, "What's that guy doing laying in the snow like that?" Ben stopped, backed up, and got out. He told Janet that if he waved to her to call 911. Interestingly enough Ben had recently had CPR training at his place of employment, and thus it was fresh in his mind. My wife, who was still inside laying down, also had been trained in CPR, though some years ago. In spite of this, I've been told it is kind of like riding a bicycle, once you learn how you never forget. My elderly neighbor at this point looked out her window, saw me lying in the snow with somebody leaning over me, and a strange car parked in the street. She telephoned my wife who did not answer because she was laying down; thus, the answering machine took the call. My wife then hears my neighbors panicked voice on the machine telling her to pick up the phone... pick up the phone... pick up the phone...! My wife rose quickly, and; thinking that our neighbor had fallen in her house and needed my help; ignores the phone and came rushing outside to get me to go over and help her. Boy, was she surprised when she got to the door! I try and imagine this whole scene in my mind and it seems almost comical in one sense, Surreal, in another.

So, out she comes in her slippers on to find Ben bent over her husband beginning CPR and asking her if she knew CPR. She answered with a "yes, but I can't think right now..."

She and "Ben" performed CPR.

The meatwagon as I referred to ambulances; took me to Rockville General Hospital, 1.5 miles away. On the way it stopped twice to use the paddles on me?

The attending physisian, Dr Gandi did what he could. At a later date he saw me at cardiac rehab and said to me. "oooohh, my my my, you velly sick young man..." the thickness of his indian accent hung heavily in the air like a thick gust of diesel exhaust. I didn't think he'd gotten the chance to know me that well, but apparently he did. His assessment was spot on by some standards. In any event, he and his team kept me alive until life star got there. I must have been stabalized enough to transport. I don't know what they did; but as I'm typing this, it apparently worked.

The "sparrow" incident I mentioned above occurred somewhere during all this. My mother in law was called and she was the one who had called my folks and had the operator interrupt "my" moms phone call. They didn't put together any significance to it until long after this phone call. That tiny frail little bird; downed, flightless, helpless and unable to move was just lying there in the cold snow. They went and looked at it and thought it was dead, they picked it up and it was still alive, for it was breathing and appeared to be just "knocked out." Suddenly, it came awake and fluttered off and was gone. They were stunned, and knew not what to make of it. They thought it was kind of neat.

Then it was time to go inside for lunch and mom was on the phone when the aforementioned call came. The operator interrupted the call and mom knew immediately that something was up and handed the phone to my dad saying something to the effect of, "here, I can't take this call." Dad took the phone and my wife's mother was on the other end and told him the very sketchy details she had and my folks bolted and came up to the little community hospital in my town, which had by this time surmised that I was in too bad a condition for them to handle so they stabilized me as best they could and the family made the decision for me to be flown to Hartford Hospital via Connecticut's LifeStar ambulance helicopter. It was my only chance. For the Lifestar helicopter to be called for you, you are beyond simply knocking on deaths door and have begun picking the lock. Those Lifestar guys are top notch in my book for obvious reasons. Since that day I have had the opportunity to meet the pilot of the flight that stormy day, to thank him and shake his hand. How he ever found that tiny landing spot during near white-out conditions is beyond me, but he did. I've seen it in daylight at ground level and it looks tiny; from the air, in a blizzard it's got to be nearly invisible.

I selected the title; in part, from a book within a book. My title selection is from the Apostle Paul's second letter to the Corinthian church, Ch 12.V.9…and he said unto me…*My grace is sufficient for thee:*

for my strength is made perfect in weakness... Whatever affliction Paul had to deal with, when God told him it suck it up and fly right, he never mentioned it again, and from all appearances in scripture, had to deal with it until his death. He believed it was better to have the issue than not have it. If it resulted in God receiving more glory from his suffering, then so be it. From all appearances the apostle Paul was all for that.

I by no means am making comparisons of this writer with that of the Apostle Paul. The inspired words of his pen seemed to fit, that is all. No matter what happens to us, the Grace of God can quite easily and without question, carry us through any and all difficulty that befalls us or that we bring on ourselves. No problem is too great for The Lord Jesus Christ. Paul was quoting the Lord Jesus in that passage, and I am quoting the Apostle Paul here. Regardless of how man thinks of himself, man is indeed a "weak" being, as Paul is alluding to in that passage. For a certainty without God we can do nothing, absolutely nothing! All it takes is somebody running one red light to find that out first hand. Man's foolish pride is easily dismantled by a supremely all powerful creator.

My reasons for writing this story are many. My excuses for not doing it sooner are like a bucket full of holes, they don't hold water. As I sit and type this, it has been ten years plus already. I am going to divert for a moment to address and issue that has come to mind that fits in perfectly with this story, so I may as well add it in. Everything will come together as I continue.

Even with my poor Swiss cheese-like memory, I can clearly recall a lifelong friend of mine asking me in the hospital bed. "Did you see a white light?" What with all the movies and television shows depicting such fictitious scenes I kind of figured somebody would eventually ask me that very question. In the months prior to my little cardiac mishap I had been attempting to memorize a variety of Scripture verses. 2 Tim 3:16 promises us that "All scripture is given by inspiration of God, and is profitable for doctrine, for reproof, for correction, for instruction in righteousness." so I knew that it would indeed be beneficial for me to tuck away as much Scripture into my mind as I possibly could. But to my shame I had not been sharing any of them as a good Christian aught to. Now, when I needed them most, they were in a place I could not access. Locked away somewhere i was unable to reach. I could only grasp onto small pieces of jumbled scripture verses dancing about in my short circuited mind.

I told him that "No, I had seen no white light, nor any light of any kind." Not even the ambulance lights. I am led to believe from a scriptural reference point that the supposed beautiful white light that some claim to have seen during similar experiences is most likely a trick of Satan. I don't want that to seem like that is just my personal opinion and I only say that because The Bible tells us that Satan himself is called an angel of light in 2 Corinthians 11:14-and marvel not; for Satan himself transforms himself into and angel of light. Verse 15 further tells us that his minions transform themselves into ministers of righteousness. The Bible tells us he was Gods most beautiful angelic creation; until pride was found in him. These minions have powers as well. Those minions are none other than the beings which became the demons and devils that were cast out of Heaven with Lucifer/satan at the fall. A quick peek at any daily newspaper can show us that. I'm not saying every "bad" thing that happens is the devils work. But he does have influence over multitudes of peoples, governments and media outlets and can easily cloud minds and judgements. Such causes people to do pretty "dumb" things, not only to themselves but to others as well. I think my answer disappointed him. Yet the truth of that passage is a clear warning not to get too caught up in angel sightings and bright light kind of sightings such as "UFO's." It reminds me of another verse, in the New Testament this time, it is Galatians 1:8 "But though we, or AN ANGEL from Heaven, preach any other gospel unto you than that which we have preached unto you, let him be accursed." So, even if an angel did appear to me and told me something "contrary" to scripture, I wouldn't have believed it based on these sample verses. I cannot discount nor discredit the things others have seen or experienced. This personal view is based on my readings of Scripture, and I simply state, that I saw no "white lights." When God says for something to be "accursed," it seems pretty clear that He means what He says. Again, all I know is that "I" did not see a brilliant white light and I believe I did not see said light because I would not have believed it based on the above verses. Enough on that.

I can only relate the event in this fashion. It was sort of like being blindfolded, handcuffed, and locked in a thickly chained steamer trunk in a bolted closet for a spell while the room was violently rearranged. If it was not rearranged to my liking, tough cookies and too bad to boot; deal with it. Have others been allowed to see angelic beings when brushing close with death and lived to tell the tale? Sure, why not. If it occurred with me, I have no recall of such. Perhaps they caught me and eased me gently to the ground? Such happened in The Bible story of Balaam in the book of Numbers where it tells of he and his donkey. The donkey saved his keester twice by turning to the right or left. Num 22:23 The donkey had "seen" the angel with sword drawn blocking their path and turned to avoid him. In the story, Balaam was on his way to do something God had clearly told him NOT to do. The Donkey turned one way to avoid the angel and Balaam smashed his foot against a wall, then the same to the other side. Then Balaam got furious and started beating the daylights out of the critter that just saved his bacon.

Then, God put words in the things mouth and he spoke. Num 22:28 and then God opened Balaams eyes and let him "see" the angel with the drawn sword that the donkey saw. So; certainly others could have seen such if God allows, I did not. That's not a great example I realize, but it shows us that our temporal eyes do not always see as clearly as we think they do. The spirit world around us is a very real thing. We are surrounded by it on a daily basis.

We can also read in Acts where The Lord struck down Saul on the road to Damascus with a blinding light and called him into service as Paul. But as for me, I saw no light, and even If I had, it has been washed from my memory with all the other items that have been omitted from my mind. Were angels present with me that day? Certainly and absolutely, I do believe that. I was held in their gracious care until help arrived. No question about that one. Do I recall seeing any? NO! Our temporal eyes cannot see the spiritual realm around us. Good thing too, if we all could see the very real spirit world around us we'd probably be unable to handle it. There are likely those who have seen it. The sprit world IS a real thing and it IS around so it only makes sense that there are a select few God has revealed it to. I am not one of them as I don't recall seeing such. Enough said.

Many people it seems, are looking for something physical or tangible to grasp onto concerning the afterlife. Faith is key, but faith in the right truth and the right God is essential. God is still God, He still works His miracles daily all over this world. Wether it's cowtown hicksville or big city USA. Wether it's on a remote island or deepest jungle. Wether it be a desert floor or the highest mountain peak, God is even there and He still works His wonders. You might not see the Red Sea part; but daily take Him at His word and you will absolutely see Him work. Why should we expect, or dare to demand a response or expect "a sign" when we have His Word; His complete, perfect and absolute final authoritative Word readily available to us like no other age in history? His Word is complete and there is no "new" revelation come down from heaven for us today as some claim. Read His Word, The Bible, Pray, believe, and just as importantly, gather with other believers to hear and see His Word spoken, taught, sang, and lived.

God's help is available. Our Creator has made His intentions very clear and obtainable to man (all men, AND women, AND children) in His Word. Sorry PETA, but Animals are not included. They are Bi-une, (Body and Spirit) Man is tri-une. (Body, spirit, AND SOUL!) The Gospel message is for humanity only. Romans 10:17, so then faith comes by hearing, and hearing by The Word of God. Animals cannot respond to the Gospel message any more than the lamp post on the corner can. That is yet another of the multitude of faults with evolutions false teaching. Man is not an animal; though many act like it. He is a uniquely created being with dignity, personal responsibility, and most importantly, an eternal soul that will live forever in one of two very real places. It is up to each one of us as individuals where we will spend eternity. It is a personal choice. That said; It is no-ones fault but their own if they end up in hell.

The problem is with us. Man! Mankind, both man and woman. Man's vision is so marred by his own wretched state that he cannot see Gods design or purpose for him until he meets the Savior. More importantly, upon that meeting, see and aknowledge his/her very real need for that Savior. Until a sinner realizes and accepts his need for a savior, he/she cannot be saved. It really is that simple. His/her pride must be broken first. You can know all about Jesus Christ. His virgin birth, life, ministry, betrayal, and death. But, until you know Him; PERSONALLY, as Savior it is knowledge without value. Until that time people are open to any and all influences, including satanic.

The age old question reads: Who am I? Why am I here? How did I get here? Where did I come from? Where am I going? Actually, that's more like five questions, but they revolve around the central idea of the meaning of life. To put it simply, the whole purpose of man on this earth is to Glorify God, not ourselves, but God. Ecclesiastes 12:13: "Fear God and keep His commandments, for this is the whole duty of man." Yes, it really is that simple. Problem is, if the god you happen to worship is not Jehovah God, The Lord Jesus Christ Himself, that's where the troubles are. God Almighty does not share His Glory with anyone. He's God and has that right. Isaiah 42:8 "My Glory will I not give to another."

The evolutionist is the one with the problem here. If the evolutionist is right, why does he get so upset? Both the evolutionist and the creationist dies eventually. Either they stand before God or they don't. The creationist believes we are accountable to a Holy God and lives accordingly.

The evolutionist is accountable to no one, so do whatever they please. In the finality of the final ending however, we are indeed ALL going to glorify God Almighty. EVERYBODY on this planet, whether they want to or not. Personally I prefer to glorify Him as a friend, rather than an enemy to be vanquished, and thus glorify Him by that vanquishing. Heaven and hell are very real places, and you do have a choice as to where you will spend eternity. Eternity is a very long, long time and each of us will spend it in one of those two very real places. This choice is up to us individually, not by our "works," or "good deeds" but by His Mercy and Grace. (Ephesians 2:9) Not of works, lest any man should boast. (Titus 3:5) Not by works of righteousness which we have done, but according to His righteousness He saved us; by the washing and renewing and regeneration of the Holy Spirit. Giving ones life to Christ is not forced. It must be real and from the heart. That's what makes it a choice of free will. You don't have to believe in Hell to go there. There is absolutely NOTHING a person can do in their own body to gain favor with God. No amount of donated monies, no amount of "penance" I believe the word is, can be offered to gain us any sort of favor with Almighty God because due to our sin nature we are unpleasing to God. You cannot "earn" his favor by any amount of "good works." Do right by all means, but do not expect to reach heaven by your own shackles. Perhaps that flies in the face of your "religious" perceptions. But it is Biblical and thus, accurate. Very accurate.

UNTIL that is, we go through The Blood of The Lord Jesus Christ and are "Born Again" and become His. That's all that phrase means. Nothing "magical" about it. It is simply transferring/ believing that Christ already suffered and defeated death and sin on Calvary's tree. That alone is where humanities hope lies. Belief in Christ's completed work on The Cross. How dare we think we can add to that by our pitiful, diminutive little "sufferings." No one has ever suffered as The Lord Jesus Christ has suffered, no one in history, EVER. Crucifixion was horrible. It prolonged the suffering and agony of the condemned indefinitely. It was not a quick and merciful death! If you were being crucified you where going to die! Period! It was just a matter of when. One endured seeming endless hours of agony. Eventually succumbing to slow suffocation and blood loss from any amount of scourging wounds. The scourging was accomplished via a leather cat-o-nine tails with pieces of bone or metal imbedded in it to rip and tear flesh as one was "whipped" with it. If you survived that complete torture, then your open wounds screamed in agony as you were laid down on a rough, sharp, splinter laden wooden cross and spikes nailed through clusters of nerves in your tender flesh to secure you to the instrument of your tortuous death. A most gruesome way to be put to death. Man is capable of all sorts of depravity due to the fall. Any nightly newscast should tell us this.

Also much beauty as some artists can paint wondrous scenes. It is simply the way our Creator wired us, each one of us individually. As alluded to above; We are inquisitive beings. A triune being just as our creator is triune. Unlike animals that are bi-une, containing body and spirit without an eternal soul. That statement will certainly irk some, but it is Biblically founded; therefore accurate. Animals do not have an eternal soul and are not equal to man. I can write that with a relative amount of certainty based on Scripture. Ecclesiastes 3:21 "Who knoweth the spirit of man that goeth upward, and the spirit of the beast that goeth downward to the earth. If evolution were true then man would indeed be on an equal playing field as the animals. But; fortunately, evolution is the lie of the ages. It was a false idea started by satan in The Garden of Eden to make Adam and Eve doubt God's promises to them. It brought a question into their minds. We can't blame it all on Eve because Adam was standing there beside her when the tempter came.

The Bible gives us the true account of Creation. Genesis 3:6 She took of the fruit thereof, and did eat, and gave also unto her husband WITH her and he did eat. All the blame cannot be laid at Eves feet because Adam was right there beside her and could have stepped up to the plate as the spiritual leader and rebuked the foul serpent; but he said nothing. Instead he took a big bite too and the rest; as they say, is history. Even if Eve didn't know, Adam DID! AND, He was right there with the authority to rebuke that foul serpent. He could have said or done something, but chose not to. In any event I suppose that's spilled milk at this point, they both bit and here we are today. You can't be too hard on them. No matter how spiritual you think you are, not one of us would have done any different.

Gen 1:20 let the WATERS bring forth abundantly the moving creature that have life and the fowl may fly above the earth in the open firmament of Heaven, and then whales and other sea dwelling mammals and fish he created out of the "waters." Land animals and insects He made from the Earth. The Earth is not the creator nor our "mother," God is the creator not the creation. The animals he made just by speaking the words. "Let the earth bring forth the living creature after it's kind, cattle, and creeping things and beasts of the earth. And it was so." Adam was special and unique, God breathed into Adam and he came to life. Eve was created from a piece of bone taken from Adams side. Thus breathed into vicariously. Sound familiar? "The twaine shall be one." This proves the sanctity of marriage is one MAN and one WOMAN, for life.

Gen 1:26 The Bible gives a very clear and specific account of creation. Millions and or billions of years simply do not fit the equation, no matter how one attempts to make The Bible "fit" into their own theory. The only "theory" is the one that is no theory at all, but is fact, and that is the account of creation in The Book of Genesis. Those days were literal 24 hour days as we know them now. They had to be, otherwise all the plants would have died because they were created a day before the sun was created, and plants won't live long without the sun, certainly not billions or even millions of years. They wouldn't last "one" year without the sun! So much for the "theory" of "evolution." A theory is an unproven guess at best. Fact is provable and substantial. Creation is clearly a fact and is altogether true. The Titanic of evolution has been bottom bound since it first left it's hideously vile dry dock of lies. Like it or not Creation and evolution are both "religious" views. Problem is, only one view; the blatant lie; evolution, is taxpayer supported and touted as "the gospel truth" to millions of school kids across America and elsewhere on a daily basis. Why should anybody be surprised when people act like a pack of crazed animals when our education system has done their best to teach them that; that is exactly what they are, animals, no better or worse than the squirrel out on the tree limb. Satan is indeed the god of this world as scripture calls him, (2 corinthians 4:4) tells us of his deceiving works: (in whom the god of this world hath blinded the minds of them that believe not, lest the light of the glorious gospel of Christ should shine unto them)

Man is unique from all other life forms in that he has Body, Spirit, and Soul, an eternal soul. After all we are created in the image of our creator who is also triune. The Eternal Father, Creator Son, and Holy Ghost. He is Alpha and Omega, the beginning and the end, the first and the last. The always and forevermore eternal three in one. In creating us as individuals God has made each one of us unique, with dignity and freedom to make choices. Unlike animals which consist of body and spirit and no eternal soul. Man is the pinnacle of His creation.

At risk of offending the offend-able, and based on scripture I have to believe that man is the only being into which God "breathed into" simply because that is exactly what the text indicates.

The God of Creation; The Lord Jesus Christ Himself, would never force a person to convert to His path by the muzzle of an AK-47. He uses the Cross of Calvary. It is an individual choice to accept the Lords invitation; it is an invitation open to all who choose to accept it, including that guy with the AK-47. Strange, but nonetheless true. Gen 2:7 God hand made Adam from the dust of the ground, and then "breathed" into him the "breath of life." God did not do this with any other of the living creatures He made; not one of them, not even Eve. It is based on this fact that I believe that animals; while under our dominion do not have eternal souls, and thus are not on the same level as man, God's very special creation. That includes every person male or female, in the womb or walking. Salvation is through faith alone in Jesus Christ and is only available to mankind. Animal rights activists will surely get steamed at that, but it is truth. Get over it. Obviously animals are great friends, and can be affectionate and show loyalty, and help us tremendously. I don't discount that at all. But, don't think for a moment that they wouldn't turn on you in the blink of an eye if their belly got empty enough. Don't feed fido for a month and see what happens when you go to pet him.

Even Eve was not "breathed into" she was created from a piece of bone from Adams side, thus a part of him, thus close to his side, close to his heart and thus being there by his side to complete him. She was not made from a heel bone, being beneath him to be trampled, nor a skull bone to be above him to rule and reign over him, but "beside" him. Close to his heart. Together. Equal. Man and Woman. Side by side and face to face. Each with parts specifically designed for each other to enjoy. This is one reason why "same sex" marriage is a big No No. Besides being disgusting and obscene; even nature very clearly tells us this. If Noah had taken two bears named Bob and Bill onto the Ark, we wouldn't have any bears today. He needed a Bob and a Betty bear. If that offends you, get over it. It is the truth. Like charges repel one another, opposites attract. Truth is Truth and you cannot change it no matter how flowery you sprinkle it.

John 17:17 ...Thy Word is Truth...

2 Peter 2:2 ...and many shall follow their pernicious ways; by reason of whom the way of Truth shall be evil spoken of... Hmmm. Sounds a lot like todays culture doesn't it.

Paul penned Romans under the inspiration of The Holy Spirit. The following verses

Romans 1:24 – Wherefore God also gave them up to uncleanness through the lusts of their own hearts, to dishonor their own bodies between themselves…

Romans 1:25 – Who changed the Truth of God into a lie, and worshipped and served the creature more than the Creator, who is blessed for ever. Amen.

Romans 1:26 – For this cause (reason) God gave them up unto vile affections; for even their women did change the natural use into that which is against nature...

Romans 1:27 – and likewise also the men, leaving the natural use of the woman, burned in their lust one towards another; men with men working that which is unseemly, and receiving in themselves that recompense of their error which was meet (due).

That is a chrystal clear warning against same sex marriages or unions or whatever disgustingly cute little euphemisms you want to attach to it. God WILL judge it. As well will He judge the nation that calls good evil and evil good. I pray we American Christians have not stood silently idle for too long. We may already have traveled too far down that very road. We have had a few "national spankings" in the recent past. Throughout history, nations that have turned their back on God to "do it their own way" have not fared well.

Within the bounds of the marriage union, sex is not fornication. It is a joyful, wondrous thing. God created order and perfection. Man messed it up. Thus, quite clearly, God did not "make" homosexuals. Mankind's sinful nature is to blame. Homosexuality is one hundred percent, a "choice." Not a "normal condition." Like it or not, God WILL judge it and those who partake in it in any way shape or form. One can easily say this also means watching it and laughing at it and not being completely disgusted by it. He already has in some ways. This includes Judges who side with ungrounded profaneness and attempt to legislate from the bench. Psalm 7:11 - The Bible tells us that "...God is angry with the wicked every day..." There will indeed be a reckoning one day.

Yes, God is merciful and extremely patient; yet He is still God, and as God He has every right to judge as He sees fit; which will be by His Word. Like it or not, the anger and wrath of God is just as real as His Love and His Mercy. His judgment will be based upon His standards which are revealed in His complete, finite, and unchanging Word. The Bible. Man's standards change on the whims of the wind. Whichever way the money flows is man's way. The patience of God is unsearchable, our own nation, more and more so in recent years has turned her back on the God that is the source and foundation of the fabric which bound her together. The Founding Fathers were not idiots. A vast majority of them were Christians, and the ones who were not at least had a belief in God to a certain degree. Obviously being a Christian and believing in God are not the same thing, not in the farthest stretches of the imagination are they any way near the same thing, even the devil believes in God.

Here's an example; though, perhaps not a great one: You've been invited to go to the penthouse of a high rise to meet the rich guy who built it. The buildings doorman guides you to the elevator and tells you all you have to do is push the green button at the top of the panel and the car will go straight to the top. The car looks like it's going too slow so you decide to get to the top a different way. You choose the stairs. That way you can show the rich guy what great shape you're in by taking the stairs and not using his electricity and saving him some money. It takes you a long time and is tough going at times and you almost quit, but you finally make it to the top only to find the door is locked and you can't get in. So, you knock... and knock... and knock. A voice eventually comes from the other side. "Who is it?" You are shocked. "It's me." you say, "don't you remember, you invited me?" The voice comes again. "You are mistaken, all those I invited have come in the way I told them to. This door does not open."

"But after all that hard work and tiring climbing and such I'm worn out, can't you just let me in? I mean, it's me!" you say. "I'm sorry I cannot. This door will not open, you must come in the way I told you to. I made it easy for you. My doorman showed you to my elevator and explained how to use it. It could not have been simpler. All you had to do was get inside." You respond, "but that's not fair, I just wanted to prove I..."

"You need to prove nothing to me, I already know all about you. You can only have access to me the way I told you to. I invited you to come here and there's only one way to get here. Goodbye."

I know that's a pretty shabby example, but that's how us people are. ME, ME, ME, Us, Us, Us, We, We, We, My, My, My, I, I, I, Selfishness and self centeredness at every turn. As exclusive as it may sound, there is only ONE way to reach your creator. It is very simple and easy to understand.

In looking at Christianity in American history it seems clear that our founders knew their creation and experiment in liberty was far from perfect. Not ALL were Christians; some were; some were deists, others unbelievers. They all, however, understood scripture enough or valued its principles enough to ingrain it deeply enough into our founding documents so that it could be undeniable. As much as satans modern minions have tried to irradicate God from America. By modeling our government after the principles they learned from scripture our founders came up with the most free and workable system of government the world had ever seen. A Constitutional Republic! It seems though as the years have passed, that the carefully crafted system of checks and balances have been twisted, tweaked and manipulated for the benefit of the "elite" in our nations capital just as the founders had feared and warned us about. Against popular sentiments to the contrary by those wishing to re-pen history to their liking, a large percentage of the founders were against slavery. They also knew from firsthand observation that a true democracy was self-destructive, in relatively short order they implode under the weight of their own flawed design. NO true democracy can long bear the heft of it's own weight. Like an upside-down pyramid, it cannot stand the strain and soon topples. When the liberals, elitists and progressives come to feed at the seemingly endless public troth of trust they soon find it empty and deplete of funds, and nothing short of downright revolt shall refill it. Unfortunate, but true.

John Adams wrote something akin. "Remember, democracy never lasts long. It soon wastes, exhausts and murders itself. There was never a democracy yet that did not commit suicide." We as individual people and as a nation desperately need Gods help and guidance.

Friendship with all, alliance with none used to be one of our nations sacred motto's. Things worked well for us as long as it was so. As soon as some politician figures out he can stick his hand in the public trough for the easy pickings within, it's all over. As Ben Franklin put it. Democracy is two wolves and a lamb deciding what to have for lunch, Liberty is a well armed lamb contesting the vote. That one is both classic, and timeless.

Many of our founding fathers were "Christians," including our nations first president. Remember him, he's the one who set the example of limiting himself to two terms. He didn't want to create a new monarchy, they just fought a long and bloody war to shed such a failed system. Neither did they want a theocracy, with some robbed pope; who is only a fallible man, in the Vatican pulling it's puppet strings. What they created was a one of a kind in the history of the world. Taking example and principles gleaned from such as the ancient Roman civilization. This was a time in our nations history when our leaders actually had a healthy fear of God. It hasn't taken too long for us to degenerate to our current situation. Many a taken-for-granted freedom has been regulated into an endless, costly, bureaucracy. I've often considered exhuming George Washington to see if he has rolled over or not and to inspect his skeletal cheekbones for tear stains. But; No, let the grand old patriot rest in peace I suppose.

Isaiah 55:8-9 gives a good view of man's deplorably shaky standing before a Holy and Righteous God. (55:8) For My thoughts are not your thoughts, neither are your ways my ways, saith The Lord. (9) For as the heavens are higher than the earth, so are My ways higher than your ways, saith The Lord. As well Isa 64:6 But we are all as an unclean thing, and our righteousnesses are as filthy rags; and we all do fade as a leaf; and our iniquities, like the wind, have taken us away... WOW, these powerful scriptural proofs reveal our wretched and rebellious state, as well our desperate need of a Savior. He can not and will not simply look the other way and let all mankind's wretchedness slide. Disney's god, and religion's god can, but not the God of The Bible. He is Righteous and Holy and there must be a payment. That payment was paid on Calvary's Cross. It was paid in full with nothing for us to add. Our lot is simple to take advantage of it and accept it while there is still time.

We are each one of us unique individuals, made in the image of our creator. Evolution is a lie! Some people are born with an aptitude for mathematics and engineering, and the wanting to know the why's and how's of the way something works based on a set of principles or circumstances, or formula of some type. This would drive another person (like me) mad and have them pulling out hair by the roots. Still others have a love of music and words and paints and thus excel in what we might call "the arts." As well there are those who see things only in black and white and right and wrong, and the way to do something is such and such a way, and there is no deviation from such. Others yet, see things with a sort of "Oh well..." attitude with a "what's good for you may or may not be okay for me so who cares." This Amoral thinking denies right and wrong and good and evil. This can be said with authority because there is an absolute source of authority we can go to for help in solving any problem and any situation we get ourselves into. The source is The Word of God, The Bible. Just keep in mind that it is the TEXT that is inspired, not the footnotes or observations of the commentators and translators. In many's view, The King James version is among the best translations for the English reader, speaker, and writer.

As people go, there are a wide variety of personality traits, and there is probably at least a little of each in every person because all mankind shares a common creator. We all are descendants of the same two people. Adam and Eve, if it wasn't for our foolish pride we would very likely all live peaceably with one another. That's the main reason why racism is so utterly stupid and foolish. Racism is born out of evolutionary thought. Why else would such ilk as Adolph Hitler have grasped it so firmly. He was a rabid evolutionist and the world witnessed the results of his false notions.

For me, the best way that I personally know of to communicate idea's and truth is through the medium of the written word. Newspapers, magazines, letters, books and cereal boxes fit into this particular genera. This last one being of least importance unless you are a dietitian or nutritionist by trade. Now, with that said; or written, rather, I propose a question.

Where does the love of storytelling come from? Is it something a person is born with, or can it be learned? I believe that much like painting and sculpting, writing is something a person must be born with. While writing skills can be learned and honed; as in painting, the "knack" and the genuine gift are not quite the same thing.

Not everyone can really write and or tell a good story. And vise-versa, not everyone can tell and or write a really good story. Only you, the reader can decide which of those two variances this particular story fits into. As you have obviously gotten THIS far, I have at least piqued your interest. Most folks however, will listen to and even read a good story. Some enjoy the fantasy of fiction. Some the allegorical melding of truth and fantasy while others still thrive on stories of real events and happenings that they can connect with on some level or another, however remotely. Experiences of others put to print to perhaps prevent another from making the same errors in life that they have made, had made, and/or are currently making. Experiences of others can benefit us. Good or bad. Wisdom can be found in experience. Words of a friend? A parent? A pastor? The errors, "miscalculations" and downright utterly stupid decisions we all so often make can benefit others greatly if they heed the results of them. These events and errors when presented to others in the form of print can help them to see; or point out and steer them to avoid a disastrous chain of events that will leave a life ruined in its wake. If only one person is positively influenced by this collection of paper and ink, it has been a worthwhile effort. The key is heeding such advice when you see or hear it.

This is not necessarily what some would call a "religious" book. Though, quite clearly there are "religious" and "spiritual" references and meanings; if you want to call them such, within the paltry sum of its meager pages. As there obviously have been already. You, the reader must decide for yourself. I am simply relaying the story. I have used the occasional scripture reference because it is very relevant to the story. Since all scripture is given (2 Tim 3:16) for mankind's benefit, it pays to use as much as possible to point out truths we all need to see. Life and true religion are often inseparable. Many of the troubles in our current world can attest to that. Actions reveal beliefs and vice versa. For instance, would a "loving and peaceful" religion murder thousands aimlessly with bombs, swords, and airplanes as a false religion surely would do? False religions thrive on hate and murder and death and fear and terror. Hence the word "terrorist". As Truth would have it, there is only "one" way and "one" way alone to reach Heavens Glory. As arrogant and exclusive as it will likely sound to the spiritually blind, that one and only way, is through The Lord Jesus Christ. His Word tells us as much in numerous places.

John 10:7 - Jesus said unto them. "Verily, verily (truly, truly) I say unto you, I am the door. John 14:6 - Jesus saith unto him, I am The way, The Truth and The Life; no one comes unto the Father, but by Me.

Revelation 1:11 - I am The Alpha and Omega, the first and the last.

Revelation 21:6 - It is done, I am Alpha and Omega, the beginning and the end.

John 10:30 - I and My Father are one. There are numerous others.

As the title I've chosen suggests I have attempted to meld both spiritual and practical truth together on this semi-short dissertation. The basic truth and point in the chosen title being that through Jesus Christ we can overcome any obstacle we get or find ourselves in, regardless of it's size and complexity. That thought brings to mind another promise in scripture. *I can do all things through Christ which strengtheneth me.* This second promise is found in Philippians 4:13. Our time on earth is rather short. In some places it is referred to as a "vapor". not much to a vapor, and compared to eternity it is just that. Psalm 90:10 - The days of our lives are three score and ten; and if by reason of strength they be four score years, yet is their strength labor and sorrow; for it is soon cut off and we fly away. On average, and barring accidents and such, that number indicates about 70 years of life. That is not a long time. At four score years old (80) you're at the end of the road and these days the majority of folks that reach that age are not up to a whole lot of anything. That short time starts at conception and gives us three main events in life.

1. We are born...
2. We live...
3. We die...

As gruesome as it is, the abortionists sharp blade and vacuum skip # 2 and force 1 and 3 to occur simultaneously. Not having a chance for life outside the womb these souls are without question alive with Jesus Christ right now. Life begins at conception, and the womb is Gods sacred domain. 2 Sam 12:23 Proves those souls are in heaven. King David understood this clearly by his statement. "I shall go to him but he shall not return to me." Clearly, the souls snuffed out through abortion are in heaven. Infants tragically killed in accidents and those dying before reaching an age of accountability are as well. As soon as one is self aware they are accountable.

In our often busy daily lives many of us tend to have no thought whatsoever of God. The average man's God is one of their own making, (Pro 12:15 in part) says just so. The way of the fool is right in his own eyes. So of course their lifestyles are easily and readily accepted by their god, and why not. Like those who bow their knee to a statue they themselves have just carved or bought in the pottery store. Such is Lunacy! It is nothing but dead rock or wood. This is idolatry, nothing else. Christ is alive! Bow your knee to Him. He is the second part of the tri-une Godhead. The Father, The Son, The Holy Spirit. Unlike animals, we human beings are tri-une as well consisting of Body, Soul and spirit. Our body is the house, our spirit gives us life, and our soul is the eternal part. The body will one day cease to function, the spirit gives life to the body and the soul gives life to the sprit and vice versa. Our soul is our eternal part, it will indeed live forever in one of two very real places. Our souls looks like us, is eternal, and by all indications will feel pain as well.

Based on a plain reading of scripture I would have to believe that animals are different in that I see no indication of them being triune. Animals seem to be made up of only body and spirit. There is no indication of an eternal soul like the one that God "breathed" into man in Genesis 2:7. In Ecclesiastes 3:21. God through Solomon says this. "Who knoweth the sprit of man that goeth upward, and the spirit of the beast that goes downward to the earth?" Verses like Job 7:9 as the cloud is consumed and vanisheth away so is he that goeth down to the grave shall come up no more can be used to prove there are no "ghosts". While there certainly are spiritual beings about us deceiving on a daily basis. A reading of scripture can tell us that people do not come back as a "haunting" spirit. Sorry if that rubs you the wrong way but it is scriptural. The "hauntings, and ghosts" this world experiences can be none another than some deceiving or lying spirit. Demons if you will. It has occurred in scripture in the past and dollars to donuts it happens in the halls of governments world wide to this very day. 1 King 22:21 in part: "I will be a lying spirit in the mouths of all his prophets." If deception in governments happened back then, it most certainly happens today, even more so and to a greater degree with greater consequences. 2 Tim 3:13 "But evil men and seducers shall wax worse and worse, deceiving and being deceived." Job 21:13 They spend their days in wealth and in a moment go down to the grave… So man is not like the animals around us, according to scripture they just "go down to the grave" Satan has orchestrated world events and has his lie of evolution firmly entrenched in the classroom and almost every other public, tax supported forum here in America. We are all paying for the liars to lie to us and our kids. Kids are taught they are nothing more than a highly evolved animal, so why are folks surprised when one is on the nightly news cast acting exactly like one. Trim out the lies of evolution and just stick to truth and science and teach away, until then don't stir more misery into the pot of lies. Teaching kids they are no different than an animal spits in God's eye and calls Him a liar. A rather dangerous place to find yourself in. Wisdom would suggest repentance. In 37 short years that is more than half of the three score and ten that scripture tells us we have been given. GONE. What of any value has been accomplished in that short time-frame.

Motorcycles can be fun and enjoyable for certain. However, one must be cautious and listen to your moms who have worked in Xray rooms for eons and KNOW... and they most assuredly do know things you cannot possibly see in your youthful arrogance. Mine worked in such an E.R. for years and saw first hand the dangers of motorcycle VS. car wrecks. She had tried to instill me to never get or ride motorcycles. There were too many idiots on the road. Unless you rode one, or knew someone who rode, most people didn't think to be aware for harder to see motorcycles. Anyway, I had bought a bike through a friend of my wife's where she worked at the time. If you ride a motorcycle, it is only a matter of time before you have an accident of some type no matter how minor. It is going to happen sooner or later. I'm not saying don't ride, just wear leather, long pants; and especially a helmet, even if it's 90+ degrees. It will help because pavement obviously does not "give" as easily as the human body does. I had jeans and T-shirt on and have a scar where the bumper of her car smashed my leg against my hot muffler on impact. The tib-fib snapped like a dried twig. I'm assuming she hit the brakes. I don't know for sure, I was too busy flying through the air on my way to the pavement. Wether she did or didn't was a moot point at this particular moment. Here is where the danger began in earnest; being sedate for so long in the cast I packed on the excess poundage. A good 20-30 pounds. Poor diet didn't help any, but just made it worse. Tick...tick...tick...

Romans 1:28 All things work together for good to them that love God, to them that are called according to His purpose...(to the faithful Christian)

2 Peter 1:9: But he that lacketh these things is blind, and cannot see afar off, and hath forgotten that he was purged from his old sins...(to the lackadaisical Christian)

It took a few years, but the constant build up of grease in my arteries from this lazy-time of life eventually caught up with me. Likely there was build up from teen years as well.

I was shocked and caught completely off guard by a letter I got in the hospital. It was from the editor of the newspaper to whom I had sent most of the editorials I had penned. Virtually one a month for a number of years. Most of them revolved around the antics of a certain despicable adulterating, deceitful democrat residing in the White House at that particular sad time in our nations history. This refined newspaper had a limit of one letter per month by it's readers. For a while there it was looking like my own personal column. About 98 percent of the time they would print my letters verbatim, even a few of the ones that went "WAY" over the word limit. One reason is because in reading the printed finals I got better at writing them and editing them myself before I would send them in. I figured out what would be printed and what would not and slightly adjusted my writing style to accommodate, or used colorful phraseology to get my points across. I attempted to express my views without appearing overly pompous or belligerent. I didn't give just my personal opinion, I attempted to seed each editorial with substantial facts, and verifiable truths. It was fun! My writing, my thoughts, were actually making it to print. Though merely an editorial section of a mid-sized local paper, I thought that was kinda cool.

Through the grapevine of people knowing people knowing other people, word got to the editor of this paper as to what had happened to me and he wrote me a personal handwritten letter in the hospital. For him to take the time and do something like that for someone he didn't even know except by my writing style, I was shocked. That letter really encouraged me to continue in writing, and even to take some courses in journalism and writing. Much to my distaste, I discovered that many, many; but thankfully not all, of our nations college campuses had sunk extremely deep into the Godless nadir chasm of far left leaning ideology; IE; socialism, more in line with the like's of such ruthlessly vile and shady characters such as Charles Darwin and Joseph Stalin and numerous others of such dispicable ilk; rather than rising above them with such unflappable Icons as Charles Spurgeon and George Washington. Such was, and is, rather disturbing to me; and I'm sure, numerous other patriotic Christians to say the very least.

I knew something of this, but found out first hand that it was far worse than I had originally ever anticipated; and this was merely a small community college I attended. A deep chasm of left leaning liberal philosophy was flowing rampant and unchecked through it's hallways like the rancid bile of a third-world sewage system. Was it any wonder I was seeing so many of the disturbing trends that destroy nations, occurring in my own (backyard) country? The state of our nation is troubling and disturbing, and grows more so on a daily basis.

This is really no surprise to the Bible Believing Christian. A sampling of elections in the 90's at least when I began penning this; shows this. Scripture clearly reveals the attitudes of mankind worsening and worsening as we near what Scripture calls The End Times. 2 Timothy 3:1-5: This know also, that in the last days perilous (savage, hard to bear) times shall come (2) For men will be lovers of their own selves, covetous, boastful, proud, blasphemers, disobedient to parents, unthankful, unholy, (3) Without natural affection, truce breaker's, false accusers, incontinent(spewing the thoughts of their vile hearts before all) fierce, despisers of those that are good, (4) Traitors, heady, high minded, lovers of pleasures more than lovers of God; (5) having a form of godliness, but denying the power of thereof: from such turn away.

The Holy spirit's insights made Tim was rather perceptive it appears. Such sounds a lot like folks today. High minded left leaning college professors not withstanding; it's a pretty spot-on definition of todays mindset. Tim was speaking of "the last days" hmmm. Kinda makes one pause and think, doesn't it? No man knows or can know that day, but we're close anyhow.

There's on old saying, I believe it's the first law of thermodynamics, that says something akin to; things tend towards disorder all by themselves. Something like that. Makes sense. If man built it, it will eventually rust, fall apart, or break down and need servicing. Whether it's a human body or a body of government, things need to be constantly checked out and maintained or a problem will soon present itself. Look at the roads and bridges near your hometown, without constant maintenance and upkeep they'd fall apart pretty quick. Lord help you if you're on that bridge when it breaks. Government isn't a ball you can roll down the hill and trust it to guide itself through, around and past every obstacle. We need God's help to guide this nation. Our founders knew this fact and did their best to instill such in our founding documents. They were not a bunch of backwoods rubes as many a progressive "historian" would like to claim. These were well educated man that put their fortunes and their lives, quite literally on the line for their beliefs and their young nation. A brief sampling of quotes they uttered is below. Like it or not God figured highly in this grand nations founding.

1. It is impossible to rightly govern the world without God and The Bible... George Washington.
2. Without God, liberty will not last... Thomas Jefferson.
3. The people never give up their liberties but under some delusion... Thomas Jefferson.
4. A gun in the hand is better than ten guns locked in the safe... Jack M. Waister.

Being a conservative, even still a conservative Christian in such an environment was not enjoyable, for if you did not toe-the-leftist-liberalized-line, your class was sure to be very difficult for you. However, I didn't mind ruffling any "liberal" feathers. I was there for fun, and not to impress any professors. The left-leaning political views of the large majority of the teaching staff was crystal clear. Christian ideology WAS NOT to be tolerated, but rather ridiculed and crushed before it spread unchecked like a wild and despised disease. If such is true in a tiny community college, what must it be like in a major university? I wondered, but understood that it must be far, far worse. I began to understand more clearly the obstacles a Christian young person was up against in going to a secular college. More so I began to understand how a Christian young person could have their faith shaken and rattled, perhaps even weakened to the point that it is all but destroyed by such an environment. This was not encouraging to me. No, not at all. I weep for my country when I consider that tomorrows leaders are being formulated under such prerequisites. Prerequisites to call evil good and good evil. That is reminiscent of another well known founding era quote. I tremble for my country when I consider that God is Just, Holy and righteous, and those traits of His Holy character, (His justice) cannot sleep forever. I added Holy and Righteous to that statement because God is unchanging. (Hebrews 13:8 Jesus Christ the same yesterday, today and forever) It being clear that the God of the Old Testament is the same God as the New Testament. By that verse it is also quite clear that Jesus Christ IS God. His Justice can only slumber for so long. His Patience does have a point where He'll say ENOUGH! and He'll take action!

He has offered His gracious hand, only to have it bitten and then spat upon by His ungrateful creations. Why should people cry out and bewail the thought that God has removed His hand of protection from our nation; when in-fact, we as a nation have fought so hard to get free of that guiding hand? Not to sound trite or to belittle such henious crimes. One reason "God" does not stop the shooting sprees in the public classrooms is because He is not allowed in the public school classrooms anymore. If a teacher where to invoke the name of God in a classroom, he or she would be sued and run out of town on a rail in tar and feathers, if not drawn and quartered. Perhaps all three, or worse. I find it quite revealing that this truth only applies if one were to invoke the name of the one and only True God's name.

Anyone is free to generically mention a "god" as long as His initials are not J.C. If you are one that worships the creation and not the creator as the pagans of yesteryear did. You along with todays batch of rabid environmentalists and their Godless philosophy's are welcomed with wide open arms in America's public schools. All paid for by the already heavily overburdened taxpayer.

Romans 1:18-32 covers a whole range of the way man's depraved, warped mind views this world we have been given to dwell on. (18) For the wrath of God is revealed from Heaven against all ungodliness and unrighteousness of men, who hold the truth in unrighteousness; (man suppresses the true truth and replaces it with his own, more palatable version)(19) Because that which may be known of God is manifest (is plain and visible) in them; for God hath shown it unto them. (we "know" right from wrong)(20) For the invisible things of Him from the creation of the world are clearly seen, (air we breath) being understood by the things that are made, even His eternal power and Godhead; so that they are without excuse: (our "cells" know what to do and how to grow) (21) Because that, when they knew God (understood there had to be a God) they glorified Him not as God, neither were thankful; (disregarded that understanding) but became vain (empty) in their imaginations and their foolish heart was darkened. (a conscious choice to not allow light in.)(22) Professing themselves to be wise, they became fools. (evolutionists, those that deny God's existence and creation)(23) And changed the glory of the incorruptible God into an image made like unto corruptible man, and to birds, and four footed beasts, and creeping things. (evolutions teachings)(24) Wherefore God also gave them up to uncleanness (vile, filthiness) through the lusts (passions) of their own hearts, to dishonor their own bodies between themselves: (homosexuality) (25) Who changed (altered to their liking) the Truth of God into a lie, (what God is not) and worshipped and served the creature more than the creator, (The environmentalist movement) who is blessed forever. Amen. (26) For this cause (reason) God gave them up unto (let them reap what they've sown.) Vile affection (improper): for even their women did change (alter, switch) the natural use (normal husband/wife joining) (27) Likewise also the men, (as if the women doing this was not bad enough) burned (desperate, uncontrollable desire) in their lust one to another; men with men working that which is unseemly, (disgusting, gross, shameful) and receiving (accepting) in themselves the recompense (payment, penalty) of their error (grave mistake) which was meet. (due)(28) and even as they (all those who do/did these things) did not like to retain (think about, know) God in their knowledge, God gave them over to a reprobate (rotten, debased, filthy, corrupt, polluted) mind, to do those things which are not convenient. Verses 29-31 are harsher still; further condemning us, including those who "know" they are wrong and still continue and enjoying seeing others do the same. (29) Being filled with all unrighteousness, fornication, wickedness, covetousness, maliciousness; full of (to the top, overflowing, great abundance) envy, murder, debate (argument) deceit (lies, trickery) malignity (evil mindedness) whisperers (talk behind the backs of) (30) Backbiters,(violent, liars, cheaters) haters of God, despiteful, proud, boasters, inventors of evil things, disobedient to parents... (In Ephesians 6:1. children are commanded to obey their parents in The Lord because it is the right thing to do, not because parents want to be tyrants. (31) Without understanding, (unable to see the forest for the trees), covenant breakers, (not keeping their word or promises) without natural affection, (cold hearted, merciless) implacable, (unforgiving) unmerciful. (32) who knowing the judgement of God, that they that commit such things are worthy of death, not only do the same, but have pleasure in them that do them. (you know it's probably the wrong thing, but you still watch it anyway.) That verse could easily translate into television and movies.

That's just a few verses covered there. It seems clear though, that through all this, God is simply telling us that we are incapable of living this life without Him. We cannot uphold "the law" of Moses. It is impossible for us. We are incapable of such. Not one of us escapes this. Romans 3:23, and 1 Kings 8:46 are just two of many verses that proves this fact to be so. ALL need Jesus, and one day, ALL will stand before Him. On that day ALL will admit to Him it is so. Not believing it is going to happen does not change the fact that it is indeed going to happen. (Philippians 2:11) And that EVERY tongue shall confess that Jesus Christ is Lord to the glory of God the father. That's kind of all inclusive and inescapable. He is the only one that led the "perfect" life, fulfilling the Law of Moses completely and perfectly. Thus pleasing God and providing a way for us to have access to Gods eternal home and rest.

The Apostle Paul penned the book of Galatians and in it he addressed such a matter. In (Galatians 4:13) "Am I therefore become your enemy, because I tell you the truth?" People don't want to hear the truth or face up to the fact that they have a need. That need is The Lord Jesus Christ. It couldn't be any plainer or simpler than that. WE are inexcusable before God.

I have added an additional item I penned no too long ago on what seems to be on a "hot" topic these days. It is a short sampling and study on the issue, or nonissue of "same sex" unions. I called it...

Dont Call God A Liar

Noah's Ark is mentioned in brief in this short treatise, it is not meant to invoke humor. Rather but to make a very direct and truthful point. Noah's ark, not the cute one depicted on children's books and knapsacks; but the real one, the one that went aground in the high peaks of the Ararat mountain ranges somewhere in Northern Turkey. Like it or not, the actual ark that God used to judge sin the first time on this earth is an actual event in human history. It did Happen. A different study covers that subject, this one is on something much more important and undermining to human dignity and even man's worship of God (who does not change by the way... (Heb 13:8... Jesus Christ, the same yesterday, today, and forever.) Yes, Jesus Christ IS God. After all, what kind of God do you wish to serve?

1. An impotent old grandfatherly god who cowtows to your every whim and says everything you do is fine and dandy and okey-dokey with Him?...Sure, he gets "sad" when you do "bad stuff" but will always look the other way and let any-and-all into His Heaven when that time comes., most people today think that's who god is thanks to television, music and movies...
2. Or do you want Him to butt out and leave you alone. Except when you want or need something then He'd better hop to it and rush to your side and cough it up right now..
3. Or do you want to serve a God who lives, who sets standards and rules and expects His most prized and dignified creation,

"Man." (the only one He has given an eternal soul to.)Ecc 3:21:(Who knoweth the spirit of man that goeth upward, and the spirit of the beast that goeth downward to the earth. Isa 14:15) to abide by them, and worship Him as He lays out on His Perfect, Holy and Complete Word. The Bible. (Indicates to us that animals have no eternal souls.)

Calling your Creator a liar is dangerous, yet that's exactly what you do when you call something "good" that our creator calls SIN. People don't like of the word "sin" today and it is considered taboo in most circles. Now-a-days man just uses the softer more innocuous word "bad" to make the filth God very clearly condemns more palatable for him and easier to swallow. The things God tells us in His Perfect, Unflappable Word are an abomination and sin, man turns around and spits in His face and says, "No it's OK, we like it, and we're gonna do it anyway. The Bible doesn't fit us today. We have "evolved", have technology and are smart. We will do as we please."

Unfortunately for those folks, God is still on the throne, He watches and He remembers EVERYTHING! He keeps count as well. Will knowing what Gods opinions are on doing and allowing and or supporting such things as gay marriage for starters, and then proving via scripture that doing such things are A FREE WILL CHOICE and "against nature" change your mind...? Either you agree with God or call Him an unjust liar and move on, Be warned however; the later of those two choices would not be a wise one.

I've only included a few proof verses for space's sake. It aught to be clear enough. The conclusion is obvious. If there's a problem with that, take it up with God. He's judge and author, I'm just the messenger.

Excessive drink, drugs, fornication, promiscuity and adultery are bad enough and will be dealt with most harshly unless a turning away and repentance comes first. Yet in this brief treatise I am referring specifically to the condemnable practice of "homosexuality." It is not normal! It is a CHOICE! Made of ones own freewill. Thanks to television, movies, music, magazines and books, it is rampant in society. Because of that, such foul practice is considered normal and acceptable today. Such an abominable thing aught not exist yet due to man's sin nature it does. Why do you think such practices are not found in nature...? Because it is unnatural! You will never find gay bears, chipmunks, squirrels, possums or dogs in nature because they don't exist. They don't have a corrupted sin nature to make them choose such. Had Noah taken two Woodchucks named Bill and Joe on the Ark there wouldn't be any Woodchucks today. Yes it really is that simple, physical laws cannot change. As in magnets, like charges repel one another, opposites attract! Clearly, God did not make the homosexual, he made himself by his rebellion to a Holy and all righteous God. It is clearly a choice! Animals don't have a sin nature, people do because we have an eternal soul, animals do not. Man is a triune being, created in God's image, with a body, an eternal soul and a sprit. Recall in Genesis 2:7 God breathed into man the breath of life and he became a living soul. He did not do this with any other creature. Animals have only body and spirit. Sorry if that offends you, it is truth! Get over it.

There are a plethora of verses both Old and New Testament that prove this fact beyond any shadow of any doubt. They are very clear and specific, there is no doubt what they are talking about. It is Gods opinion on homosexuality:

The God of the Old Testament and The God of the New Testament are one and the same and He does not change. Like it or not, His opinion is still valid.

{HEBREWS 13:8 Jesus Christ, the same yesterday today and forever} hmmmm.

LEVITICUS 18:22...thou shalt not (don't do it) lie with mankind as with womankind, it is an abomination... (putrefying, disgusting.)

LEVITICUS 20:13... if man lie with man as with a woman, both committed abomination and shall surely be put to death... (wow, sounds like God means business to me)

LEVITICUS 26:16... a burning ague... consume the eyes... (hmmm, sounds like a horrid disease of some type... Aids? could it be God is serious?)

Oh now that's just mean, Besides that's Old Testament. God is all love, He would never condemn anyone to the literal flames of an eternal Hell for doing those sorts of things today, right? (HEBREWS 13:8!) Jesus Christ the same yesterday, today and forever.
OK then, how about the NEW TESTAMENT? oops... It's even clearer. Guess God's True to His Word after all.

ROMANS 1:27...and likewise also the men, leaving (its a freewill choice) the natural use of the woman(self explanatory) burned in their lust one towards another...men with men woking that which is unseemly (disgusting) and receiving in themselves the error (big mistake) of the recompense (payment) that was due.(deserved) (hmm disease...?)

1 CORINTHIANS 6:9... effeminate... abusers of themselves with mankind...?

hmmm That doesn't sound like something a Holy and Righteous God is pleased with.

Jesus Christ came and judged sin once for all when He suffered horribly on the cross for us. His death burial AND resurrection is proof that He was who He claimed to be. God Almighty Himself. His atonement for all sin we have and will ever commit, past present and future, is not a blind blanket that covers us so we can go ahead and live like the devil however we want. No! It is true that Salvation is freely given. All one need do is ask. Its a personal choice that takes humility and admitting to yourself and or others, and more importantly to God that you are incapable of "gaining favor" with God of your own accord and asking Him (Jesus Christ) to save you. He'll clean up all the filth afterwards. How can the Christian claim Christianity and also claim that what God calls an abomination is really good and normal? What

God calls Sin we aught not call righteous and good. What God calls abomination we aught not make a law legalizing such. Sin is sin however we disguise it and whatever lofty cloak of idea's and words we dress it up with.

Homosexuality is the begging of the end for a country. History is proof of this. If one were to violate a natural law there will always be a consequence...always. It has nothing to do with being Spiteful or hateful. It is about right and wrong! The Bible is Right in all it shows us. From word one to the very last word. Which, incidentally are, In The Beginning GOD, and AMEN. It has been given to us to show us and guide us in the paths of righteousness. Like the acronym mentioned, BIBLE is simply Basic Instructions Before Leaving Earth. What The Bible tells us about homosexuality is clear in the above verses.

If you see someone speeding down the road and YOU know the bridge is out and certain death awaits them unless they STOP IMMEDIATELY, it is kind of your duty to warn them. Sure part of you wants to say "who cares, if they're gonna do something that dumb let them fall to their own folly." But, part of you wants to shout a warning and tell them to stop. If they choose to ignore you and continue on in their folly, then you are guiltless. The road to freedom from past guilts starts with repentance. God is willing to forgive any and all, but you have to go to Him on His terms not your own. 2 peter 3:9- The LORD is not slack concerning his promise, as some men count slackness; not willing that any should perish; but that all should come to repentance.

It's still a choice one has to make individually.

It all comes down to one of two choices.

1. Either you believe God.
2. You count Him a Liar.

You can't have it both ways. It's either one or the other. Forever is a long time.

So, as far as school went, and regardless of any liberal feelings being hurt and their leftist egos bruised, I asked my questions and wrote my papers from my heart. But more importantly, I enjoyed the writing process. I tackled such fun and "controversial" or "non-issue" subjects such as gay marriage. THEY chose the books and topics, not I. I would have made wiser choices. As the above states quite obviously, scripture has plenty to say about the topic; both Old and New Testament alike. You don't have to seek Gods approval for something He has already very clearly given His absolute disapproval of. The class was fun for me; and I attempted to glean from such whatever constructive criticisms were aimed at just the writing; and not what were just shielded attacks on my religious beliefs or personal political leanings. Such was not an easy task in such an environment. But, that is what writing is really all about, putting your heart to print. That is what the Bible is. In essence, it is Gods heart in print. If you want to know Him. You have to begin with, and do it through The Word. His Word. His Way. By His Son, Jesus Christ. John 14:6: No one cometh unto the Father, but by me. The truth of that verse tends to leave out all but True Biblical Christianity. The Buddhist, the Muslim, the jungle pagan, the (cultists) the (fill in the blank). Any way that is not the way set forth by The Lord Jesus Christ in His perfect, complete and Holy Word, is the wrong way! Period!

It is that simple. Scripture is very clear. Like it or not, it is the truth. That may appear arrogant or exclusive. It is neither. It is Bible and it is Truth. Better to find out now when you can still do something about it than to trust some other means and find out you were wrong only when it is too late and you can do absolutely nothing to change it. Hell is a terribly real place. Your body will be prepared in such a way as to never be desensitized to the searing flame. Memories will haunt you. Pain caused to others. Miseries and deliberate wrongs brought to others by you. Every harsh word uttered by you, in secret or shouted will be known to all. Each opportunity and each denial of Jesus that you've had throughout your life will be made known. Complete darkness, complete loneliness, complete fear, utter hopelessness, no rest, real pain, real flame, real fire, Forever. Hell is not just a euphemistic burning thirst for God as some have called it; though that may well be a part of it. Telling folks Hell is just a dark ages mentality sounds good and comforting and it fills the pews and coffers on Sunday mornings, but it is slightly askew by Biblical standards.

That being said, Hell is very real. It is a literal place that Christ Himself spoke of and warned of. Luke 12:5 But I will forewarn you whom ye shall fear; fear him, that after he hath killed hath the power to cast into hell; yea I say unto you, Fear Him. Life and death is in Gods hands, no one else's. People are sinners in need of a savior, it's that simple. Do what you will with this knowledge. (John 14:6) I am the way the truth and the life, no man comes unto the father but by me. Saying such a thing in todays climate will likely get you jailed on a hate speech charge. I've heard it put that BIBLE stands for Basic Instructions Before Leaving Earth. I by no means am intending to trivialize Gods Word, the acronym fits, is all. No one gets out of life alive.

I want to look back just a few years.

God knew that I would one day come to the realization of His Lordship and that I would cry out and claim Him as my personal Lord and Savior. He gracefully spared me much harm, including certain death on more than one occasion. There was the lessons that only the professor of pain could teach, but death was kept at bay each time. Before I knew Him or even had any inkling of wanting to know Him, God knew, loved, cared, for and about me. Some of the below will explain such.

Years ago, My dad had a friend with a cottage on Cape Cod. We normally rented it for a couple weeks each summer. My sister got to bring a friend with her and I got to bring my buddy Mike. This year Mike and I had brought some fireworks with us, nothing big mind you, just some packs of bottle rockets and those little "black cat" firecrackers. You could actually buy em in the 70's and early 80's. It was cool lighting them off on the dunes. Especially with our little plastic army guys we were playing with in the sand. It added a measure of realism to our rather vivid imaginations. We were having a great time, shooting off bottle rockets and blowing up little sandcastles. Harmless fun for a couple kids. Like I said, you could buy them, but USING them was often a different story. Our mistake was making our launching point directly at the bottom of the dune that connected to the parking lot.

Had we walked down the beach a ways where wind and waves could have masked our activities we might have fared better. Oh well, in everything there is lesson to be learned. Hopefully, to be learned the first time, or preferably by watching others folly and taking the learned lesson to heart and thus not doing it yourself and falling into the same pit of shame and possible pain.

I had just put the bottle rockets launch stick of another rocket I intended to launch into the sand and set the angle at ninety degrees. I only had a few left and figured I might as well use em up, we were going home in a couple days. Mike turned and looked up towards the parking lot. "Hey, there's somebody up there." He said. I turned and took a quick peek. Sure enough, there was indeed someone standing at the dune-top. He was silhouetted by the parking lot streetlight. He was just standing there looking down at us. My glance lasted about 2 or 3 seconds. I looked back at Mike and said. "Who cares." or "So what." and lit the wick. The rocket launched straight and true. Whoosh... POP. Cool! We looked back up the dune. The shadowy figure was now charging down the dune with a flashlight on; the bouncing beam of the flashlight proved as he made a bee-line towards us. He was already halfway to us. Panic rushed in! "RUN" Mike shouted and off we went in a flash.

It's not easy to run on sand as it is, and we still had our sneakers on. If you've done it, you know what I mean. It kinda felt like I was running in place, and I don't know that we got more than five steps before we heard. "FREEZE, POLICE!" From behind us. We both watched the TV show "chips" and knew the routine. So we froze and turned around. I don't remember if we put our hands in the air and "reached" as the term goes. The guy was still about 20 yards away and rapidly closing that short distance and I said to Mike. "That's not a cop, he's just trying to scare us." My heart was still pounding like crazy, however.

How many reading this have ever been dead wrong about something they were so dead sure of? With wavering and utterly false confidence we waited for this individual to reach us. Sure enough, the closer he got the clearer he became and the sound of his keys and cuffs and holster jingling came to my ears. Then he was standing in front of us. Yup, he was for real all right. I could clearly see the badge and gun and uniform even with his mag-lights powerful beam blazing through my cornea's. He "confiscated" the paltry amount of fireworks we had remaining and marched us up the dune to meet our doom. There sat his cruiser. He led us to the back of it. He frisked us quickly and put us in the back of his squad car. He got in behind the wheel and without turning around he asked if we were there on vacation and where we were staying. After a sullen spoken "yeah." I showed him how to get to the cottage 1/4 mile away; all the while whispering to Mike, "my dad's gonna kill me..." over and over again, which of course was a complete exaggeration. He was an engineer and not a hit man at that point in his life. Neither is he now, he is a retired pastor. Just gotta clear that up.

At this point, Dad was enjoying a quiet and quite peaceful evening by himself, all by his lonesome in the solitude. That was about to change. Mom had gone out with my sister and my sisters friend. He and Kimo, our faithful Husky were at the cottage kicking back and "chillin out" before that phrase was even known or popular. The cop let us sit in the back of the car and went up to the door. I could see them; the cop and my dad, and even kimo peering out the lower screen, but I couldn't hear them. Then the cop came back and got us out of the car, and marched us to the door. He told dad he was leaving us in his "custody." Loudly enough for the two of us to get his point. He told the three of us that fireworks were illegal in Massachusetts and to enjoy the rest of our vacation. I think at that point in time the only thing that wasn't illegal or taxed in some way in the Democrat controlled Utopian State of Massachusetts was walking and breathing. That has probably changed in the last thirty years since then, but chalk that one up as another lesson learned, I suppose.

A few years later Mike and I were at home in the neighborhood enjoying the summer, shooting baskets, building tree forts, riding our bikes and even more fun; riding go carts and mini-bikes. Yes, that was illegal too, but it was grand fun indeed. Mikes dad had built both the mini-bike and the go cart. He was a town engineer and one of those kind of guys that could fix, weld or build literally just about anything. Mikes mini-bike was kind of like a tiny Harley Davidson motorcycle. It was big and burly, grey and black. Wide stance, big tires, 10 hp tractor engine wedged uncomfortably in the hand made frame. It looked cool, like something out of a "mad max" movie. We both wore crash helmets so at the very least we'd be somewhat safe when we drove or rode our illegal, unlicensed motor vehicles on the public streets of our sleepy little neighborhood. I stood in the culdesac and watched Mike go down towards his house just 5 houses down and turn the corner and disappear. The motor was running normally when all of a sudden it revved, wined, popped rather loudly, then abruptly stopped. I chuckled, thinking it had stalled when he tried to pull a wheelie. All was silent. He didn't start it up again. When it didn't start after a minute or two I started jogging down towards his house. A fuel line? A flat tire? What happened? I was about to find out.

When I got there the mini bike was laying half in the driveway and half on the curb. The chain was in the street as well was a portion of the clutch. Mike was exiting his house holding a bloody cloth over his eye and his mom was right beside him. "What Happened." I shockingly querried? "The clutch blew up an' got me." was all he said, and off they went to the Emergency room for stitches.

I knew nothing of prayer at this point in my life, I mean, I never prayed. I never even thought of it, why should I? My youthful arrogance and indestructibility made me; so I thought, invincible. I therefore never considered just how very frail and destructible I really was. I had never thought too much about the fragility of life. I simply took things like eyesight and hearing and walking for granted. Evolution was touted as the one and only truth on every public and tax paid for forum around. From the schoolroom to the newsroom the state would not allow us; the public, to learn or believe any other. We were all once nothing but pond-scum and now look at us, oh boy. Bigger and better everyday. Look what we can do. We can do anything. We can probe the oceans depths and land on the moon. We're awesome. Pretty impressive for some goo that oozed out from under a rock one day a zillion years ago wouldn't you say?

He'd be Okay, I assured myself. I scooped up the mini-bike and walked it back to his garage and then played basketball in the circle until I saw their car return. Then I went to see Mike. His eye was all bandaged up. But, he still had it.

Apparently the clutch "slipped" out of it's housing. These type of clutches have four metal "shoes" held together with a large coiled spring. They spin more rapidly as the throttle is applied and the "shoes" grab the metal housing acceleration occurs. When the shoe assembly slipped out of the metal cover the four shoes expanded, and not having the metal housing to contain them and give them something to grab onto, simply "flew" apart in all directions. Mike was looking directly at it and one of the shoes caught him right in the corner of one of his eye sockets near the eyebrow. He needed stitches, I forget how many. His dad fixed the mini-bike and engineered and welded on a hand fashioned clutch shield to prevent a return of the clutch failure. Done and done! Thoughts of vision loss never occurred to me, he had been "lucky" is all.

I suppose my close call with potential vision loss came to visit me during "target practice" with my BB gun. Thinking on it now, it reminds of the movie "The Christmas Story" when "Ralphie" got his Red Rider BB gun and was shooting it in his back yard. A "ricochet" off an icicle went through his glasses and freaked him out. In somewhat similar fashion, target practice with the pellet/BB Gun was a fun and often daily amusement I engaged in. For whatever reason, I was extremely close to the targets this day. Point blank, is the term used for this range of distance. Perhaps five feet, if that. Certainly closer than I should have been. My target was a row of empty soda cans I had placed atop my tree house. Seeing the carnage to those cans at such close range was gratifying, yeah, I know, I was an odd kid, perhaps. Said tree house was three tiers high, constructed of a pile of nails of every sort, size and variety, scrap plywood, nails, old wooden shutters, nails, pallets, nails, ratty 2X4's I found in the woods, and did I mention nails? It was constructed down on the hill by my parents house. It made a great backstop for BB's and a semi-decent backstop for arrows. My neighbor much to his chagrin found many a "missing" arrow with his lawn mower. Anyhow, without me even realizing it or knowing it, one of the earlier experiences with the protecting hand of God on my life was a ricochet that hit me dead center between the eyes, right over the bridge of my glasses above my nose. I had a nice little red welt there for a couple days after that.

The BB had apparently hit dead center one of the thousands of various sized nails used in the forts slipshod construction and decided to bounce directly back at my face, striking me dead center between the eyes right above the bridge of my glasses! Having learned a quick and uncomfortable lesson, I shot at a slight angle and an increased range after that experience. A fraction of an inch to the left or right and I'd have lost an eye for sure. That was a close call. I didn't think a whole lot of it at the time and after rubbing the impact site for a moment or two, I foolishly cursed the inanimate nails and went back to shooting my row of cans. Boy, I sure got even with those cans for that near miss, let me tell you. I thought nothing about God having protected my vision. I had just been "lucky" is all. The only evidence was a tiny red welt that rose quickly and faded in a day or two. My thoughts of God at that juncture in life were "afar" off, not to mention afar off in completely the wrong direction. My own direction with my own views of God, who He was, and how to reach Him. It certainly wasn't a Biblical view, but I didn't know that, how could I. I was too busy doing my own thing and God was on a high shelf. I, like many folks I'm sure, assumed God was like the genie in a bottle that you could take down off the shelf and uncork when you needed Him and then put Him back in there after He had done your bidding or got too embarrassing to have around. Wrong! Wrong! Wrong! Very Wrong! Also very wrong is the white haired impotent old grandfather type who gets sad when His creations do "bad" things but still accepts any, and all into His Heaven, regardless of situation or circumstance. Just live a good life and everybody will be okay. That's a view many hold and have held throughout history, but according to The Bible, such thoughts are a lie.

Mankind in and of himself is NOT good, and cannot do good or please God apart from Him. Any way other than Gods way, is the wrong way. Period! To get to Gods Heaven, you have to do it Gods way. The way He tells us in His perfect Word. He created the place and thus He can make the entry rules and He alone gives the entrance exam. We humans, being vile, reprobate sinners cannot enter Gods perfect and Holy Heavenly Home of our own accord. Never, no how and no way. In John (10:7&9) Jesus reveals to us that He; Jesus Christ, is the door; the entrance, to Heaven. We cannot even look upon Him without complete and utter shame. Unfortunate for us, but Fortunately Jesus Christ has already passed the entrance exam for us. Only through Him and His way can we ever hope to enter in. No other individual in history has so willingly sacrificed Himself for you. You may be very genuine and sincere, but you are sincerely wrong if you believe you can make it to God's Heaven any other way other than the one and only way He provided by The Lord Jesus Christ Himself. Doing a lifetime of "good works" and living a "good life" is worthless, and is of absolutely zero value apart from Christ. This is a truth I never learned until much later in life; and after much pain and misery that could well have been avoided. Even the jungle heathen can look around the natural world around him and see there is indeed a creator... (Acts 17:23 For I passed by, and beheld your devotions, I found the alter with this inscription, TO THE UNKNOWN GOD. whom therefore ye ignorantly worship, him I declare unto you.) Paul then showed them the truth, and the one and only true and living God, Jesus Christ.

Friends normally come and go throughout our lives, normally making long lasting impressions for good, or bad. All of life's experiences go into our memory banks whether we want them to or not. Thus is one of the blessings of having "short-term" memory loss. It can be a double edged sword, however. A pleasant experience can be relived as if new, and an unpleasant experience, easily forgotten, and vise versa. The key to success is "repetition."

Have a routine to follow and do it over and over and over, be deliberately redundant. Leave important items such as wallet and keys in the same place every night. Attach them to your belt via one way or another. A chain or keyring loop of some type. If you don't, you're going to be in for an unpleasant surprise when you awake. For sure, whatever you need will not be where "you left it" but more often than not, in the place you left it before that, or even before that, wherever that place might happen to be. It can be maddening, and so very frustrating. Without repetition or a routine to follow, it WILL happen.

I again want to go back in time for moment here to relay a couple of things that have relevance on my characters formation. Above any thing else, perhaps the biggest thing that made high school a real blast was the fact that during my freshman year a curvature of my spine known as scoliosis, was discovered. The curvature was two fold, causing me to "hunch" forward and also causing one shoulder blade to be a tad lower than the other. This dual curvature confined me to a cumbersome plastic and metal contraption that gave my entire upper body the movements of a nineteen fifties Frankenstein movie monster. Logically, this of course was right in that timeframe of that odd, "uncomfortable" time betwixt boys and girls where the skin depthness of physical appearances seems to be foremost in the minds of 97 percent of teenagers. Such do not seem to consider that all it takes is one wrong step or one missed stop sign and that all important physical appearance can be permanently and forever changed. In less time than it takes to snap your fingers.

Television and movies did nothing to discourage this, but rather the opposite. As things tend to get worse with time, not better, today it is far, far worse. I wrote a story about betrayal and vengeance. I penned a joyful twisted little tale I wrote about the now defunct Bradlee's department store chain and the back brace I was confined to for 23 hours a day for the growing curvature in my spine. After being hired by a lower level manager without the brace on; but disclosing that it existed and I had to wear it. I appeared for my first first shift at work with the brace on; and was summarily let go by a higher ranking manager. Understandable to a liability degree I suppose. This was to be my first "real job." But no. So, I made up a Waister story about a kid with a peg-leg and let Him take care of the matter for me.

1 Corinthians 2:14 - but the natural (unregenerate) man receiveth not the things of the Spirit of God: for they are foolishness unto him: neither can he know them for they are spiritually discerned. Waister dealt with the situation with quite a bit of pent up anger. The Non-Christian Waister did not understand the Biblical reference showing that anger rested in the bosom of fools he just pushed through and said it like he saw it. It was excellent stress relief. The non-Christian

Waister is quite the ugly, vile, reprehensible and rather profane creature which makes sense because it shows the true genuine nature of the unregenerate man as I was at the time I wrote it.

Unless I were in a swimming pool or shower, this back brace had to be worn for 23 out of the 24 hours we are given in a day. As you can well imagine this was a big plus in hooking up with the ladies. After all, it was every high school girls dream to be seen with turtle boy and his metal and plastic shell, right? (I am being facetious in case you were wondering) I would not understand until much later in life that this experience was actually a very great and tremendous blessing that I would not now trade for all the tea in China; and I like tea. However, at the time I was living it, I began having doubts about who God was and if He cared at all. I wrote a "statement of faith" for the youth group at the Congregational Church I attended then, concerning God's existence; who He was; and wondering at that point of life if He was indeed a loving God and if He cared about me at all. Listening with a pliable, soft, and hearable heart would have revealed such to me, but I had to learn the hard way. Typical stubborn New Englander, right?

Besides all that I went to a technical high school, and in those days most girls that went to technical high schools where kind of scary. There was three in my graduating class and perhaps 15 in the whole school if that many. Slim pickings with prospects few to none for a guy that hated drink and cigarettes and was wrapped in a metal and plastic shell.

I would find out later in life that He does indeed care very, very much. So much so that He spared me untold grief and pain by not being "Mr. popular." Wearing that confounded, confining, despised-by-me, brace might well have kept those scary kind of girls away. Not being Mr. popularity was a blessing-in-disguise. It meant not being invited to the "parties" that high school kids foolishly seem to think are so vital to their social well being. Not being part of this party-crowd-mentality meant not having the peer pressures and temptations of drugs and cigarettes and alcohol and premarital explorations with the opposite sex. I am tremendously, beyond thankful for this today. But back then while I was living it, I was completely miserable. I hated my existence. I would fly into fits of rage over the smallest things. I would get mad at

God and stupidly shake my fist at Him. If He was so good, then why was all this happening to me? Again my focus was on "self." I was not a Christian; and did not know God at that point in my life. I thought I did, as many think they do today, but my understanding of God at that point was in error as well. (1 Corinthians 2:14) "But the natural man, receiveth not the things of the Spirit of God: for they are foolishness unto him: neither can he know them for they are spiritually discerned." I had no understanding nor concept of who God really was and why, if at all, He could ever have a use of someone like me. My view of Him was in complete error. A view molded by soft preaching, wrong films and wrong music. It is only by His inexplicable Grace that I avoided the multitude of temptations that bombard kids in the public school system and life in general. Unfortunately, Satan is alive and well here in America. Fortunately, his time is very short.

Unfortunately, he knows it. He hates your guts too, especially if you are a Christian. Just being a human is enough, because your triune make up of body, soul, spirit reminds him of God; Father, Son, Spirit. (Gen 2:7) Why else would things be moving so quickly towards deeper ruin and disaster? Since satan is in control of the world system both militarily and financially, such is to be expected.

Of course, I was not a Christian in these days. I THOUGHT I was; but that didn't make it so.

Besides; what did all that mean? All religions are the same right? Don't they all point to the same God? Sure, people do bad stuff but God is Love, is He not? Yes, that is true. He even tells us as much (1 John 4:8 God is Love) But He is also many other things. Including Righteous and Holy. (verses...?) As well as Counselor, Creator and Savior, and one day very soon, Judge.

I, being a sinner, could not stand before Him as Judge on my own haunches or baubles. In Isaiah 64:6 through His prophet God informs us of His opinion of our "goodness." "But we are all as an unclean thing, and all our righteousnesses are as filthy rags; and we all do fade as a leaf; and our iniquities, like the wind, have taken us away." Well, that's a pretty bleak assessment of mankind by our Creator. But it is dead on target. Watch any nightly news cast for 30 seconds if you disagree and it will be proved to you. Mankind is not getting progressively better as days and years progress but the opposite. 2 Tim 3:13 clearly gives us mans wretched state. "But evil men and seducers shall wax worse and worse, deceiving and being deceived." Pretty bleak and terrifyingly accurate description of todays political realm isn't it? Not to mention people in general.

Yet again, I rectified my frustrations and masked my anger in writing. The masses of Freudian Fools littering our cultural landscape would surely be terrified and quaking in large puddles of their own making at this "escape" tool, as such crackpots would surely call it. Such people are the cause of much grief in our society. Sure, my temper was explosive and my fuse extremely short, quite often next to none-existent. But it didn't drive me into a tower with a rifle because I knew that wouldn't do me any good. My tower was my typewriter and my rifle was my writing, each word it's own projectile. The character I had created; Jack M Waister, had life anew and continued to right wrongs and even the score. His way. I have no idea what hat I pulled that name out of, but he is with me to this day.

As stated, in high school; my best friend got a job at a local Bradlee's department store in town, so I went down and applied. I was hired by the assistant manager. Alright! I'd be working with my best friend, this would be cool. I showed up for work the next day and met with the general manager to get my uniform shirt and work schedule. He told me that I could not work there with the brace on because of liability reasons. End of story. Bye! As I remember, my dad was furious and went down there to "talk" to the guy. I suppose I could have pursued some legal matter with this issue but I was too upset at that moment to even think like that. This was the 1980's and frivolous lawsuits did not clog the nations courtrooms as they do in these gimme, gimme, gimme, greed-filled later days of ours. Besides, what would that have proved? I ended up getting a job with the grocery store down the street. They didn't have a problem with the brace at all, and I worked there all through high school and it paid my gas and insurance. Today that grocery store is still in business while the department store went belly up years ago. Not that that means anything, but it simply shows that if such attitudes and fears of lawyers and lawsuits prove anything it is that such are quite costly in more ways than one. There WAS an alternative to the brace, and that alternative was a metal rod being welded or fused to my spine. Boy, that sounded like loads of fun. As you can well imagine, I elected to go with the removable back brace. The first three years of high school were spent 23 hours a day in the ruthless clutches of my own personal body armor going from the waist and up around my neck. I have to admire the creativity of some of my classmates who nicknamed me Roll Cage Russ. Yeah, it could have been far worse!

My point in relaying this is that it is an example of how I used my writing to deal with difficult situations. I wrote a Waister story about a kid with a peg leg whom a similar thing happened to. In my story, the hero "Waister" and the villain; "the store manager" whom I had named Winston Chashwarnagetts, yes; oddly enough I actually remember that fictitious moniker, had a "confrontation." Waister saw this kid with the pegleg come out of Chashswarnagettes office and being the observant fellow that he was, noticed that he was visibly upset. Waister stopped him and the kid told him that the manager fired him because the job required walking and he couldn't walk fast enough. Well now, Waister could not let such an injustice go unchallenged, and as his blood pressure was rising he marched into the guys office and confronted him. I don't recall their verbal exchange but the manager was quite belligerent and unreasonable, not to mention downright nasty and rude. I think I also mentioned that he was a foul democrat, political persuasions being ingrained in me even then. Waister ended up coaxing Chashwarnagetts to take a poke at him. Waister smiled and, being an eight degree black belt, was able to thwart the feeble, wimpafied attempt and quite easily break Chashwarnagetts frail little arm with very little effort; in not one, but in three different places. Of course, I realize now that such a display would have been in conflict with the mentality of a true martial artists discipline and self control. When I wrote that story I was not training in the martial arts as I have since done. I wrote it from a vendetta and settling a score mentality. A true martial artist has self-control because he knows what he can do to another human being. True to human nature, everyone likes to see the bad guy get what WE feel he deserves and Waister liked to pass out the award certificates. He felt it is duty to his fellow man. Neither Waister, nor I, knew at that time the scripture that said "vengeance is mine, I will repay sayeth The Lord. (Rom 12:19)

He was and is his own entity; Jack M Waister. He is reminiscent of a Chuck Norris/Clint Eastwood/Monty Python/Jackie Gleason type of a character just to drop a few names. If the four of them were morphed into one entity, it would be a close approximation to Jack M. Waister. Waister has changed and grown with me over the years. Just for kicks one day I typed the word "Waister" into my computer browser and found it to be the name of some kind of Swedish brazier strap that secures around the belly hence the name, Waister. Odd, but it may explain a few things, or nothing at all. It was also the name of a British sailor of yesteryear who's job it was to remain in the deepest bowels of the old wooden vessels. I presume to ward off any hull leaks.

Anyhow, with a little help, Winston Chashwarnagetts winded up "accidentally" falling through the mirrored security panels located on the second floor of his office. He landed on a row of carriages, breaking his other arm. He lay there staring at the ceiling, twitching and convulsing. As the ambulance took him away, Waister shouted to him… "Hope your resumes in good order, you'll surely be fired because your job requires you to write and you can't write with two broken arms." Waister then took the kid with the peg leg out for ice cream to celebrate their victory, and gave him a job working in his gunsmith shop.

Sure it was an utterly ludicrous and ridiculous story, but it was fun to write and it was stress relief for me. That was the main way I dealt with difficult situations. Some folks lock themselves into a room, others hit the gym. Some eat (this last one is not recommended). I wrote. Surely all the sinister witchdocto… I mean psychologists of the day would have labeled me with one of their "conditions" and attempt to pump me full of some of their noxious potions to "cure" me of the fictitious disorder they would gleefully have sentenced upon me. No matter, I just kept writing. After all, I dreamed of one day becoming a writer and that is what writers did, was it not, they wrote!

Just for kicks one day I penned out a bunch of one-liners Jack Waister might and occasionally uses.

Waisterisms: Words of Wisdom by Jack M. Waister

The citizen who shirks his duty to contribute to the security of his community by packing heat, is little better than the criminals and thugs who daily threaten it.
                Jack M. Waister.

A gun in the hand is better than ten guns locked up in the safe.
                Jack M. Waister.

A liberal is an utterly useless life form which contributes nothing but grief and heartache to any unfortunate society it so attaches itself to.
                Jack M. Waister.

The creeping death-rot of socialism is the weeping arbuckle(boil) that renders a free society undone(impotent)
                Jack M. Waister.

Why waste paper on target practice when a liberal is handy?
                Jack M. Waister.

A liberal and a leech share the same common purpose.
                Jack M. Waister.

Liberals are like itching powder... they irritate whatever place they get into....
                Jack M. Waister.

An armed man is a free man... a dis-armed man is a subject...
                Jack M. Waister. (Not original)

A regulated man is a slave...
                Jack M. Waister.

Liberalism is a cancer destroying and sucking the lifeblood from the American dream.
> Jack M. Waister.

The purpose of a liberal is to stir the blood of the slumbering patriot and re-awaken him to his duty as a citizen.
> Jack M. Waister.

Two guns are better than one, and three are better still.
> Jack M. Waister.

Liberalism arises when Patriots slumber.
> Jack M. Waister.

0A gun without bullets is a dog without teeth.
> Jack M. Waister.

If you eat fried grease, expect a short life.
> Jack M. Waister.

Venison hamburgers are delicious and healthy.
> Jack M. Waister.

I love animals, they taste great.
> Jack M. waister (not original)

If you don't brush your teeth, don't offer kisses.
> Jack M. Waister.

If you can't shoot straight, practice more.
> Jack M. Waister.

Learn to shoot with both hands, and even your feet if possible, your very life as well as the lives of others may depend upon it one day.
> Jack M. Waister.

Oppose big government, embrace liberty.
Jack M. Waister.

Assume that your fellow man has mayhem in mind for you and yours and you will be ever vigilant.
Jack M. Waister.

When the vessel is blown from the water beneath you, your wounds are bleeding profusely, the waters are shark infested, your lifeboat is leaky, has no oars, a snapped sail mast, a torn sail, an outboard that has fallen overboard, an inboard with a blown head gasket, no floatation cushions, no fishing lines, no flare gun, no medical kit, no water, no food, no signal light or mirror... Never, Never. Never! quit the battle. Fight to the very last breath escapes your lunges.
Jack M. Waister.

That is a very brief taste of the fictitious persona of Jack M. Waister.

Around this time era was when I was in the "youth group" of the congregational church I went to with the rest of the family. About this time the "statement of faith" is something the teens penned in our particular congregational churches "youth group." Mine was by and large an allegorical scribbling about my back brace. I was not sure exactly what I believed of, and, or, about God at that stature of life. I believed in God as many wise folks do to this day. Unfortunately, MY god was like many others peoples, he was the one I had conjured up in my mind. Hey, I believed; I was sincere; but I was sincerely wrong. Like many today my god served me well, soothing my conscience with soft lies. He didn't convict me about all the attitudes, language, actions and things (sin) I had been doing. Not one time can I recall "feeling bad" about my actions or attitudes. My god was my pal that agreed with all I thought or did. This was the time of the aforementioned Back Brace and oohh was it a time of questions. All the "why's" in my head and doubts I had of God. Questions looking back now it reveals to me a searching or a longing for something unseen or unreachable. A "girlfriend" was unattainable for a guy like me; or so I thought. Being so pre-conditioned to think I had to have a girlfriend at my young age or there was something "wrong with me"; by society, by music, by movies and television. The homosexual/sodomite crowds feed on thoughts and confusions like these as ravenous wolves do on a dead deer carcass. Disgusting but true in both cases. Such a debauched lifestyle is not normal, it is very clearly a choice; (lev 18:22-) the guilt brought on by it destroys a life just as quickly as any disease normally associated with such a lifestyle. There is guilt because deep down these folks "know" it is altogether, absolutely, 100 percent WRONG. Life left little room for waiting on God and allowing Him to bring the right girl along. And, I most assuredly wanted a girl by my side, no question about that one. True to my born in human nature. I was impatient and wanted everything MY way, and I wanted it "NOW."

I did not yet know nor understand the principle of "waiting on God". That is still a concept that is hard to grasp; even for a well seasoned Christian. Impatience is a nasty streak to overcome. God is right there when we need Him. Jeremiah 23:23. Am I a God at hand (right here) and not a God afar off. God is never late. He is always on time. Psalm 37:34, Zephaniah 3:8, Pro 20:22, Ps 27:14, and many other verses plead with us impatient human critters to simply excersize patience, and wait. Wait? For how long? For who? How could you wait on someone you didn't even know? What did that mean exactly anyhow? Wait on God? How? Did He go somewhere and isn't home yet? Reminds me of the new testament example when The Apostle Paul was speaking to the heathen, he's gone on a long journey and isn't home, shout louder, cut deeper! That is a very brief paraphrase of Acts 17:16-34. Paul says that these folks were "wholly given" to idolotry, and like people today, want it OUR way. Thing is, it won't work. Never has and never will.

When we decide to push God into our idea of what His will must be for our lives, we will come out short every single time and God will still be glorified. He loves us and is altogether interested in the absolute best for us. He is outside of time and space, time and space are for us not God. He spoke it all into existence and tries His utmost to have us understand what is really important. Jonah is one good example of this. He ran the opposite direction when God told him to go preach to the Ninevite's. These folks were his peoples avowed enemy. Jonah didn't want mercy shown to these critters, he wanted them wiped out. No way did he want to give them a message of God's grace and forgiveness. They were ripe for it. God knew this. Jonah had too much hate in his heart for "those people" to see Gods mercy; or the true need of the desperate Ninevite's.

To back that thought up, I included a brief Bible Study of mine I penned a ways back on the Book of Jonah. It is certainly not exhaustive and much can be added. But, at the time of it's writing, I simple entitled it Tools! It is written from a singular point of view and I have seen others that approach the book from a different angle and they too are loaded with good thoughts. Just one more example of the wideness and greatness of Gods Inexhaustible, Holy, Unsearchable and Perfect Word.

TOOLS: A brief Jonah study.

God sometimes brings a storm into our lives to get us right with Him, as well as getting those around us (through our example, good or bad) right with Him as well…

God chose Jonah, to serve Him with glee…
Jonah chose not God, but instead rose to flee…

TOOLS:

Even the old, rusty, broken, twisted, bent, and relatively "worthless" tools (people) can be used greatly by a Great GOD. Even the ones that have become tarnished or rusty and are lying in the bottom of the box for lack of use, might, and could still be used in a great way by a great God. That's how patient and loving He is. God likes using tools it seems, He is a creative God, He walked Earth as a carpenter after all. Just like a guy who can't let himself throw away that rusty old screwdriver because it can still be used for some job he might have to do at sometime in the future. God doesn't wish to put aside any of His tools either, such seems to be the case with a tool called Jonah. Jonah was the son of a lesser known prophet, but a prophet just the same. Maybe God had spoken through his dad once or twice, certainly not a lot or we woulda heard more about him. Jonah was following in the family business it seems. Here's a guy, that, on the surface seems to be kinda ordinary. We aren't given a whole lot of info on the guy other than he was a prophet, and that he was the son of a guy named Amittai. And the only mention of Amittai I can find in scripture is in 2 King 15:25 which stated that he also was a prophet and the region he lived in. From what I can find it is somewhere around what is known today as the Dead Sea, but in Biblical times it was called the Salt Sea. So it seems that Jonah was simply an ordinary guy, as I. From an ordinary town, as I. But God wanted to use him, and God prepared a bunch of things in order to prepare reluctant Jonah. He easily could have prepared Jonah for the task he was giving him had Jonah simply obeyed from the get go. We aren't told exactly "how" The Word of the Lord came to Jonah, but it very clearly did. As well Jonah apparently knew exactly what it was, and it certainly was not his imagination, nor to his liking for that matter. So, as Jonah made his preparations to disobey, God was making some preparations of His own...

He prepared a fish… just one…

He prepared a gourd… just one…

He even prepared a worm… just one…

God had also prepared the Ninevites, much to Jonah's dismay.

All these preparations to prepare His reluctant prophet.

I don't think it is as important an issue as to HOW Jonah got the message, but that he did indeed GET the message and understood it, clearly and completely. Jonah knew "exactly" what God wanted him to do. As there was no UPS service in those days one might only speculate that perhaps God spoke to his prophet Jonah in a dream? We aren't told, we also aren't told what Jonah "did" before this episode? We don't know so it must not be important or relative. he only indication is that he was apparently was following in his dads footsteps, and was also a prophet. Don't know for certain because we aren't told. Any guessing on our part is just that, guessing. However, Jonah IS mentioned briefly in the Gospels, by Jesus himself when discussing the events of the crucifixion shortly before He willingly went to the cross and literally "became sin" for us. So, apparently, something a bitter old crab named Jonah has to teach us must be rather significant. Yes, we understand now, that the three days in the fishes(whale) innards was in comparison to Christ's 3 days in the grave. We can also know by this that the tale of Jonah is not a cute little childs story; but that it actually happened just as described!

The Bible simply says that the LORD (all caps) indicating God The Father as the speaker, came unto Jonah "saying", so we know it was audible. In verse 2 of chapter 1 God gives Jonah very clear instructions. ARISE! GO! PREACH! 3 explicit commands. God even gives Jonah a reason… "Because their wickedness is come up before Me." That God told him to Arise, Go, Preach should have been enough; without the reason. God doesn't have to tell us "WHY" all the time. It's not for us to know why, and most of the time it is better that we DON'T know "why", but simply to obey. That is hard to understand, but that's where Faith comes in I suppose. How much do we (I) really trust God? Asking "Why" seems to indicate that we don't trust Him…? I don't know, but even after God gives Jonah the reason, what does he do…? Does he jump on his horse, donkey, camel (if he had one) and gleefully run to do Gods bidding…? Nope. He very clearly knew Gods will, and he blatantly disregarded it and downright ignored it altogether.

Ol' Jonah goes the opposite direction as God had commanded him. God said go "this" way and Jonah purposed in his heart to say NO and went "that" way. We can read the whole story and know the ending, but are we any different today concerning our own obedience? Just as we cannot see tomorrow for today, neither could Jonah see the outcome, he only knew what "Those people, Those rotten Ninevites" were like and went on his assumption of their uselessness without considering Gods view of the lost soul. Hmmm, interesting, how closely does our (my) eyesight resemble the Lords…? Or is it closer to Jonah's…?

Today The Holy Spirit reveals to us through prayer and the reading and preaching of Gods word the direction we should go. But do we (I) heed (listen, follow, obey, His leading.)? Likely, not as we should be doing it. The more you are in The Word of God, reading and studying it, the clearer you will hear God Speaking to you through His Holy Spirit.

I find it interesting how it says that Jonah "rose" up to "flee" to Tarshish "from" the presence of the LORD. Now, I find that wording odd. Jonah is a prophet. His dad was a prophet. He of all people aught to have known that there is no place he could flee to, that was beyond Gods reach. For God is ever, always, everywhere present. You cannot "get away" from God, especially when He has called you and told you to do something important for Him. One way or another, you WILL do it. Jonah is soon to get a quick refresher lesson on just how far Gods grasp is. It appears that Jonah is somewhat far from God at this juncture in his life. We are not told if something had occurred just prior to this that soured Jonah's relationship (at least from his standing) with God. Had he been on the shelf for a while? Unused and dormant? Making him more bitter than he had been for God to have put him there to begin with? Had he been lazy in his walk with God? Had his prayer life been weak? Whatever his reason for doing so, (disobeying that is) It was unjustified. For God is good. All the time! Any communication problem, was Jonah's. Likewise, with us. The communication problem is ours, not Gods. Either we "don't wanna." or we "ask amiss" James 4:3 "Ye ask and receive not, because ye ask amiss, that ye may consume it upon your lusts" or our attitude is wrong. God won't help us if we're carrying hatred in our hearts, or holding a grudge against somebody. That harms no one but ourselves, so what's the point. Jonah learned this the hard way. It must have been a huge disappointment to him and probably embarrassing too.

Jonah is soon to find out first hand that such blatant disobedience to the creator of the universe has it's costs. The first thing it did was cost him some money. Money in any day and time is hard to come by and likely was for Jonah as well. He obviously had some money because we are told that he "paid the fair thereof" when he bought his boat ticket to Tarshish. He didn't even barter. In his haste to flee from Almighty God, he just paid whatever they were asking, and climbed aboard. Already his disobedience has wasted his time and his money and he isn't even out to sea yet. He goes down into the "hold", or lower deck or whatever it was in that day. He went down into the darkness and lay down, silent and inactive. Maybe he thought God wouldn't see him if he put his head under the pillow in a dark corner and didn't move? Not a wise move on Jonah's part. He likely knew all too well that even the darkness is light to God. But, just like a little child when he wants to hide with the cookie he has swiped before dinnertime, Jonah is cowering from the perfect illumination of God in a dark corner of some cramped, musty, perhaps even questionably seaworthy craft. Not a good move on Jonah's part. He went down into the hold of a tiny ship to hide from Almighty God. Twice in verse three alone we read the words "from the presence of the LORD."

That is kind of a scary thought. I don't want to be away from Gods presence, but I know it isn't hard to put myself there. First thing Jonah did was say to himself, "No way, I'm not doing it, I don't like those people, I want God to wipe them out. They're Israel's sworn enemies. They hate us, and I hate them. Even you hate them God? What are you thinking God?" Next thing he did was act on those thoughts and tried and run. It's bad enough he had the thought, but then he dug the hole deeper and acted on that thought.

God however is not going to let Jonah off so easily. We don't know how far he got, just out of port, or miles out to sea but pretty quickly a rather large, and unexpected storm hits virtually out of nowhere. We can know this with a relative amount of certainty because the sailors would not have set to sea had their been any inclination of bad weather. We read a few verses deeper and see that they are not novice seamen. Before long, the ship is being thrown around most unpleasantly apparently for we read where the sailors were "afraid." These are guys that had certainly been in some storms in their time and knew what they were doing and how to maneuver their vessel, but they're absolutely terrified. This was no ordinary storm. It says that each one of them "cried unto his god" to save them. Apparently nothing happened. They try and lighten the ship by chucking their cargo into the sea. They wouldn't do this lightly because there was certainly a lot of money involved and would cost them. They were truly terrified for their very lives to be willing to do something like this.

Their own personal gods didn't save them…

Their own efforts didn't save them…

Had it been an ordinary storm perhaps doing these "things" in their own efforts might very well have helped, but the LORD had sent out this great wind and made this storm for a special purpose.

It also says, "But" (during all this) Jonah was "fast asleep"… he was completely unaware of anything going on around him. It's probably safe to speculate that it was not too quiet aboard and was not a calm ride at that moment, yet he was sound asleep, oblivious to his surroundings, sailors no doubt yelling, the boat being thrown to and fro. Cargo flying around about Jonah's head. It's not easy to sleep on a boat as it is, but one that is being tossed around like a cork in a bathtub doesn't compute good in the human brain that Jonah could be so "dumb" as to not be aware of his surroundings and his predicament. But then, how often are "we", "I" in similar Jonah-like circumstances of our own design and in exactly the same place as he…?

The captain comes running down to Jonah and wakes him up and has what could almost be a comical kind of exchange with him. "Good grief man, what are doing, get up and pray to your own god like everybody else is doing. Maybe that god will do something for us and we won't die." That is an obvious paraphrase of Jonah 1:6.

Apparently, Ol Jonah had put in with a band of heathen in his haste to flee from the one true God. Of course, Jonah didn't care, he just wanted to "get outa Dodge" as the saying goes, and did and said and paid whatever it took to accomplish his means. So here he is standing there on a storm tossed ship, rubbing the sleep from his eyes only to open them and find a bunch of panicked, superstitious sailors staring wide-eyed at him. They decide to draw straws to decide who's fault this storm is. Now, games of chance are not exactly a Godly persons past time but God used these guys superstition to nail Ol Jonah. Because we read that "the Lot fell on Jonah." I kinda wonder if he drew first or last and how much tension was in his heart as the lots got tossed or straws picked or however they did it. It must have been somewhat comical in an odd sort of way. Jonah knew better. He likely knew he would be chosen but didn't fess up before hand. Did he somehow think that God was not at work? NO! He knew because he told the other guys as soon as he picked the short straw. He fessed up right quick, "Oh yeah, heh heh, it's me guy's, I'm the one."

Now suddenly all these sailors seem to want more info on their passenger, and start asking him twenty questions. Who he was, what he did, where he came from, and the like. Apparently his money was the only language they had been concerned with when the ship sailed. I can imagine the look on their faces when he told them he was a Hebrew and served The Lord God who had made the dry land the seas. There's a big "oops" moment huh, yeah.

These guys are at a loss as to what to do. They even asked Jonah "What are we supposed to do with you so the sea will be calm?" Jonah, seeing his way out, smiles and said. "It's my fault guys, throw me in the ocean and you'll be fine." This is another paraphrase, of Verse 1:12.

I can only imagine Jonah's expression and thoughts as he said that. He might have been thinking that he had won, and pulled one over on God. Ha, what can you do know God, they throw me in and I drown and I don't have to go to Ninevah, OR, the ship sinks and I drown and I don't have to go to Ninevah. HA. Either way, I win. Jonah's rebellious, sinful attitude has now endangered more than just his own life and he couldn't care less. Ouch.

But the sailors turned away from ol' selfish, smug-faced Jonah and tried even harder get the ship turned and manageable but they couldn't do it. The storm got even worse. Then we have these guys moment of truth, and perhaps even salvation? Where apparently they get right with the one True God. They cry out to Him and ask Him not to lay Jonahs death on them because He sent the storm for His own purpose.

Then they pick up Jonah and toss him over the side. Instantly, the storm stopped. And right here in verse 16 of Chapter 1 we see conversion take place in these guys hearts and minds. Their gods had done nothing for them. We read that, they feared God exceedingly! Pretty strong wording, almost indicates a reverential quaking with terror. I wonder if they went back to port scratching their heads as to why this Jonah guy would ever want to willingly run away from an all knowing, all powerful God like that.

Then we see Jonah in the water, happily resigned to death and, apprently pleased that he had spoiled God's plans. Then a big fish swallows him whole. There's not much detail other than that God had prepared this fish just for this purpose. Now, the Bible doesn't say "whale", but it likely was for they are air breathing mammals and Jonah would get occasionally resupplied with oxygen for the duration of his trip. He was in that fish for three days and nights and would need air. Whales are sea dwelling mammals that breath air and it is common sense to come to the conclusion that the "great fish" in the story of Jonah is a whale.

Jesus pointed to this example in Mathew 16:4 when the Pharisees came with their accusations and pompous questions they didn't really want any answers to. They weren't prepared to listen and especially hear what Jesus had to say. They wanted to trick Jesus, they wanted a sign from heaven for Jesus to "prove" that He was who He claimed to be. Jesus answer shocked an offended them. "A wicked and adulterous generation seeketh after a sign; and there shall no sign be given unto it, but the sign of the prophet Jonah." And He left them, and departed. It appears by this statement that Jesus also expects us to know His Word. Jonah and the whale is as real a story as there ever was. It apparently was being told, or at least the story of it was known in Jesus time for Him to use it and expect the religious crowd to know exactly what He was talking about. Jesus spoke to the "Religious Leaders," not a bunch of children. While Jonah and The Whale is often used as a children's story. It is far from a simple children's story. Tremendous truth and lessons can be learned by a read through it's inspired pages.

I can only imagine the hideous stink inside of a large fish's belly. The outside of a fish smells bad enough, but the inside has to be far worse. Not to mention the darkness, the cramped space, the stale air, no food, no fresh water, probably hot and quite humid as well. Most unpleasant I'm sure. Not a place for a vacation. Needless to say, it was very likely extremely uncomfortable. It's enough to make a sane man scream for mercy in three minutes let alone three days. Three days being in that kind of environment would do things to a man that could never be undone. Three days! What gets me is that Jonah waited three days before finding enough humility to admit to God that he was wrong. Talk about stubborn. It is baffling. But we are all the same way, if not worse. His attitude change, however temporary it was, can be seen in his prayer in chapter 2 verses 1-9. God knew Jonah's level of stubborn hardheadedness and exactly what it was going to take to break it, and break it He did. I don't think I would have made it three minutes, let alone three days.

The three days is important though in reference to the New Testament account of Christ's resurrection on the "third day"! Hence Christ's comment about the "…sign of Jonah…" when the pharasies where questioning Him about signs. They apparently knew exactly what he was talking about, and hated Him even more over it.

Then Jonah is literally "barfed" out of the whale, and it seems that instantaneously, God tells him yet again, and a point is made to say it is the "second" time, to go to Ninevah and preach what I told you to preach. God didn't speak to Jonah in the whale, in fact He had to wait three whole days before Jonah finally dug down deep and found enough humility to call out to Him. God knows exactly what, and how much it takes to get the attention of His creations.

So, Jonah goes from the shoreline straight into Nineva. From what is written it appears he did so without stopping to eat, drink or bathe, and does Gods bidding. Considering where he'd spent the last three days, he must have been quite a sight. He would have gotten folks attention for sure. We don't know if he preached with a spirit of gratitude to God for being given this opportunity, or an attitude of vengeance towards a hated enemy. However he did it, Jonah preaches Gods message to the Ninevites. And, to his utter shock, the Ninevites repent and plead with God to forgive them. Many politicians pass laws for "the rest of us" and then sit safely and dominantly above them, watching all the "little people" the laws are meant for. But the Ninevites didn't do this. Even the King repented and made a law saying people were to call on and pray to Jonah's God for mercy and deliverance. He set the example and the people followed suit in repenting. It certainly seems like true repentance from a casual reading of the account. That is what God desires, true repentance and not lip service. Perhaps America should take a lesson from that king, and return our course to the straight path we once trod before it is too late. The judgment of God is still a very real thing. Often times it is our own folly befalling us, but it can also be something far worse. I've heard it said that the wheels of Gods justice may turn slowly but they turn surely.

Ol' Jonah finished his "preaching" and then he goes outside the city gate and gleefully waits to see the hailstones start falling. But nothing happens, and so Jonah has a little pity party. He's mad because the Ninevites sought, and then received mercy from "HIS PEOPLE'S" God. He's mad because it's hot. He's madder still because God isn't bringing judgment on a people whom he feels are worthless, wicked, and deserving of Gods full blown wrath. Yet because God is ever merciful to His servants; and any who call out to him for mercy, He makes a little shade tree grow over Jonah's head to keep him cooler. Then, unbeknownst to Jonah, and to make a point to His bitter servant. The tree gets ate by a worm that God also prepared, and it dies and Jonah gets all mad again. It's almost as if he is trying to make God look bad by citing many positives about God, such as His loving, caring, forgiving ways. The way he told God that he knew He'd forgive them because He is so merciful is almost like he is trying to butter God up. Then God tells Jonah and gives a number of how many lost souls there were in Nineva before Jonah preached. I would think Jonah would have felt honored and pleased and grateful that he could be used in such a tremendous way by God, but, he isn't? Reading the account in our day, these things are clearer for we can see the beginning and the ending and the results of the players actions.

Our own hearts, how grateful? Do we often flee to our own version of Tarshish; whatever it might be, to avoid Gods direction and then fight the course change when He brings it along. Do we need the whale to swallow us before we "get it"...Don't we understand that our will, is not going to prevail? Having a new puppy is kind of like that. It is a task to teach him that "my" will is going to prevail and that his will is going to be in submission to me. I don't want him doing it out of fear but because he wants to. It's not easy, but he'll get it. It might take a dozen times, but staying the path will pay off. It's a similar type of thing with God and His creation, man, I suppose. How much do I/We fight the leash of His will? Do we even hear Him when He says "NO"? What does He have to do to get our attention? I don't want to get "swallowed" by a "whale" for God to get my attention.

Perhaps by replenishing, sharpening, and cleaning the tools in my own "toolbox" I can begin to learn how to avoid the whale. Many times it is difficult to see the coastline for the waves and I'm unsure if it is Tarshish or Nineva and whether or not I should keep sailing without knowing for certain my exact heading. I suppose by keeping the toolbox close at hand and the tools cleaned and sharpened the course will take care of itself. Faith.

We don't know if Jonah ever did anything else, or if he ever repented of his actions and his foul attitude. It appears not, for his usage by God seems to end with the dying of that little shade tree. Certainly Jonah had much to think on and consider as he made that long journey home. God loves people! That He knew the exact number of souls in Ninevah is proof of that. He would rather forgive than judge His creations. All His creations need do is ask, just like the Ninevites did. 1 John 1:8-10: "If we say we have no sin, we deceive ourselves, and the truth is not in us.(9)If we confess our sins, He is faithful and just to forgive us our sins and to cleanse us from all unrighteousness.(10) If we say that we have not sinned, we make Him a liar, and His word is not in us. It applies equally today. The worst offense and the worst of offenders God want's to, and will forgive when they ask Him to.

The New Testament reference is given by Jesus Himself when being asked for "signs" by the unbelieving Pharisees. Christ uses Jonah in reference to his 3 days in the Grave VS Jonahs 3 days in the belly of the great fish. Our Lord said, as Mathew recalled. Math 16:4 "A wicked and adulterous generation seeketh after a sign; and there shall no sign be given unto thee but the sign of the Prophet Jonah." Remember, Jonah was in the fish's belly for three days. After Christ's resurrection most of them still didn't believe. It's strange how Gods simple plan of salvation can be so hard for people to grasp, most especially for those who "should" know to begin with. Mainly, the "religious" leaders in the community. Same goes for today, All the multitudes of learned scholars that write papers and books and give long lectures but still miss the simplicity of the message of The Cross.

You absolutely must believe what God says about you before you will believe His Word. Like it or not. God made man and He makes the rules. Like it or not, A loving God would indeed have created a place called Hell. He doesn't send people there, people send themselves there. Forget about blame placing, there is only one way out of this fix and that is through the shed Blood of Jesus Christ. The fact remains, because of Adam, mankind has a very large and befuddling problem called sin that each one of us must deal with while there is still breath in our lungs. Hopefully sooner than later. Yeah, it stinks, but get over it and deal with it. A solution exists. If you heed my warning and accept Christ you can meet Adam one day and ask him how many tears he's shed over the millennia watching the antics of all his generations of offspring, and knowing he was mostly to blame. Each of us is accountable, Yes. But his silence echoes loud and long throughout history.

Romans 3:23 For ALL have sinned and come short of the Glory of God...

Romans 5:12 Therefore, as through one man (Adam) sin entered the world, and death through sin, and so death passed to all, for all have sinned.

Romans 6:23 The wages of sin is death...

Every single person born into this world, save for The Lord Jesus Himself, has a sin nature and a flesh willing and all too eager to go along with it. It can be looked at in this way. If you have One birth (physical) equals 2 deaths (physical and spiritual) Two births (Physical and spiritual) equals 1 death (physical)

1. your physical death when your eternal soul leaves it's human shell...
2. your spiritual death when that soul is cast headlong into eternal torment.

1. your physical birth when moms water breaks and you breach the womb and enter the world.
2. Your spiritual birth when you come to the realization that you are a hopeless, no good, dirty rotten smelly Ol' sinner and call on The Lord Jesus Christ to save you.(BORN AGAIN)

Seeking vengeance in and of ourselves is always wrong, regardless if the outcome is actually a good thing. In an unsaved state, Waister dealt with all problems with vengeance, even the most minor occurances that came his way were normally dealt with to a certain extreme. Waister's view was not so much shoot first and ask questions later but shoot first and pick up the shell casings later.

Luke 9:54 James and John saw this they knew their old testament and wanted to call down fire from heaven like Elijah did in 2 Kings 1:10-15... 2 Captains and their entire contingent of soldiers was seared to a crisp with "fire from Heaven" when they came one after the other and "demanded" that Elijah go with them. Guy number three was a tad smarter, it was obviously well known what happened to the last two guys and their men, so he humbled himself before Elijah and God and was thus spared, along with the guys with him. Just another proof that God hates pride in any way shape or form. All those guys dead just because the king had gone a different route and not sought the one and only true God. Had he simple gone and sought Elijah himself and not made foolish, proud and boastful demands from afar things might well have fared differently.

Pride always costs. It costs money. It costs time, and often human lives. Because of pride 100 guys were seared to dust. They were just soldiers obeying their leader. A good lesson in being careful who you listen to and who you follow. Attention teens! Because of pride, Nebucadnezzer lost seven years out in the woodlands living like a wild animal. Daniel 4:16-37 is the account of King Nebuchadnezzer becoming like an animal for seven years. No hair cuts, no shavings, no nail trimmings, no baths for seven years would certainly fit the description given of him in Daniel. He ate grass for sustenance, His hair grew like eagle's feathers and his finger nails grew like birds claws.

If you didn't shave or trim your hair or chop your finger and toe nails for seven years how do you suppose you'd look. Such a definition sort of defines a condition known as lycanthropy, an altered state of mind and physical appearance. Whatever "we" call it today, Nebuchadnezzer was not quite himself for seven long years. Not possible, you say? How do you suppose you'd look after seven years in the woods without so much as a comb touching your hair?

God is not willing that any should perish, but that ALL should come to repentance. (2 Peter 3:9) God uses people, even reluctant people. It took Jonah three full days of being in a cramped, wet, smelly environment, with no food, no water, little, if any sleep, before he cried "uncle" and God placed him right on the doorstep if you will, right on the very shoreline of Nineva and simply repeated His earlier command to Jonah. He did and the Ninevites repented and God spared them. Unbelievably, after all this Jonah STILL had the wrong attitude and went and sat on a hill outside the city to pout and watch God destroy it. Bad attitudes are like flat tires. You go nowhere till you change them. Even in this vengeful state God still had compassion on Jonah and grew a little shade tree for him to cool him a tad. Then fed it to a worm! Then God touched Jonah's heart with a rebuke in that he cared more about a dumb plant and losing his shade than all the lost souls in Nineva… OUCH…! If Jeremiah was known as the Weeping Prophet, then Jonah might be called the Pouting Prophet.

Besides all that, I didn't have the slightest inkling or understanding of God at that point in my life and I was trying to force it, or Him to be like what I wanted Him to be like. Such erroneous thinking leaves one susceptible to all sorts of circumstances. As I said earlier I couldn't stand the drink, drug, party scene because I had seen what it did to people by watching a relative. I was disgusted and turned off by the actions and attitudes of "those people" and wanted no part of that kind of life.

In a way, I am thankful for that because I was spared untold grief. I "hated" that kind of lifestyle, but "everybody" seemed to be doing the same things. And, boy oh boy where they having "fun," so it seemed. There had to be people out there who didn't do those things. There just HAD to be. I couldn't be the only one. So, why couldn't I find them. Of course, I wasn't looking in the right places, I wasn't really looking in the wrong places either because I didn't care for that type of environment. So I just kept on going, for the most part, alone.

I went to a congregational church at this point in my life. Mom was an artist and Xray tech and dad an engineer. I had one sibling and we had a dog, a cat, and I even had a seemingly schizophrenic gerbil. The mostly, semi-normal American family I suppose.

Part of the difficulty we have in our culture is that we are a sex crazed society and are brainwashed into thinking that waiting to get married is crazy! From cradle to grave, Television and music of our vast cultures promote this. Undeniably, it is worsening from generation to generation. Virtually every magazine cover on the newsstand smacks of sexuality in some way.

Our sin nature gleefully says "OOOHHH whats that?" And reaches for it. You can't even reach for the candy bars because the "fitness" magazines are right below those and are often times just as pornographic as the other right next to it.

Proverbs tells of the young man devoid of understanding; in other words he is STUPID, to put it mildly. So in he goes and gets snared. The fool goeth his way to her house and is caught. (snared, trapped, dead.) Sin might be fun (and it is, temporarily, VERY temporary), and death is it's ultimate payday. (reward)

The live for today mentality is nothing new. The Bible strongman, Sampson lived by this credo and it eventually cost him his eyes, his freedom, and ultimately in the end, his life. It is a selfish attitude that has been around since that first fateful bite in the Garden. A biblical parallel in Luke 12:19-20 and I will say to MY soul, Soul, though has much good laid up for many years; take thine ease, eat drink and me merry. Sounds like fun, but read on and see that God calls that man a fool because he's going to die that very night and all his stored up wealth will be absolutely worthless. It won't help him one iota (v:20) though fool, this night thy soul shall be required of thee. Much to the errors of the pharos of old because you sure can't take it with you. Scripture even says so in (1 timothy 6.7) for we brought nothing into this world and it is certain we shall carry nothing out. The only things that will last are things done in Christian love such as giving a glass of cold water in His name as Mathew and Mark say. You can't take it with you so why not use it to benefit others. People are free to what they want with the fortunes they have made, But thinking it can go with you as the hight of foolishness.

Noah's Ark is mentioned in brevity in this treatise, it is not meant to invoke humor. Rather but to make a very direct and truthful point. Noah's ark, not the cute one depicted on children's books and knapsacks. Like it or not, the actual "ark", or big barge shaped craft, that God used to judge sin the first time on this earth is an actual event in human history. It did Happen! A different study covers that subject, this one is on something much more important and undermining to human dignity and even man's worship of God (who does not change by the way) After all what kind of God do you wish to serve?

1. An impotent old grandfatherly god who cowtows to your every whim and says everything you do is fine and dandy and okey-dokey with Him? Sure, he gets "sad" when you do bad stuff but will always look the other way, most people today think that's who god is thanks to television, music and movies...
2. Or do you want Him to butt out and leave you alone. Except when you want or need something then He'd better hop to it and rush to your side and cough it up.
3. O do you want to serve a God who lives, who sets standards and rules and expects His most prized and dignified creation, "Man." (the only one given an eternal soul) to abide by them, and worship Him as He lays out on His Perfect, Holy and Complete Word. The Bible?

Calling your Creator a liar is dangerous and it's exactly what you do when you call something "good" that our creator calls SIN. People don't like of the word "sin" today and it is considered taboo in most circles. Now-a-days man just uses the softer more innocuous word "bad" to make the filth God very clearly condemns more palatable for him and easier to swallow. The things God tells us in His Perfect, Unflappable Word are an abomination and sin, man turns around and spits in His face and says, "No it's OK, we like it, and we're gonna do it anyway. The Bible doesn't fit us today. We have "evolved", have technology and are smart. We will do as we please."

Unfortunately for those folks, God is still on the throne, He watches and He remembers EVERYTHING! He keeps count as well. Will knowing what Gods opinions are on doing and allowing and or supporting such things as gay marriage for starters, and then proving via scripture that doing such things are A FREE WILL CHOICE and "against nature" change your mind...? Either you agree with God or call Him an unjust liar and move on, Be warned however; such a choice would not be a wise one.

I've only included a few proof verses for space's sake. It aught to be clear enough. The conclusion is obvious. If there's a problem with that, take it up with God. I'm just the messenger.

It cannot be said enough, or warned of enough. be cautious; Excessive drink, drugs, fornication, promiscuity and adultery are bad enough and will be dealt with most harshly unless a turning away and repentance comes first, yet in this brief treatise I am referring specifically to the condemnable practice of "homosexuality." It is not normal! It is a CHOICE! Made of ones own freewill. Thanks to television, movies, music, magazines and books, it is rampant in society. Because of that, such foul practice is considered normal and acceptable today. Such an abominable thing aught not exist yet due to man's sin nature it does. Why do you think such practices are not found in nature...? Because it is unnatural! You will never find gay bears, chipmunks, squirrels, possums or dogs in nature because they don't exist. Had Noah taken two Woodchucks named Bill and Joe on the Ark there wouldn't be any Woodchucks today. Yes, it really is that simple, physical laws cannot change. As in magnets, like charges repel one another opposites attract! Clearly, God did not make the homosexual, he made himself by his rebellion to a Holy and all righteous God. It is clearly a choice! Animals don't have a sin nature, people do because we have an eternal soul, animals do not. Man is a triune being, created in God's image, with a body, an eternal soul and a sprit. Recall in Genesis 2:7 God breathed into man the breath of life and he became a living soul. He did not do this with any other creature. Animals have only body and spirit. Sorry if that offends you, it is truth! Get over it.

There are a plethora of verses both Old and New Testament that prove this fact beyond any shadow of any doubt. They are very clear and specific, there is no doubt what they are talking about. It is Gods opinion on homosexuality:

The God of the Old Testament and The God of the New Testament are one and the same and He does not change. Like it or not, His opinion is still valid.

{HEBREWS 13:8 Jesus Christ, the same yesterday today and forever} hmmmm.

LEVITICUS 18:22...thou shalt not (don't do it) lie with mankind as with womankind, it is an abomination... (putrefying, disgusting.)

LEVITICUS 20:13... if man lie with man as with a woman, both committed abomination and shall surely be put to death...
(sounds like God means business to me)

LEVITICUS 26:16... a burning ague... consume the eyes...
(hmmm, sounds like a horrid disease of some type... Aids? could it be God is serious?)

Oh now that's just mean, Besides that's Old Testament. God is all love, He would never condemn anyone to the literal flames of an eternal Hell for doing those sorts of things today, right? (HEBREWS 13:8!)

OK then, how about the NEW TESTAMENT? oops... It's even clearer. Guess God's True to His Word after all.

ROMANS 1:27 and likewise also the men, leaving(its a freewill choice) the natural use of the woman(self explanatory) burned in their lust one towards another...men with men woking that which is unseemly (disgusting) and receiving in themselves the error (big mistake) of the recompense (payment) that was due. (deserved) (hmm disease...?)

1 CORINTHIANS 6:9 effeminate, abusers of themselves with mankind...?
Hmmm That doesn't sound like something a Holy and Righteous God is pleased with.

Jesus Christ came and judged sin once for all when he suffered horribly on the cross for us. His death burial and resurrection is proof that He was who He claimed to be. God Almighty Himself. His atonement for all sin we have and will ever commit, past present and future, is not a blind blanket that covers us so we can go ahead and live like the devil however we want. No! It is true that Salvation is freely given. All one need do is humbly ask. Its a personal choice, But that takes humility and admitting to yourself and or others, and more importantly to God that you are incapable of such of your own accord and asking Him (Jesus Christ) to save you. He'll clean up all the filth afterwards. How can the Christian claim Christianity and also claim that what God calls an abomination is really good and normal? What God calls Sin we aught not call righteous and good. What God calls abomination we aught not make a law legalizing and glorifying such. Sin is sin however we disguise it and whatever lofty cloak of idea's and words we dress it up with.

Homosexuality is the begging of the end for a country. History is proof of this. If one were to violate a natural law there will always be a consequence, always. It has nothing to do with being Spiteful or hateful. It is about right and wrong. The Bible is Right in all it shows us. From word one to the very last word. It has been given to us to show us and guide us in the paths of righteousness. What The Bible tells us about homosexuality is extremely clear in the above verses.

If you see someone speeding down the road and YOU know the bridge is out and certain death awaits them unless they STOP IMMEDIATELY, it is kind of your duty to warn them. Sure, part of you wants to say who cares, if they're gonna do something that dumb let them fall to their own folly. But, part of you wants to shout a warning and tell them to stop. If they choose to ignore you and continue on in their folly, then you are guiltless. The road to freedom from past guilts starts with repentance. God is willing to forgive any and all, but you have to go to Him on His terms not your own.

It all comes down to one of two choices.

1. Either you believe God
2. You count Him a Liar. you can't have it both ways. It's either one or the other.

Forever is a long time

The normal marital relationship is; One guy + One girl for life. That is the masters plan. It was from the creation. Inside marriage the sexual relationship is a perfection of completeness between husband and wife, face to face and altogether enjoyable. It is not simply a spontaneous hormone release between unmarried guys and gals. Scripture calls such, fornication. Part of the problems we have in our nation today is that we are conditioned by the majority of the music, media, and film industry to think that if you have not had some time of sexual experience by the time you leave high school, that there is something wrong with you. The homosexual and lesbian crowds and other such debauchery based groups prey on this idea like ravenous bloodthirsty vultures. Both young men and young women are targeted, snared and ultimately destroyed by it. Many such youth snared by, and in this "lifestyle" turn to drugs, drink and tragically, even suicide. Such a lifestyle is not an "alternative" lifestyle, it is an abominable lifestyle. Plain and simple.

Not only is sex alluring, But power is alluring, witchcraft and other similar "dark arts" are out there lurking after our younger generations. When I was growing up it wasn't as strong or widespread as it is today, and when my parents were growing up it was even less prevalent. The craze for witchcraft based books and movies and television shows are luring; it is safe to say, millions, into the dark void of the occult. Really now, what teenage girl; even secretly, would not want to be able to conjure up some kind of a "spell" or "potion" to make themselves more popular or prettier, or get a certain boy to pay attention to them.

Likewise the guys, which one would not want to be the strapping musclebound guy that get's all the attention and is great in any sport he tries. That's like a dream come true. If it's fast end easily available many jump on said bandwagon without giving thought to the consequences. Again, movies and music support this self-indulgent promotion.

You can't play with fire and not get burned. Proverbs 6:27 speaks specifically to this, "Can a man take fire in his bosom (to his chest) and his clothes not be burned?" Interesting question, the answer of course is NO. If you touch or play with fire you will get burned. End of story.

Waister would refer to such vile reprobates as carnivorous human soulless leaches as well as or instead of gutless cowardly slime-sucking commies. Waister enjoys using colorful phraseology whenever possible to better grasp hold his readers attention.

Pride is the enemy here. Pride is perhaps one of satan's favorite tools. After all, it's what got him in the beginning. Proverbs speaks volumes of pride, here's just a couple that come to mind. Proverbs 11:2… when pride cometh, then comes shame. 29:23… A mans pride will bring him low. 1 Tim 3:6… being lifted up with pride he fall into the condemnation of the devil… 1 John 2:16… goes on about the lust of the eyes, the lust of the flesh, and the pride of life.

None are good. Unfortunately when discussing pride, scripture always seems to indicate a negative connotation. Rather Thank God for allowing you to win that trophy or award. When taking it all in for ourselves it only builds us up. Not much good can be said of the foul "emotion" called pride. It's not so much an emotion as an attitude. Proverbs 16:18-Pride goeth before destruction, and a haughty spirit before a fall. Proverbs 29:23: A man's pride will bring him low. Satan is loving it! He's having a field day with that ugly entity we call pride; and why not. That's what did him in. It's one of his most used and favorite tools. Maybe not today, or tomorrow, or the next day. But your pride WILL bring you low.

As well does satan love the public school system we have here in America because humanism; one of his favorite false religions, has successfully infiltrated America's public school systems very fabric at virtually every stitch. It is a breeding ground for untold debauchery which is thriving in such an atmosphere. There is no fear of God before our eyes as a nation as a primary. Psalm 36:1 in part says as much. (there is no fear of God before His eyes.) Perhaps He has removed his hand of protection form off of us? I don't know, such is speculation, considering the last number of years, what else might what one think. America was founded on Christian principles and beliefs, and Christians have willingly allowed our Godly heritage to be chiseled and chopped away at without much of a struggle; despoiled at every turn and now we have an enormous battle on our hand. Most Christians have sadly gotten out of politics and the result is clear. A nation that allows such abominable things as abortion, rape and other such murderous acts to run rampant with little or no punishment, is bound to have God remove His hand of protection from it. A nation that allows and trumpets the joys of the homosexual and sodomite lifestyles and even applauds the marriage of homosexuals is in for a rough ride. Such a nation will certainly not have Gods hand of favor to guard, guide and protect it, as it once did. But rather His hand of judgement will instead prevail and attacks of all sorts will be allowed to take place, whether they be man made or "natural." As I write this there is a glimmer of hope that a constitutional amendment is in the works to protect marriage. Though it is completely unnecessary; and even if it does get passed and we have it in writing for future generations: unjust, activist judges and politicians will stop at nothing to get it recanted and removed. Interestingly, but not surprising, these type of folks belong to the same crowd that viciously protects the "right" they think they have to perform abortions. Psalm 58 deals with unjust judges. What's that you say? How dare I write such archaic and unenlightened things? There is coming a day when all such workers of such abominations and inequities will stand before the Most Righteous Judge in the entire universe. All mouths will be silent on that day, no argument will be given.

 I can say and write such things because of Psalm 32 and 51. Both deal with David's thoughts after the babe resulting from he and Bathsheba's murderous lust-filled trist, died at birth, but still went to heaven. He wrote those psalms expressing his guilt and seeking and then receiving Gods forgiveness. I shall go to him - David's cry - The unborn ARE alive. Life begins at conception; period. If the child is not alive then how can he grow? Anyone who clings to the claim that it isn't alive is fooling no one, not even themselves. To say that he can't survive on his own is utterly ridiculous, of course he can't. Neither would you survive if you were dropped without clothes in the arctic tundra. The abortionist has no escape from God's Word. How about Isaiah 44:2 thus saith The Lord that made thee, and formed thee from the womb. Jeremiah 1:5 Before "I" formed thee in the belly, "I" knew thee. Life is a gift from God Almighty, and it begins at conception, end of story. In light of these truths abortion cannot be justified under any circumstance. If you're intent on killing someone; kill the rapist.

Enough on that little rabbit trail, moving on. At that point in life I was feeling nothing but despair. What was wrong with me? Did I have no hope of companionship, of the warmth of a woman at my side? Was there no hope of finding female companionship, any female companionship? In one sense, YES! In a certain way I can understand how the sickness of the homosexual crowd is able to suck in so many in their youthful naivety. These same vile persons prey on these very thoughts and struggles that young people are bound to have. Growing up is hard enough without such vile sickness pulling one astray. Peer pressure absolutely plays a roll in this shaping. The choices are A and B, black and white, right and wrong. That is why making the choice to become a Christian early in life is so important. You will be protected from much of these foul influences and able to walk away from them with victory. Drugs and alcohol will not be as alluring, fornication (un-married sex) while certainly an extremely potent and strong lure, can be overcome. You can walk away from these lures without being a Christian, yes, it is possible. As well being a Christian does not necessarily prevent you from being caught up in it all. But, it most certainly does help considerably because being a Christian gives you the means you need to be able to fight temptation, and fight it successfully. Doing so as a Christian makes it much easier to bear than simply going it alone on your own shackles simply because you cannot keep up the battle on your own for very long. No matter how strong you are, the enemy is still far stronger.

I am convinced the main reason I stayed away from drink and drugs was because of all the "so-called" friends of my older sibling. I was the second of two children, my older sister was 4 years my senior. I got my extreme dislike for alcohol, cigarettes and the party-type-crowd mentality from her lifestyle and the kind of people she called "friends."

I watched them when they came around the house; when my folks were away, of course. The way they acted and talked. Rude, obnoxious, belligerent, foul-mouthed, disrespectful. Such should not be surprising. Alcohol flowed in abundance at these gatherings and who knows what other stimulants were responsible or the culprit for such behaviors. I understand NOW the reason, but back then, even as a non-Christian I was thoroughly disgusted. That is exactly how an unregenerate person before a Righteous and Holy God might, and does act. Whether or not it was complete ignorance or outright rebellion didn't really matter, because both attitudes and reasons are an abomination to God and flat out wrong. There will be a day of reckoning. On that day all will be laid bare and uncovered for all too see. Nothing will be hidden. "Neither is there any creature that is not manifest in His sight, but all things are naked and open unto the eyes of Him with whom we have to do." (Hebrew 4:13) That clearly says we are all, every single one of us, accountable to a holy and righteous God. I had no clue about such then, I just hated and despised the drink and cigarette crowd. I had wisely decided it was not for me.

So, it is no surprise that in a few years when I got to high school I wanted no part of that crowd. Not that shunning drink and drugs makes one better, for in Gods eyes (before salvation) we are all equal, (condemned sinners) and (saved/redeemed) believers after salvation "for we have all sinned and come short of the glory of God, there is none righteous, no not one." Romans 8:28 tells us. Being Biblically saved does not make one "better"; just "saved."

As well; Hell is not simply a garbage dump where "bad" people are to be tossed. There will be plenty of "good" people in hell simply because their goodness was based on a false image of God and what His standards of righteousness are that require any of us to be "right with Him"; as well their complete unwillingness to see Him as anything but loving, overlooking and turning a blind eye to all our filthy vile wickedness. Thus, sadly, because of such, most do not see themselves as sinners in need of a savior, as we all so desperately are. Our idea's of "good" and "bad" are not the same as Gods. Isaiah makes no bones about this truth and makes it crystal clear. Isaiah 55:8-9: "For My thoughts are not your thoughts, neither are your ways my ways, saith The LORD (9) For as the Heavens are higher than the earth, so are my ways higher than your ways, and my thoughts than your thoughts."

"It is not of works of righteousness which we have done, but according to His mercy He saved us." Consider The Bible as a mirror, and the sinners reflection is dog ugly to use a term. The more you read Gods Word and understand what He is telling you, the more your true reflection can be seen. You will come to realize that you are indeed a no good rotten sinner with zero hope in and of yourself of ever rectifying the situation. Most especially will it be rectified with some meaningless "good work" of your own design. Good works are fine and the right thing to do, for sure. But they do not and cannot save a soul. No matter how well meaning and "good" your "work" was. God would be perfectly justified in hurling you headlong into the raging inferno of the pit. At the moment you are ready to receive His FREE gift of Salvation offered and available ONLY through His Son Jesus Christ. Eph 2:9 again: It is not of works of righteousness which we have done, but according to His mercy He saved us. When you accept this gift is when you become a Christian. It is a personal decision. Sprinkling water on the head of newborn is not baptism and does not make one a Christian. That is a personal choice one makes as they hear and understand the Gospel message.

Don't get offended and stop reading! God IS love, and because of this, He has made a way for us to be rectified to Himself. The best part is, it costs us absolutely nothing. It is free to any and all who want it. Your average run-of-the-mill politician could never imagine something so fantastic being "free," but it is. You don't have to do anything to take advantage of it either. It is as simple as this:

Realize that you are indeed a wretched no good rotten sinner completely deserving of the raging flames of an eternal hell for an endless eternity.

Admit to God that you are a sinner. Everyone who has ever lived; aside from The Lord Jesus Christ, is. There are no special words. It has to come from your heart. Just tell Him you are sorry and ask Him to forgive you. You are confessing your unworthiness to the creator of the universe. It is between you and God. There is nothing shameful in it. It is a step of faith. In one example Christ simple says to a blind man, "Receive thy sight, thy faith has made thee whole." Luke 18:42.

Trust Christ ALONE for your entrance into heaven. Ephesians 2:8-9 For by grace are ye saved through faith; and that not of yourselves: it is the gift of God (salvation) (9) and not of works lest any man should boast. In us is no good thing, only what Christ brings into our lives is of any value. In Luke 7:6-10 is an account of Christ healing a Roman Centurions servant who was terribly sick, the text indicates near death, the centurion tells Christ he isn't worthy enough for Jesus to set foot in his house, but if Jesus just speaks a word he knows his servant will be healed. Here's a guy who's not even a Jew, but a gentile, from Israel's enemies even, coming to Jesus because he believes Jesus can and will heal because he believes Christ has the power and authority to do so. He understands the authority structure. He apparently understands exactly who Jesus Christ is and that He has the power and authority over life and death itself.

Becoming a follower of Jesus Christ; A Christian as we are called, is the most important decision you will ever make in your entire lifetime. This decision must be taken on faith. Numbers 21 tells the reader of the time when the Israelites were in the dessert and God sent fiery serpents (venomous snakes) into the camp and started biting them and killing them. They complained to Moses (again) about no water and no food. Then they complained about the KIND of food God did so graciously give them. Then He gave them quails for meat to eat. Then they wanted to go back to slavery in Egypt, and Boo Hoo, Boo Hoo, complain about this an complain about that. I for one am glad God is so incredibly patient and will always make a way for us and supply our needs. Then more complaints and venomous vipers came into the camp and started biting people. God made a way to be saved, and again it was by faith. He told Moses to make a large metal snake and lift it up high on a pole so it was visible from anywhere in the encampment. He told Moses to tell the people that whenever anybody was bitten, all they had to do was "look up" at the snake, and they would be healed. It seems like an odd request, but it was a test of faith. How is looking at a piece of metal on top of a big stick going to do anything for a venomous snake bite? I mean, come on now, those things have a bite that is full of poison that will kill you in just a few short minutes, if not sooner. Yet, that was the way God said to do it at that time. Faith! If they did it, they lived. Those who looked up at the snake were healed, those seeking healing of their own wits and ways, did not. That passage is even alluded to by the Savior, The Lord Jesus Christ when he was talking about his impending work on the cross to His disciples. John 3;14-15: And as Moses lifted up the serpent in the wilderness, even so must the Son of man be lifted up. And key verse (15) That whosoever believeth in Him should not perish, but have eternal life. Again belief in Jesus's death, burial and resurrection alone, with nothing added or taken away is what saves. Belief that His cross death is all that is needed to clear a path to heaven for us as individuals.

In Moses day there where those who "spake against God." Who are we to complain against the graciousness of our Creator? But they did, Verse 8 and The Lord said unto Moses, "make thee a fiery serpent and put it upon a pole; and it shall come to pass, that every one that is bitten, when he looketh upon it, shall live." Verse 9 shows us that is exactly what happened.

Skip ahead now to our day and time. God indeed IS love, but He is also many other things, including righteous, and His righteousness cannot allow sin of any kind to be in His presence which brings us again to His Son, Jesus Christ. John 3:14 And as Moses lifted up the serpent in the wilderness, even so shall the son of man be lifted up(15) that whosoever believeth on Him, shall not perish, but have eternal life. Belief, or "faith" is what is required to take advantage of Christ's finished work.

It is never, never, never, a good idea to follow the "popular" or "party" crowd mentality. It's end is always, always, always destruction and despair. Many times, even death. Don't do it.

Not believing in Hell does not make it any less real. Many hold to the old wives tale that if you can't see it or touch it, it isn't real. That's an utterly ridiculous notion. I've never seen an oxygen molecule, but I know they exist and are real because I breath. Foolish memories from the past haunted me and I wrote a little ditty about such. There was a ski trip I went on in 8th grade. It has no meaning whatsoever but I remember it clearly. Like most 8th graders I had an adversary. I'll call this kid, Stephan. Your typical know it all punk with a big attitude and an even bigger mouth:

I wasn't paying attention and was just standing there mid-mountain looking around at the scenery that Connecticut's tiny "mountains" offered. When, seemingly out of nowhere, "Stephan" skied by and ran over the fronts of my skis. He was close enough that a quick shove would have sent him crashing away, but I hadn't been paying attention and didn't see him approach. I moved on but foolishly yelled curses on his name all the way down the mountain. I could hear it echoing back to me. All that accomplished was prove a had a loud mouth and was acting the fool. He probably never heard a word of it and I went home with a sore throat and raspy voice. Pretty dumb I know. Yet again, I used this type of thing in my writing. Attitudes and actions of individuals became part of the despicably unlikable characters in the stories and tales I would spin. Waister dealt with these punks most effectively, efficiently, and more often than not, permanently.

I love to write, and have wanted to be a "writer" for as long as I can remember. It all began in grade school English class. I hadn't dwelt a whole lot on the subject of English, my relatives were English, I liked the muffins, and I spoke the English language; America's "official" language by the way. Just as you'd have to learn Chineese to live in China, or Russian to live in Russia. Speak as many languages as you like, but to do business and function in the American society, learn our language. America is a Melting Pot where all become as one, a blend of many cultures, not a Multi-cultural society. There is a vast difference between the two. In a melting pot all become one. Multi-culturalism is a fantasy land. It is divided and just that, divided. No unity, division upon division and a mess. My grandfather and a whole bunch of his buddies arranged it so we all didn't have to speak German or Japanese and I for one appreciate that our language is English. Like it or not, it's true. Check the news headlines if you disagree. Enough on that rabbit trail for now, and that was indeed a rabbit trail.

Since I love to write I asked a writer one day. "How do you get published? How do you get people to look at your work and take an interest in it?" With the multitude of different books being printed each year, there had to be a chance of something I might write making it to print.

This man settled back in his chair, which creak-squealed in momentary protest at his abrupt change in position. He rubbed his grizzled chin momentarily and squinted at me. Then, steepling his fingers, he tapped his chin, and then pointing the steeple at me, uttered the phrase.

"Write what you know.... Write what you know...." Okay, on his advice, here goes.

This writing portion of this tale begins somewhere around sixth or seventh grade if I recall properly. It was during that somewhat peculiarly odd time frame known as "the seventies." It was a time period when people everywhere it seemed needed brush-up courses in the proper uses of the English language, not to mention fashion and music choice. But, those are each separate issues altogether. Such is included only to acquaint you, the reader with a brief indication of what was endured during my childhood and early formative years.

So, in continuing, my English class had an assignment in creative writing to do. There were the usual grunts, groans and mumbled complaints from a bunch of kids. But I quietly started thinking. This sounded cool. The teacher, Mr. C, had given us a blank page. There was no framework, no specified guidelines to follow, we were just to "write." He wanted us to create something. This was a first, and it sounded kind of cool to me. I hadn't thought much about writing creatively before. Not at all really, I loved drawing pictures and painting, but the opportunity to "write" in this way had never before been presented to me. This was going to be fun.

I want to sideline briefly for a moment of retrospection to paint a contrast for comparison. Mr. C was one of only a handful of teachers from those days who made lasting impressions on me. Impressions both good and negative were ingrained in me during these early, formative years. An alcoholic math teacher, Mr. K, for example, is one of the negative ones. Mr. K. constantly and consistently sipped vigorously from his thermos of "coffee" during class. All I remember of him is that he was old and yelled a lot. He tended to slur his words together and babbled on endlessly about the square roots of mathematical equations that had no place or meaning for us unless we were involved in the space program or some other high level college level classes. I didn't recognize fully back then that he was sloshed or hammered most of the time. Though, in his defense, there were those times nonetheless; however infrequent, when he was sober, that he seemed to actually care how we students were doing and was more in tune to our level of understanding. During these brief interludes of staidness; as I recall them now, he was not slurping robustly from his stainless steel "coffee" thermos.

Star Wars' Yoda would have said it this way. "The Jekyl and Hyde of math teachers was he!" Perhaps that is one reason why I dislike math so much to this day.

While Mr. K. left a lasting "negative" impression on me. My English teacher however, is one of the only other educationalists I can remember well enough to put briefly to text. Mr. C was tall and thin with a slightly emaciated and incredibly pale complexion. He was not yet bald, but approaching that future reality at near breakneck velocity. At the moment he still retained a relatively significant number of jet black folicals upon his ghoulishly opaque and squeamishly narrow dome; but for how long, was anybody's guess. They were normally combed over to one side and slicked down heavily with one of the men's hair products of the day. This was the nineteen seventies after all; a somewhat gruesome time for fashion, and this gentleman did his utmost to fit in I suppose. He failed miserably, but that is beside the point. On a scale of one to ten I would give him a very generous seven for effort. The inventor of certs breath mints must have gotten inspiration from this man. His breath; in a word, was HIDEOUS. Looking back on him now, Mr. C. was a terrifying figure really, tall and lanky, he reminded me of "lurch" from that old television show, "The Adams Family." He had a tendency to "hunch" his large, gaunt form over the desks of his victi… I mean students. While there, his intense halitosis left its mark on not only his students young, impressionable minds, but their desks, books, pencils, paper, and clothing as well. Students with severe allergies had to burn their clothes after his class. No, not really, but it was horrible. I don't know that the man was even aware of it, but every student and faculty member was for certain.

While the sourness of that horrendously sharp breath no longer lingers. There was one other item I must not neglect to include. Mr. C had one memorably unforgettable feature. A Glass Eyeball! Yes, he really did, he had a glass eye. A brown one. I don't recall if it was his left or right eye, but it was kind of cool in a weird sort of way; to look into those eyes of his and see one that would never move. The eye stayed fixated wide and unblinking upon you wherever you were, and every time you looked up, there it was. It was kind of creepy in reality. It was only an optical illusion for certain, but kids didn't seem to be looking out the windows and out the door all the time as I recall. For, Mr. C's portentous crystal peeper would follow them like the shadow of an imaginary apparition down a dark hallway. For certain, he would catch anybody who was daydreaming. If that happened, your doom would be sealed. He would hover over your desk expelling his noxious exhale upon you while giving his rebuke and make you rue the day that you dared not pay attention and daydreamed in his class. Shudder!

He would begin his class by sitting at his desk and noisily rifling a thick stack of papers. He would do this, in part, to get the attention of the class, and to get them looking in his direction so eye contact could be made with us. Today was not unlike any other, but there seemed something different with Mr. C. He appeared unusually jovial, totting an almost unnaturally pleasant disposition. I don't recall his exact words but the following is a close enough approximation for the sake of this story. "Today, we are going to do an experiment in creative writing. I want it at least a minimum of two pages in length. You may write about anything you want. It can be a real event, or something made up. Just, be creative, and write me a story."

The class set to work, and Mr. C. meandered the aisles of students, looking at their papers and checking the progress of our work. Occasionally he would pause and point out a spelling or grammatical error of one fashion or another before continuing his dark, troll-like stroll of death-breath amongst our midst. My paper, with its virtually nonexistent punctuation and creative spelling put a lot of strain on his good eye I'm sure.

He was getting closer to my desk. I could feel the weight of that glass eye closing in on me as he loomed closer. Then, I heard the darth-vader type breathing and caught the aroma. It was like last weeks socks left in a closed car under the noonday sun. Perhaps even the aftermath of last months cabbage and beans dinner down at the Elks club or even The Possum Lodge. In any event; I did not wish it to linger. He was right behind me! The hairs on the back of my neck stood up, and a few curled in protest. I could feel the weight of that cloistered pupil pressing on me and shivered. Then, suddenly, he was right beside me! Leaning over me! Almost as if it had a life of its own, the eyeball glared at me and seemed to sparkle. Creepy. I could feel the heft of it. It was, as if there were, an almost invisible yet physical pressure on the back of my head. I began perspiring. I imagined a brain surgeon smiling gleefully with drill in hand. Such a notion was silly I know, yet that was a feeling that most; if not all, students in any classroom across the land have experienced at one time or another in their lives. One-eyed teachers not withstanding.

The sourness of his horrendous breath wafted around my head. ("please move") I said to myself. ("gotta breath, please move") The aroma hefted weightily upon my shoulders, like moldy wet wallpaper paste or month old damp gym socks. I choked back the urge to gag, and held my breath. Please move, please move, my lungs weren't that large. I had to breath, hurry, please move…move, move, move… I started to get light headed from lack of breathable air, but then, he pressed on. In his wake, was the fresh air my young lungs so desperately craved. I gulped it in.

"Write me a story." Was what he had said. I could make up anything I wanted. So, I did, I remember rather enjoying it too. I even remember what it was about, and I don't have the slightest clue as to where it came from, so don't ask. He had given us the assignment later in class and the remainder of it was to be our homework. Cool! Mr. C. moved on to the next desk without a word but the dampness of his last rancid mouthful of exhalation still clung heavily to the air about my desk, it's damp reek dissipating ever so slowly. But, I wasn't really that bothered by it. Suddenly, I was encouraged. A spark had been ignited in me. A spark that would soon become a raging conflagration. I began thinking about the story I was going to write. Mr. C was a guy that knew how to inspire his students, at least me anyway. He probably didn't even know it.

The story I had made up was about a doctor who's last name was Waister. Jack M. "Waister". I don't know what hat I pulled it out of, but I clearly remember it. You've seen that name above and here is it's origin. Dr. Jack M Waister was on duty in the operating room the night his younger sister; and only living family member; of course, had been rushed into surgery after a terrible car accident. She had been mangled in a car wreck by some drunken teenaged driver, who incidentally also had been brought into the hospital with a small cut on the chin, a broken wrist, a few bruises and the mildest of concussions. He carried a miserable attitude and demeanor towards those trying to help him to boot. My despising of alcohol was quite clear to my readers.

Jackie Waister's internal injuries were massive and quite numerable, and, for the sake of this story, Dr. Waister was unable to save her and left the hospital with the machine's flat line sound still echoing in his mind. He never returned to the hospital again. In fact, he vanished altogether and was simply "gone."

He disappeared for a number of years and then turned up at some small mountain hospital out west. It was northern Colorado If memory serves. The air was clean and brisk, and those dark memories of distant death haunted him not in this high, desolate place. It was peaceful here, and Dr. Waister had begun anew. He had successfully moved on with his life it seemed, until that is, a bunch of college kids came into town on a skiing trip. He was picking up a loaf of bread at the local market when they came in. They were loud and rude and gave no concern whatsoever for other patrons of the establishment. They bought beer and cigarettes, and I think a box of chocolate cupcakes.

Waister approached them, preparing to rebuke them on their unseemly public attitude, when he suddenly recognized one of them. His hair was longer, but it was him, alright. He could never forget those contemptible eye's. His sister's killer! The night in the hospital flashed by him in a moment. Anyway, he went off the deep end and followed this guy and his pals around and then makes his move on a ski slope. I remember writing that he had used a seven inch machete to do the deed, not taking into consideration that seven inches is not really all that large for a machete, four feet, yes, but not seven inches. Oh well, If you recall me writing, I was terrible in math. Waister had left a note at the scene of the last grizzly execution. "Revenge Never Ends." That's how the story ended. Revenge never ends!

The implication had been quite clear I thought; meaning, that if you set out on a journey of revenge, you are setting out on a path of perpetual misery and heartache that will have no end and give you no rest and very likely end in your own destruction as well. I did not delve into the psychological and physiological ramification of seeking a path of revenge to settle scores, but made such a statement in that three word sentence. Revenge never ends. Of course, at that age, I doubt I really thought that deeply on the subject, it just sounded cool, but there it is. I left the ending open for a possible sequel.

Anyway I turned it in, and went on as usual. A day or two later Mr. C. approached my desk. His atypical glass peeper appeared larger to me for some reason, and perhaps shinier. It fixated unmovingly upon me. It was eerie. I half expected a laser beam to flash from it and incinerate me on the spot. All eyes were on him, and also on me. His voice was expressionless, pale, flat, and his halitosis, characteristically horrendous. I had the urge to turn away and "gag" but I; like the other students in the class whom this gentleman towered over and breathed the exhale of decay upon, dared not. He held my paper high in the air and rattled it loudly. He blurted out for the whole class; as well those in the hallway to hear, almost accusingly. "Did you write this!?"

I was kind of shocked, and somewhat terrified as well. Who did he think wrote it? Just what was it exactly that he was implying? What eighth grader has a room full of ghost writers at their disposal to give their homework assignments to? I nervously looked up at him. The singular lifeless optic locked on me, unblinking, unmoving, cold and dead! The weight of that cloistered pupil bore deep into my very soul. It was eerily unnatural! He awaited my answer. His breath damp and heavy. The longer I lingered on a reply, the longer the musty aroma would linger. I shrugged. "Yes, I did…, why…, what's wrong with it?" As Darth Vader breathed, I anxiously awaited the response, expecting the worse. His momentary pause seemed longer than it was I'm sure. "Nothings wrong with it, it's good, I liked it." Then he left it on my desk and moved on to his next victi…, I mean student. A brief gust of his overly fusty halitosis followed in his wake.

I let out my breath and looked at the large "A" he had put at the top of the paper in red ink. It obviously made an impression on me. The spelling was quite horrendous I'm sure, because it still is, and I've heard that things are supposed to get better with age? That was long before I had an electronic typewriter with an erase ribbon. Even longer before home computers and spell check. But Mr. C. had looked for the content, not the atrocities committed upon the English language by me. He made notations on spelling, punctuation, and grammar of course, but in an encouraging way. A teacher a couple of years later went through boxes of "red" pens in "correcting" my papers. I was probably the reason she needed carpal tunnel surgery later in life. Well, probably not, but I'm making a point here. Like in construction, you build the foundation first, then the structure. This first teacher understood that. The creativity was there, his encouragement helped to solidify the foundation.

Summer days were long and hot for me as it is with all kids of this age, and to handle daily grind of humdrum duldrums my best friend was Mike, and lived a few houses down from me and we used to walk or ride our bikes to school. We lived a few houses apart and he was about a year older than me. To this very day he still is older than me. It was the beginning of fall, and Mike and I were peddling to school. I must have been between seven to ten years of age; that I was struck by the city bus. The school was about a mile from my house and Mike and I usually rode our bikes or walked to school together. That was back when bike helmets were non-existent and school buses didn't pick you up if you lived within walking distance of the school; taxes where cheaper too as I recall, and I didn't even have to pay them back then.

Anyway, this day began no differently than any other. It was early fall, and a beautiful morning at that too. I stopped at Mikes house to collect him and pretty soon we were on our way. Three quarters of the way to school we rode up the little hill just as the city bus passed us. This was not a new happenstance, for the bus did this each morning at the same general time. It stopped at the top of the hill a few yards ahead. As this was also a city bus stop, there were normally two or three passengers waiting to board the fume belching beast atop that little hill where it stopped. Environmentalists were not as rabid as they seem these days or that old heap would have been pulled out of service years, perhaps decades and maybe even eons earlier.

Today however there was a slight alteration from the norm, for there was an old beat up station wagon parked next to the stop sign at the hilltop. The bus could not stop directly by the curb as usual, but had to swing out and beside the station wagon. Parking at such an angle that the space between the car and bus narrowed as it went down the length of them. At the rear it was a generous four feet or so, but near the front of the two vehicles it shrunk to a meager two feet, perhaps less. The handlebars of the bike I was riding were wider than two feet, but less than four. Even with my meager mathematic abilities I understood that this was going to become a problem rather quickly. I did not stop, not because I didn't want to. I did not stop because I COULD not stop. For you see, my bicycle was a number of years old, pieced together from other hand-me down bikes. It was a fine bike, except that it contained little or no braking ability whatsoever. That's why my sneakers wore out so quickly I suppose. The sneakers doubled as the "emergency" brakes of my bike. It was okay, it had worked each time prior to this event and I saw no reason why it shouldn't work again. Another hindsight moment was about to introduce itself to me.

In any event, I was approaching the hilltop. I could hear the bus coming over the hill behind me. It was no big deal, it had done the same thing many times before. It passed me and stopped a short distance ahead to pick up a few passengers. The bus was parked beside the aforementioned car at the hilltop. Mike had wisely diverted up onto the sidewalk via the last driveway apron we had passed. For whatever reason, either lunacy or lack of wisdom, perhaps even a little of both. I sort of involuntarily chose to keep going forward. I squeezed the handlebar brake lever. Nothing happened. This didn't surprise me, it had not worked for some time now and why it should suddenly begin functioning now was beyond me. When I say that nothing happened it isn't altogether true. SOMETHING did happen, it just wasn't the bike stopping. I couldn't turn, there was no room, I had to keep going. The quarters were so close I couldn't even get my feet down to apply my "sneaker brakes." The bike continued forward and the handlebars wedged between the parked car, and the side of the bus, gouging them both considerably as I recall. Well, I had almost made it. But now I was wedged betwixt a rather large smelly bus, and a beat up old station wagon. And, I was off balance and fell over. The bike was now half under the bus' large rear double wheels and I was still half intertwined in the bike with my arm and part of my upper body under the rear tires as well. Had the infamous Darwin Awards been around back then I would have been in the running for a possible runner up, easy.

Making matters worse was the fact that the bus driver had not seen me and had begun moving again. As he did, I felt the rear tires on my bike and then on my arm, it was almost a slow motion thing you see in movies. My elbow was seconds from pancake city and I either pulled it free or it was somehow "pinched" free. However, by the Grace of God, which I knew nothing about back then, my arm was yanked clear. Still screaming I looked up the side of the bus and saw faces looking down at me. I was screaming STOP, NO, or AAHHHH, or something to that effect. The driver was alerted either by my screeching or by the passengers and he stopped the bus. It seemed like a long time but was probably more in the neighborhood of three to five seconds, if that much.

I got untangled from my bike and stood up.

The folks in the house who's car I had so absentmindedly "scuffed" allowed me the use of their telephone. The telephones had dials back then, and real bells, no electronic beeps and no buttons. I called my mom, and with shaky voice and through tears, told her briefly what had happened. Within a matter of literal seconds; remember I was about a half mile from home, I heard the familiar sound of her Volkswagon beetle. A very distinct rattling sound came from those air cooled German power plants. It sounded like it was really cooking too, and when it came around the corner on two wheels that suspicion on was confirmed. Well, not really but you get what I mean.

The police came. The firemen came. The paramedics came. The bus driver was off the bus and checking to see if I was okay. The poor guy was pretty shook up. If anything came out of that event it was that I got to stay home from school that day and had something exciting to tell my dad when he got home that night.

I suppose looking back on it could be a lesson in not spreading or listening to rumors. My sister heard about her brothers run in with a greyhound bus at school via the school rumor mill. From what she could gather I was either headless, dead, a pile of shattered bones, or worse. In reality I was only scratched up a bit. My faithful old bike however was no more. It paid the ultimate price for my utter stupidity. The back half of it looked like it had been steamrolled. Those buses are pretty heavy I guess and had it been my arm and not the bike I doubt I would have use of it, or even still have it today. But, I had gotten even and gouged the side of the bus pretty good, the car too. The lesson they learned was not to park their car in front of a bus stop, it must have stuck too because I never saw the car in the street again.

I had heard the bus coming up the hill behind me and it hadn't fazed me. However, to this day when I hear the same sound behind me on a bike I instantly remember that day. It is a very loud, very distinct sound, something not easily forgotten. Kind of like people remembering their first dog bite. As I am finding out through all that has transpired, the odd things our memories store away and bring to recollection can be both uplifting or humbling. Our minds are incredibly complex and profoundly created. How any intelligent, thinking person could actually believe that the unproven, lie-pandering "theory" of evolution is an actual fact, is mind boggling. It is ludicrous to believe that our brains could have "evolved" from pond scum, or anything else for that matter. Although the blatant foolishness of certain politicians bring this pond scum portion into question. Proof of evolutions falsehood is clearly found in Psalm 139:14 "I will praise thee; for I am fearfully and wonderfully MADE." That emphasis is mine. It does not say fearfully and wonderfully evolved.

At school, my buddy Jeff asked, "Hey, where's Russ?" There were a whole slew of kids in the neighborhoods in those days, and you could actually walk to school in relative safety back then, and some kid who had seen me in the ambulance at the crash site, said, "Oh, he got hit by a bus on the way to school." Jeff's reaction was shock. "WHAT!" I'm told is all he uttered. I was more upset that my lunch was pancaked. It took a direct hit from that bus' double rear wheels. Peanut butter and jelly, smashed toll house cookies, Freetos and an apple came squishing out the paper sides. It was my favorite lunch too. Had it been my head which was also my favorite, I surely would have been dead. Either that, or the bus would have busted an axle on the thickness of my coconut. But, more than likely the first of those two. This was not the first time I had kept my "guardian angel" busy and it definitely would not be the last.

Before all this, at about age 3 or 4 at the then Pratt and Whitney aircraft tennis club. I had gone with mom and close friend "Aunt J" and inadvertently was "left behind" whilst wandering around in club gift shop. My Uncle Don, Aunt J's husband, had an old green pick-up truck. They actually tracked him down and found him by the description of his pick-up truck that I gave them. It was a late fifties or early sixties model. No air bags, only lap belts, no emissions control or other similar power robbing devices on board, all solid metal, no plastic and 8 big thirsty cylinders, in other words, a REAL truck, the only plastic in that baby were the knobs on the radio. AM/FM, no tape, and the radio was American made. Definitely no CD. CD's didn't exist. Even eight tracks hadn't yet reached their zenith, and those were the latest and greatest hot item to have in your car, if anyone can even remember those things.

I had no clue of the consternation I was inadvertently causing, I was too busy having a grand old time eating cookies and talking to the ladies at the club's front desk. I didn't know mom was a nervous wreck. I hadn't even know she was gone. She had been playing tennis with my Aunt J and each had made the incorrect assumption that I had gone home with the other. Aunt J had a pool and two kids my age and she and mom had talked about it but apparently not been clear in their communication with one another. In any event, I went looking for them and couldn't find them. The ladies behind the counter finally figured out that mom and my Aunt J had left. This was way before cell-phones and even before pushbutton phones. All I knew was that that my Uncle D worked across the street at Pratt and Witney and he drove a cool old green truck. They called across the street and were able to find him by that description alone. Man, if that were to happen these days, some nazi-like government agency would goose step in and snatch the kids away and arrest the parents for neglect or some other foolish nonsense like that. It was an innocent happening that worked out just fine.

Yet again we were with Uncle D and Aunt J and their two kids up in Vermont, and the moms and dads were out at the time and the four of us kids were at the rented house. Me being the youngest and the only boy put two strikes against me right from the get go. I don't recall how exactly it happened, but somehow the girls were outside and I was inside. I think a 3 on 1 snowball fight drove me inside, where I promptly locked and bolted the door on them, then ran to the back door and locked that one. I could hear them banging on the doors and windows while I went into the kitchen, got a chair and retrieved the cookie jar from atop the fridge. I got a cup of milk and went and turned on the TV. All the while the girls were banging on the doors and windows and trying to find a way inside. The whole time I sat smugly on the couch finally getting to watch MY TV show and not that dumb "girl stuff," AND I was eating all the Double Stuff Oreo's to boot! A huge mug of milk to dip them in at my side. Oh yeah baby, this was a TREMENDOUS victory for any little brother. I had GOT them ALL, not just one girl, but all three of them. My victory quickly faded however, when they found a way inside, I think it was through an upstairs bathroom window, but it was fun while it lasted.

Then there was the time when my folks went away for the weekend and my older sibling had planned a gathering of "friends" at our parents house. I eluded to this above and in a way, I am thankful for this because it taught me a valuable lesson in the foolish perils of smoking and alcohol and who knows what. I watched the way alcohol affected these kids. The loudness, the belligerence and the disrespect they spewed forth from their very vile inner beings. I was disgusted in my heart. I grew to hate and despise drugs, cigarettes, and alcohol. In a way, I am grateful for this because I avoided all the grief such things bring and cause in a life. My payment for this avoidance? I was not a "popular" guy and was the brunt of many crude and "insensitive" jokes. I can understand, though not condone how some kids can be pushed over the brink and kill their classmates and or themselves. There is certainly no excuse for such selfishly insane acts. Everyone that has ever lived will stand before their creator one day and give an account of their lives. Paul paraphrases Isaiah 2:10-11, in Romans 14:12: So then every one of us shall give an account of himself to God.

Places that served as a kind of escape would probably be the cottage at the cape our family rented each year. It belonged to a friend of my Dad and we usually went for at least a week each sumer. We all brought pour bikes. This was before lawsuits required ALL to wear bike helmets. I don't recall seeing ANY helmets on kids in those days and we all managed to survive. You learned NOT to fall by falling a few times. Anyhow, I was peddling along on my way back to the cottage and I glanced down for just an instant to adjust the bag of goodies I had purchased at the "general store." CRASH! I smashed full speed into a parked car and right over the trunk and on the ground. Ouch, that stunned me. The thing I crashed into was an old beat up jalopy of late sixties or early seventies vintage. It's color was green and rust with a fresh "red" dent from my red ten speed. My fondness for older model vehicles I will reiterate here with this description. That was back when they made "real" cars out of metal and not plastic. The only plastic was found in the knobs that controlled the radio, and even that radio was made here in the USA. They were big and heavy and had V-8's for engines and got 8 to 10 miles to a gallon. A behemoth among auto's. That's the second time a big vehicle and a bike tried to do me in. A number of years would pass before number three occurred and that would be a "biggie". Third times a charm; almost. Anyhow, I flipped over the trunk and the stuff I had just bought at the "GS" (what I called the General Store) there in S. Wellfleet where we stayed on Cape Cod; went scattering across the roadway. Some old lady looked out the door and asked if I was okay as I got up, shook myself off and said. "yeah." I was kind of worried because I had scratched her car and left a red mark and a tiny dent from my red bike on it. I Must have been moving at a good clip. I guess I was in a hurry to get back to the cottage and use the new cap gun I had just bought. Which thankfully had not broken upon impact.

Even though there was the occasional victories in school like the one I mentioned above, my schooling experience in total, really was no picnic. In fact, it plain and simply, stunk. I hated it, I was not athletic and did not fare well in sports of any kind. Baseball, Basketball, hockey, I tried them all more than once and I was lousy. It was not for lack of trying, but I simply was not "a natural" as the saying goes. Even the aforementioned ski trip fell amongst the sporting mishaps of my youth. Towns didn't have football leagues for kids my age where I lived in those days and today the only sport I really enjoy watching over all others, is football. Most likely because I never had the opportunity to bomb out in it? As is the case in most instances like this, I was not the most "popular" guy in school. I preferred reading and writing over throwing and catching. My dad was a good hockey player and did his best to get me involved in it. As I couldn't stand on skates, let alone actually move and skate on the things, he was in a loosing battle. Tying a pair of what was essentially butter knives to my feet and going out on a frozen lake, was not my cup O' tea. Even floor hokey at the local YMCA didn't go to well. I'm sure it drove my dad nuts because he was a good ice hockey player back in his time. His dad; my grandfather, was an all star football player while in college in Massachusetts. That was back when they played "real" football, with little or no padding and those little padded dome-shaped helmets were optional. Even so, "sports" in general was really not my thing. I picked up the artistic abilities of a sort from mom's side of the tree rather than the athletic or mathmatical abilities of my dads.

Then there was a day when moms car was broken down and dad had gone to work in his. We may even have had just one vehicle at that time, I don't recall clearly. This was president Carters era and gas prices where rather high; kind of like today; only adjusted for the time frame of the 70's. Bad either way you slice it. Mom had to run to the store for something so she called our friends down the street. They agreed to let her use their car. Said car was a 1969 Ford Galaxy 500. A big heavy behemoth of a car with a monstrous engine and a posi-traction rear differential. Once again, this was a REAL car. All metal, Big 390 C.I. V-8 with a 4 barrel carburetor and no emissions garbage on it to rob it of precious horsepower. This was back in the day when they built cars that had speedometers that went up to 120 plus MPH. Nearly everything was a V-8 and all the Japanese cars were embarrassing to drive and shameful to be seen in, not to mention downright unsafe. If a car like the Galaxy 500 was in a head on collision with a little Japanese car; especially todays Japanese cars, it would go through it like a freight train going through a pile a pillows. Yeah baby, a REAL car. Sadly, those days are long gone. But at least we had cool stuff to drive.

In any event, mom and I walked down the street to borrow the car. We chatted for a little bit and I saw my buddy Mike and then we had to go home to get ready for our errand running. She started the car, put it in reverse and backed down the driveway and into the street. I stayed and talked to Mike. That's when it happened. She seemed to be having trouble with the column shifter getting it into "drive". She fought with the gear selector lever for a moment or two before it popped down quickly and then suddenly the 390 cubic inch engine was wide open and the old Galaxy roared up the street the short distance to the dead end we lived in. Trailing twin black strips of rubber and a cloud of white smoke. Mom was on the brake with both feet the whole time. What a racket, it sounded like a drag strip. Wow, MOM...! It was cool. At least to me, she was freaking out though.

Somehow the engine pivoted onto it's side and the 4 barrel carburrator was jammed in the full throttle position. In an instant, all the horses were loosed and wanted out of the barn pronto, all at the same time, too. Mom is in a panic and the car is tearing up the street toward our house. Not to mention the telephone pole at the end of the culdesac, directly in said vehicles line of flight. White smoke from the burning rubber poured out of the rear wheel wells in a massive cloud. She pressed firmly with both feet on the brake. Yeah, right!

Mrs. C asked Mike what that awful sound was and who was racing up the street like that. Mike replied calmly, "That's Mr's T in our car." Mom got into the circle and was in a panic and was trying to move the gear selector back up to PARK. She fumbled with the key and the gear lever and somehow got it in either park or neutral. The engine was still screaming but either by the key or perhaps a blown head gasket, she got it turned off. Needless to say, we didn't make it to the store that day.

All Mr. C. did when he got home and was told the tale was laugh. The mental image of my mother roaring up the street like that; in his now ruined car, was most humorous to him. He was a town garage engineer and could fix or build or weld and repair just about anything mechanical, he fixed his car. Turns out, a motor mount had broken and the engine had flipped from all the torque and jammed the throttle open. He had it fixed fairly quickly and it was and is still a running joke between the families to this very day.

The only sport I wasn't bad in was skiing and had even joined the skiing club in eighth grade. Even in this endeavor there was the occasional miscreant tormentor who would do their best to either cause me embarrassment or even harm while skiing. But, being up on the slopes, alone, enjoying the view and the "ride" I could put away any thoughts of unhappiness. To this day I love the mountains. Not that there were any real "mountains" in my home state. The mountains we have in Connecticut are really just oversized hills. We call them "mountains" but when you have seen a real mountain, there is no comparison. I have been to Colorado skiing once in my life, and I am glad I took the opportunity to do so. The occasional trip to the White

Mountains in New Hampshire keeps that need in check here in New England.

I'm trying to make a point about "teasing" here. While teasing may appear harmless. It is not. It is even worse these days than it was twenty plus years ago. It is no doubt that our fallen human nature drives us to harm one another; any way we can. Words often hurt worse than any bladed weapon. They cut deep and leave longer lasting scars than any fist or thrown rock could ever leave. Broken spirits are much harder to heal than broken bones. Oddly enough, I can understand to a certain extent why some kids resort to suicide thinking it is the answer to all their ills, when in reality it is only the beginning of them. No matter what the problem is, no matter what the reasons or the who behind the thoughts of suicide are. It is definitely not the answer. No, No, No, a thousand times no. I recall hating getting up in the morning to go to school. The reason I did not go to the regular high school after grade school was to avoid being with the same crowd of kids I had been with all those years beforehand. I applied to, was accepted, and went to a local tech school. I just barely squeaked in on the entrance exam as I recall. It wasn't really my thing to do technical type of stuff but I didn't want to go to the regular high school and sought any route to avoid such. I didn't really want to there and "I knew it" from the get go and even switched trades while there, but to no avail. I foolishly wasted those valuable formative years in essence, "running" from my past and the troubles I foolishly thought I could leave in the dust. This was the same time frame as the back brace. A handful of kids from grade school went to this tech school as well, but not many. Although, they were not as bad without all their cronies around them to embolden them. Which is normally the case, an audience gives the bully his boldness, alone they are cowards. I didn't really want to go there, but I knew I didn't want to go to the town high school with all the kids I had been in grade school with. It was pretty miserable. I changed trades twice while there and finally settled on something I have no desire for today. Had I gone to the regular school perhaps I could have done something with writing back then. But I didn't and that is that. Be careful your decisions, you live with them a long time. It was not all loss, however.

Today I have the greatest friend a guy could have. If I had not gone there things would surely be different. Many people might call that a waste. I don't. It wasn't a waste at all. As I said, I came out of there with the best friend a guy could ever ask for or have. He knew what he wanted for a trade when he went in and now is superb in it. I gave him the nickname The Belch because he could ring doorbells and telephones by cupping his hands over those devices and "belching." I know, it's kinda gross, but, in high school, it was cool and impressive. They don't make guys like The Belch anymore. They are few and far between.

Left in a normal state, things usually tend towards disorder and all things will eventually fall apart if left alone or untouched. This goes not for just man made mechanical devices, but people as well. Such an existence builds up stress in a kids body and they need an out. Some kids to turn drink, drugs and the cankerous, lying mask of the party life. I knew an individual who lived that life and saw first hand what it did. I grew to despise and hate drink and drugs by watching what it did to people. I am ever grateful today that I did not go that spineless, self serving easy road. Wide is the path that leads to destruction and many there are who are on it. Please heed a warning and take the narrow path, don't go for the easy wide way, you'll be sorry if you do.

Problems come from this also, constantly being the butt of jokes and picked on makes kids, If I can use this non-term, "self-conscious" and they lock themselves in a shell and it is hard for them to interact with other kids. Hard but not impossible. These types of kids may not be all that great at sports activities. All of this factors in, especially so when it comes time to start looking for a future wife or husband it can be devastating. Constantly being "ranked" on was no walk in the park. Especially with the brace. At that age and timeframe of a persons life, words slice like a hot razor. Peers, especially girls, can be intensely viscous towards one another. Sorry ladies, but it's kinda true. Most outgrow that stage as hormones and such change. Some gals who don't find the self control to deal with with these issues tend to wind up in politics somehow. Me? I just stuffed it all down deep and kept it locked inside where non could see and applied the internal bandaids.

I used writing to "fix" my ills. I started to write more stories, and grew Jack M Waister into plain old Waister. He was kind of a Chuck Norris/Clint Eastwood/Monty Python/Jackie Gleason type of character all rolled into one. Waister took care of things for me in a self gratifying harmless kind of way. I often would sit at my typewriter late into the night and laugh over my typings. I would sit there for hours tapping madly away at the keys and then look outside, notice that is was dark and that I had missed lunch, and sometimes dinner as well.

To this day "Waister" is still with me. He has changed along with me. Everybody needs a way to let off steam, one method I use is by writing. As the years passed, I began writing editorials and sending them in to a local paper. One paper in particular apparently enjoyed my work, for they printed nearly everything I sent them. I even got used to the way editorials should be written by studying what they deleted from my drafts and what they actually printed. I learned how to "self-edit" and It made me a better writer. I took care for word count, but on one occasion they printed one that filled nearly the entire editorial page without many deletions. I guess they liked it. All the points I made needed to be addressed and I trimmed it as much as possible, and they liked it. The editor of this refined newspaper even sent me a hand written get well note in the hospital after the heart attack which I thought was kinda cool.

I said before that I was not a great, or even a semi-good athlete and didn't really care about sports that much. Even today I only will sit and watch football, sometimes basketball, and on the rare occasion they can be found, a hunting or fishing show; and almost any kind of auto race except formula one cars, something about them just doesn't appeal to me. Probably an American thing. Stock car, NASCAR, monster trucks and even an occasional dirt track or smash up derby are this boys forte.

I was not the "outgoing" type. I came to be thankful for this in later years, but at the time I was living it I was completely miserable. Not knowing the intended purpose for this trial, I blamed and even hated myself for it. Making matters worse, during these high school years of my life I was found to have a curvature of the spine. Because of this curvature, I had to where a plastic and metal back brace for most of these highly impressionable high school years. The plastic portion came from my hips and up to the center of my chest, and cold metal bars rose up from that and formed a ring around my neck. It made me move like a wooden Indian. After a month or two, you get used to it and find ways to deal with the nasty rashes the things can give you and It did, especially in the summer. I got fairly adept at putting it on by myself as well. You have to reach around behind you and buckle and unbuckle the device. Nowadays it is probably all velcro. Surely this was likely a factor in the above mentioned paragraph. Really now, what girl wanted to seen with a guy who looked like he was wearing a stunt car roll cage. As a matter of fact that was even my "nickname" around school as well. Roll Cage Russ, funny huh. Yeah, hilarious. This was high school after all, the place where kids are always nice to each other and never ever mean, hurtful, spiteful, or vengeful. One time in-particular I was walking down the hall minding my own business; as was always my intention, and I could hear them whispering, loudly and obviously on purpose. Then I felt something "hit" the back of the brace and bounce off. I stopped, turned around slowly and looked at them. I tried to give them a Clint Eastwood kind of squint but without a Colt .45 holstered at my side it was rather ineffective. Boy, that was hilarious. A laugh riot.

I had an older sibling growing up, she's always been older than me, and still is to this day. She and I were on completely different ends of the spectrum. She would be the one going out and doing the party scene and getting in trouble. I watched how her "friends" acted and talked, as well as the things they did when no adult supervision was around, and grew to despise it. This is certainly the reason I avoided that crowd, their alcohol, cigarettes and whatever else they did like the plague in a few years when I reached that point in school. Then there was a time when my folks went away for the weekend and my older sibling had planned a "gathering" of "friends" at our house. In a way, I am thankful for this, because it taught me a valuable lesson in the perils and downright stupidity of partaking of drugs and alcohol. I watched the way alcohol affected these kids. The loudness, the belligerence and the disrespect they spewed forth from their very vile inner beings was like a visible poison. I was disgusted in my heart. I grew to hate and despise drugs, cigarettes, and alcohol. In a way, I am grateful for this because I avoided all the grief such things bring and cause in a life. My payment for this avoidance, I was not a popular guy and was the brunt of many crude and "insensitive" jokes. Having been there I can understand in a way, some kids can be pushed over the brink and kill their classmates and or themselves. Though there is certainly no excuse for such acts. Everyone that has ever lived will stand before their creator one day and give an account of their lives. Paul paraphrases Isaiah 2:10-11 in Romans 14:12: So then every one of us shall give an account of himself to God. Like most families, there was occasional tension and some difficulties between mom and dad, but nothing that wasn't eventually worked out. Such being the case I spent a lot of time alone and didn't talk much about it. I did a lot of writing in this time frame. Waister's character and persona flourished, and he's as much alive today as he was back then, even more so in some ways. He has changed along with me. When I became a Christian; he became one as well. However, but in many ways, he is still the same.

Mom was an X-Ray tech working at Hartford hospital, and as a result saw all sorts of accidents involving "motorcycles." She told me never to get a motorcycle and I didn't; as long as I lived at home that is. In a rare bout of rebellion though, I broke her heart, for about a year after moving out I bought an old Yamaha 440. To be certain it was a real piece of junk that couldn't get out of it's own way if it had been dropped off a cliff, and that was probably one reason I got clobbered in the first place. You cranked the throttle and there was at least a good second or two of hesitation before the lousy thing reacted in any way. Any rider will tell you; that is too long. When it did react it was like an ancient snail on sleeping pills racing a dead turtle up a 70 degree steep incline.

It is safe to assume that this paperweight on wheels was not the most responsive bike on the road. Anyhow, here I was, going through an intersection in Rockville Connecticut and the light was green in MY favor. This meant that the young female driver who "T-Boned" me had a red light. Although; she likely did not see her light; or me, for that matter because her hands were covering her eyes and mouth. I know this for sure because I recall seeing her clearly as I quickly passed the windshield on my way over the hood of her car and onto the pavement. Maybe she didn't see her red light because her hands were covering her face, I don't know for sure. Most likely she was flapping her gums to her friends. I can't blame cel phones because they were not as popular or mobile as they are today. Only folks with limo's and Mercedes had them, and they were a big box attached to the car with a cord. It was the 80's. In any event, I landed on my head and shoulders and came to rest in the intersection on my right side in the fetal position, clutching my left thigh in a death grip because of the searing waves of numbing pain rocketing through it.

I looked at the leg and noticed that a brand new "joint" had suddenly appeared between my knee and ankle. It did not feel very good either. For some reason, looking at it made it hurt more. Some guy comes running over and says; I still can't believe he actually said this after witnessing the accident, but he did. Picture it spoken with mellow hippie-like tone of voice.

"Hey man, are you alright?" I responded through pain-filled, clenched teeth, "Yeah, but my legs broke." If I had been a little quicker I might have come up with a snappier response, but I was in too much pain to think as sharply as all that. Really now, think about it. You see some guy get creamed in an intersection and thrown off his motorcycle and the only thing you can think of to say is "Hey man, are you alright?" It is actually kind of funny when you think about it. My junky little bike had rolled it's last, I wasn't going anywhere fast either at the moment.

I was only about a mile from the hospital to the east and even closer to a donut shop to the west so both the police and ambulance were there in a New York minute. I'm sorry, I shouldn't poke fun at the police like that, they all did an awesome job and I am glad they were there. In fact I noticed one of them waving off a "clergyman" in flowing black robe-like trappings bolting over from the huge cathedral-like church on the corner. In his hands were the beads and gold plated trinkets of his trade. Thanks again guys. Guess he wanted to chalk another one up on his scoreboard for that mere man who lives in Rome. Not me and not yet.

They proceeded to transfer me from the pavement to a backboard and I heard them discussing my helmet and how to get it off. I told them my neck felt just fine and took the helmet off slowly and handed it to them. I later saw the big "rip" out of the top side of the helmet. I'm glad I had it on. I was just going about a mile from my home and it was a hot day, but I still wore my "pail." I deemed it too hot for leather though, so I only wore a t-shirt and jeans and can still see the spot on my leg where the bumper of her car smashed my leg against my hot muffler, and a red scar on my shoulder where I first hit the pavement, although the shoulder scar has cleared up as the years have flown past, the leg burn scar will probably remain, no biggie, it could have been far, far worse. Besides scars are kinda cool, they are like badges of honor or reminders to be more careful next time. Every time you look in a mirror you are reminded not to do something, or at least be more cautious the next time around.

We arrived at the hospital quickly, and though I was still in tremendous pain I frantically asked the E.R. crew to contact a friend of our family who did volunteer work there. I had no idea if she was even there or not but I figured she could break the news to mom easier than a cold call from some ER staff member. As a parent I can attest that is the call every parent dreads getting. Thankfully she was indeed there, and came down. I was relieved. She did break the news to mom as gently as possible. I was alive and had learned my lesson. I still like motorcycles, but I don't have one anymore.

They set the bone and let me pick a cool camouflage cast from an assortment of colors they had. It went from my toes to my ankle to my hip and then they sent me home. It was a challenge learning to move around a tiny little 500 Sq foot apartment on crutches, and then a wheel-chair. I was in my early to mid twenties when this happened and no thoughts at all of death were even in my mind. At that age, who really thinks about the fragility of life. From stories I've heard, even though it's always in the back of their minds, soldiers on the battlefield think it will be the other guy and not them. Had death come that day, I most certainly WOULD NOT have been ready. Death is a shameless enemy, and often comes sneakily and extremely quickly, with barely enough time to say "oops" before he attacks. Even as I saw the car coming and knew it was going to hit all I had time to do was grit my teeth and squeezing the brakes. If I didn't tense up perhaps I might have fared better. But the normal human reaction is to tense up for the collision. Ever wonder why a fool drunk driver can be relatively unscathed while his car is totally mangled and the telephone pole is cut in half? Or worse, the people he just murdered are mangled and broken beyond recognition or repair?

It was all so quick. All of a sudden there was the car, Then CRASH, a sudden jerking motion as I left the seat, a second or two of weightlessness as I took flight, then a sledgehammer like blow to the head as my helmet made a dent in the street, and finally laying in the fetal position on my right side with both hands clamped tightly around my left thigh. Waves of pain rocketing through my leg with eyes locked on and staring at the brand new "joint" that had appeared between my knee and my foot. The lower half of my left tib/fib hung dangling out of my jeans, my foot appeared to be turning to look at me as my sneaker was pointing at a very unfamiliar angle. It felt numb and throbbed at the same time. Ouch! Yeah, that hurt. The pain didn't even register at first until I released some of the tension coiled in my body.

I wasn't expecting death when I left the apartment that morning, nor, as I would one day learn, was I anywhere near ready for death had it come for me that day. That is a perfect example of Gods kindness. Before I knew Him or even had any thought of Him, He cared for me, and spared my life in that accident. Had it been a truck, or had she been going faster, or had a been a foot or two either way the outcome would have been quite different I'm certain. People think they have plenty of time and can get "right" with God "a little later" and that they really are not all that bad. In Romans 3:10 God says. There is none righteous, no not one. That is in line with the old testament because He also says that The day of Salvation is at hand, or "right now." a quick saunter through the pages of the New Testament reveals to us that we are not at all "right" with God in our natural state. No one is "good" in and of themselves. Any thought contrary, are deception.

I did not lose consciousness at all but just lay there in the street; in numbing pain, jamming up traffic until the "meat wagon" as my grandfather liked to call ambulances, arrived to scoop me up. I don't know where he came from, but a town police office was suddenly there. I remember telling him as I was on the ground and he was kneeling over me. "I had the light! I had the light! It was green! It was green!" I also recall admiring his sidearm. As a shooter, and firearms pistol instructor; I had an interest in firearms of all sorts and so it was a natural distraction for me to focus on something like that. It kept my mind off the searing pain in my leg anyhow.

I remember looking down at my leg. It both hurt beyond measure and was also numb. Those two feelings are opposite of one another and I can't figure that one out, but that's the way it was. I was on my right side in the fetal position with both of my hands clamped tightly around my left thigh. When I let go it hurt, when they rolled me onto my back it hurt, when they gently laid my leg out straight it hurt even worse. Every movement of the gurney hurt, even the straps that tied me onto the gurney hurt. I remember asking the EMT if he could give me something for the pain. I also remember my voice was raspy and strained. "We're almost there." Was all he said. I guess that meant "no."

My heart was racing and the stress my body endured was no doubt intense. I was taken to a little hospital about a mile from the accident site. If I had felt better I probably could have hopped on my good leg and saved on the cost of my deductible. The ambulance crew wasn't too keen on that idea, and, frankly, looking back, I wasn't either. After all, I wasn't the hitter, I was the hit'ee. I was just hoping for something to counter act the pain. Get me there quick, my leg was beginning to hurt quite considerably. At the hospital they set my leg in a long cast from my ankle to my hip, kept me a spell and then cut me loose. It felt good to be home in my tiny apartment.

Not long after this, I took a tumble in the john. I was standing near the bowl and a sudden dizziness swept over me. That had never happened to me before. The room literally started spinning and I felt myself falling backwards. That was the first and only time I have ever blacked out. I can imagine my eyes rolled into the back of my head as I keeled over. I landed against the corner wall and partially in the bathtub. I'm sure it was kinda loud. It was a terribly small bathroom. Just big enough for the tub, potty and sink, and that barely. No closet.

The room itself wasn't much bigger than a closet. Certainly lacking the space required to turn a leg with a full length cast on it. My wife came charging in to see what was up and found me coming to in the corner. I was in a cold sweat and shaking. Turns out it was some type of flue virus. In any event I spent the next few days in bed on only my pain meds, toast, saltines and ginger ale.

To make matters worse, every time I got out of bed, or sat up or stood up. I could feel the bones pop, shift and grind against each other inside the cast. It's hard to describe the feeling unless you've experienced it. Pressure and tension and then a quick "thop" as it sounded through the cast. I told my wife to "C'mere, check this out." She put her hand on the cast. When I moved a certain way she could feel the bone "pop" and "grind" back and forth over the break site and she would cringe and pull away with an "ewe gross." I thought it was kind of cool, but that's probably just a "guy" thing. However, it sent a quick shock of pain through my leg and hip every time I did that, so I tried to avoid moving in such a way as to cause such to happen. It made sleeping a bear.

After a week or two of this type of thing, nothing was setting properly. My leg would be an uneven twisted mess today if the cast had stayed on and it had healed "normally". We elected to go with a rod inside the leg. I have since seen that exact same operation on one of those cool cable television operation shows. Good grief, it's no wonder my leg hurt after the surgery. The drilling, the pounding, the twisting. Ouch. Man, it may be unpleasant but I am so ever thankful to be living in America. God Bless the USA! These kind of operations are not available everywhere. Far, Far to many Americans take it for granted how truly blessed this nation has been. Had I been living under a socialist medical system, theres no doubt I would undoubtedly have either lost the leg or had a crippling limp for the rest of my days had I been living anywhere else. Thank God for our medical system, and thank God for our free market society. The only remnant I have left from it is that accident is that the toes of the left foot are slightly more "pulled back" than the toes of the right. I'll take full blame for this in not pushing myself hard enough during the physical therapy to regain the full range of motion in that leg.

For a while I had a plaque hanging in the house as a "reminder". I had taken the three screws that had been taken out of my leg which had initially been installed to keep the rod from shifting inside the bone until replacement bone marrow could grow back. It was risky in that they could easily have snapped the head off the bolt and then, AND THEN, well, I don't know, they all three came out without a problem, good thing too, they where bothering me so much I'm glad they're gone. I even made up a plaque with the three screws and a little "trophy" motorcycle on it. It had an inscription "First place in bone snapping from the CT Bust-a-Bone society" or something foolish like that.

For Christmas that same year I gave my mom a customized, personal gift; I little trinket from her sons rather peculiar sense of humor. It was a little Playmobile policeman toy on his motorcycle. Only I had bought some model paints and painstakingly repainted him to look like me. I chopped off the appropriate leg with a hacksaw and superglued it back on at a twisted angle. I even painted the year on the helmet. It is a favorite ornament for all the kids to hang when it comes time to trim the tree. I am sure it also serves as a reminder to something she can never forget anyway. What a nice guy, huh.

Being inactive and sedate with the leg began to take a toll on me. I couldn't bike or excersize for so long that I got "lazy" and lost the initiative to get moving. Over the next couple of years I put on twenty five plus pounds or so easy. Man, I look at pictures now and am shocked. No wonder there was such an even more unpleasant event awaiting on my horizon in the not too distant future.

Soda and fast food was quick and easy and relatively cheap. Plus, it tasted yummy. Hindsight! Forget that it was loaded with sugars and salts and poisons I could well do without.

As I had done landscaping work in the past I decided to take the insurance settlement and invest it in a truck, trailer and equipment to start a landscape business. I learned too late the way I did the business was not the proper way. I had jumped in both feet, full bore, 100 percent gung-ho all the way. I didn't build the business up slowly and thus did not have a large customer base to rely on for constant work to keep me afloat. I needed more than just lawn cutting jobs. I needed at least 8 to 10 of those a day plus other yardwork such as hedge-trimming, yard edging, gutter cleaning, and other odds and ends. You had to account for rain and other weather reasons for missed days. I had no where near enough work to keep busy with a steady work load from week to week. If not for a large amount of snow that first winter I would have gone belly-up sooner than I did. I hooked up with another local landscape crew and subbed out plowing parking lots for them.

The most fun I've even had was working for myself and being out on the road at 2:00 AM. plowing driveways and parking lots in a blinding snow storm, it was a blast. I had the roads all to myself except for D.O.T. trucks and other plows. It was like being in some futuristic world were I was the last human left. The only other living thing I ever saw were those strange graveyard shift employees when I pulled into the 24 hour burger joint drive through window. Sitting in my pickup truck scarfing down burgers and fries or some sort of deep fried chicken particles. My excuse? Nothing else was open, and it was quick and filled the hole. I had jobs to get done by a certain time and I needed fuel. The time bomb in my chest continued to wind tighter and kept ticking away. Each time I ate that junk I wound the clock on that bomb tighter and tighter. My worst consumption record was 2 chicken sandwiches, 3 supersize fries and a jumbo soda. Most of the time it was only 2 large fries. I would dump all the fries into the bag and sit the bag in my lap. I opened at least 2 or 3 of those little salt packages and dumped them on the fries and then shook the bag for a minute or two to disperse the salt evenly. I tore the top of the bag off and sat it in my lap between my legs and made a nice little "bucket" of yummy grease and salt to gobble down as I drove home. The sandwiches each had their own perch on my left and my right thigh. Then I would wonder why I was so thirsty after guzzling a liter of Pepsi Cola with my meal of grease and salt. Tick tick tick....

I had an interest in police work and the landscaping work had helped me trim down and I was; I thought. In great shape. I applied for and passed the first portion of the state police exam, the written portion. The next step was a three part physical test consisting of weight lifting, stretching and reaching, and a run. The weight lifting went fine,

I passed without difficulty. I passed the stretching test in like manner. I was getting exited now, I was actually going to make it. Cool! Could a dream really be this close? Apparently not. I did not make the run, and was terribly winded afterwards too. Tick Tick Tick... I went home determined to make the next batch of tests that was coming up in a month or so. I trained every night to try and increase my time and distance for the run and increase my weight lifting. When the next test came up a month later I went for a second try. My results were the same. I passed the weight and stretching portion with a slight increase in both. I even did better on my run time, but still fell short. One had to be able to be faster than the low-life in a foot chase. I couldn't do it over the long haul. I still had no thoughts of my greasy diet plugging me up. Don't forget, I was never good at math so it didn't add up for me.

So, I hung that dream of being a policeman in the back of the closet with some others I'd had, and took an armed security job in the very bowels of Hartford's infamous North End. I had hoped this security experience and the "in yer face" Kempo Karate lessons I was now taking would boost my chances of making it as a State Trooper. During the karate lessons I experienced shortness of breath and occasional coughing bouts. Again, I had never even heard of a "cardiac cough" and I assumed I was just "out of shape" and continued to push myself harder and harder. TICK TICK TICK...

I never thought there was anything "wrong" inside of me and that I was just "out of shape." Not once did I ever take into account that my family history put me at serious and increased risk of heart disease. My garbage food diet was no help and Like a true fool, I arrogantly assumed that I could worry about that stuff then I was seventy, never even considering I might not even make it half that extremely short distance.

I had to do something to put food on the table so I began servicing alarm systems in homes and businesses. Then I began installing alarm systems in the same places. I still had hopes of one day trying again with the state police, or any police department. Thinking that the security and self-defense backgrounds I had acquired would be a benefit to me on a resume. This security system installer job is the one with the hour to hour and a half long drive on an almost daily basis. The junk food rations continued and worsened in this job. Many times a long drive ahead, I had to get up early and drive one to two hours to get to the job site. This meant that if I had been too lazy to pack myself a lunch the night before, it was a grease bag lunch, and likely the same for supper too. Our two kids at this point where very young and very close in age, 14 months apart. My own foolishness and determination to make ends meet and keep bills paid and mouths fed left me blind to issues with my wife. Had I known or been wise enough to "see" the difficulties my wife had begun experiencing, perhaps things would have gone differently. Again, that hindsight thing. I figured it was something with me so I pushed myself even harder to make amends for whatever offense I had inadvertently committed. Or thought I was committing.

I gave no thought whatsoever to checking out the "ticker" and summed it up to being "out of shape" and would push myself even harder in any activity I was involved in. I didn't like the idea of quitting. Through this whole ordeal I had never even considered death and what would happen if I had not made it. I was young and not ready to die. More arrogance on my part in thinking such a decision was actually up to me. Besides, when you die, you die and that's it, right? Wrong! Very wrong. Very, Very wrong. Many teach that, but it is utter, complete and extreme error. Life continues when this frail clay shell we temporarily reside in ceases to function. The SOUL is our eternal part. Where it ends up for eternity is completely up to the individual it belongs to.

No one knows how many breaths they have. The Psalmist; generally speaking, when he in Psalm 90:10 writes, the days of our years are threescore years and ten; and if by reason of strength they be fourscore years, yet is their strength labor and sorrow; for it is soon cut off and we fly away. To the rich fool, God said in Luke 12:20 But God said unto him, though fool, this night thy soul shall be required of thee, then whose shall those things be, which thou hast provided...? Hebrews 9:27 and it is appointed unto man once to die, but after this, the judgment.

These verses tell us that we cannot "Die" and then come back. Nor as the Pharos of old believed, could they take all their "stuff" with them. It is because of verses such as this these I don't believe I was technically, completely, "dead"; meaning my soul had not left my body, I may have been locked in the closet for a while, and about as close to "dead" as I could get. I saw no white lights or "heavenly" beings. If such did indeed happen, then that is lost in that portion of memory that is "gone" from the events of that day. I am by no means ridiculing or discounting any experiences others may have had. I simply base my personal experience and belief in Scriptures such as these.

John 1:18 No man has seen God at any time: and later the same author reiterates...

1 John 4:12 No man has seen God at any time: Even John the Baptists parents Zechariah and Elizabeth, did not see "GOD" In Luke 1:7-13 we see the event told to us plain as day. Zach got panicked thinking he was a dead man because he had seen "God". Turns out it was "only" an angel. Elizabeth and Zechariah in Luke 1:7-13 gives the account of John the Baptists birth. The angel calms him down and then tells them the news of John's birth. Here was a case where a guy who served God in The Temple thought he was a dead man because he "saw" God. He was well aware the scriptures that said. "no man has seen God at any time and liveth..." His wife was a bit more level headed and calmed him down. "Hey Zach, think for a minute, why would The Lord tell us this good news if He was going to kill us on the spot?" That is obviously a paraphrase, but essentially that is exactly what she said. Did an angel catch me and hold me sustained until help arrived? Likely, but I don't know. All I know is help got there fast. I'll get to see that moment of my life some day and find out all the behind the scenes things that transpired. As for now, it is what it is.

Aside from the time when Christ Himself walked the very earth He created, there are plenty of other instances recorded in scripture where God quite literally came down to either talk to, communicate, or interact with and be seen by His people. I don't know what others have experienced. I only hold to what I can plainly see in scripture and of my own personal account. Angels may very well have been at my side that day, and probably were. One day I'll find out. Did I see them? No. But I have no doubt they were indeed there.

It was in 1994, after The motorcycle accident and I had started the landscaping business with the proceeds of what the insurance company had given me from the motorcycle wreck. I wasted it on frivolities and not on things of value such as a house for my wife and I, and though it was not even in my thoughts yet, for children.

I am reminded of many of the words of Solomon when he attempts to warn youth about the pitfalls and many snares that grasp hold of so many in their youth as it did him; and me, and everyone else.

My memory couldn't recall the house until we turned the corner, then the lights came on. I had pictured a completely different house in another part of town and a different color, it was another house that we had actually looked at but ultimately decided against. The house we chose needed a lot less work, but sat on a much smaller parcel of land. It was also more secluded and had the heart attack occurred in that location there would not have been nobody there to give aid. Just another proof that God directs even when we don't aknowledge it.

Memory glitches appeared right away in small ways, for instance I didn't remember having a vasectomy and while in the hospital after my kids had visited me I said to my wife. "Let's have another" Then she told me that I had been "fixed." In disbelief I replied. "I did…? Me…? I did that…? Me…? No way…? …I did not!" Seemed more to me like something got broke, not fixed. But alas it was true.

Then was more fun stuff. Rounds and rounds and rounds of endless testing. Neurological and cognitive testing stuff. Trying to work on ways to improve memory. Trying and testing different strategies to see what worked best. There is no easy answer. You just need to try different things and see what works best for you. Each person is different I suppose. Repetition is essential. The flow of continuos repetition in this short missive has shown. Without the repetition, lessons tend not to "stick." When that happens then buckle up because you're going to be back in class again before too long.

God is ever patient however and He even causes the rain to fall on the just and the unjust. Math 5:45 tells us this. So why should the Christian be immune from problems? Far from it, the contrary is true. God can only use what He has tried and tested and proved. Don't fight the leash, rather bide your time and learn from it. We are told in Proverbs 10:17 that he that refuseth reproof (correction) erreth (makes one whopper of a mistake). Also in 13:18 poverty and shame shall be to him that refuseth instruction. So listen up and pay attention when wisdom "speaks." to you. It speaks every day, listen up.

One particular time when mom came for a visit I shouted. "Hey ma, thanks for coming…" they were pumping me so full of happy-lala potions that figmints of the fictitious Easter Bunny and Santa Claus could have danced an Irish jig across the room in pink tutu's and top hats and I wouldn't have noticed, known, nor cared.

I didn't learn until far too late that Gods way is best. One of the most important rules; for guys anyway, is don't touch the girls unless you're married to them and whole heaps and heaps and heaps of heartaches, problems and troubles will be avoided. God's way is always best. ALWAYS.

Maybe someone reading this right now is thinking, "yeah right, I can't wait! Man." The hormones are just as strong for guys and girls alike no matter what anybody says. You need to wait. But, if it's too late already there is still hope for you to redeem yourself and shed any guilt you may feel, God is willing and waiting to forgive. Come to Him, His way.

Television, movies and music are no help. Our hedonistic society is so inundated with sensuality at every step it's hard though not impossible to avoid. Virtually every magazine add is sensual in one way or another. Images attack our eyes and enter our brains daily from all directions and it effects the way we think and act whether we like it or not.

Not going to college but to work instead was probably an error on my part as well. Oh well, that hindsight thing again. I had a multitude of jobs over the years from grocery store clerk to shoe salesman at a big department store. From dry cleaner to landscaper. From car lot jockey to armed security guard. From appliance repairman to lawn and garden man at the local big box chain store. There were others as well. A jack of all trades and master of none I suppose.

It was sometime around 1994-1995 that I was invited to go to a revival meeting. For one reason or another I accepted. I believe it was the fact that the preacher had been a combat marine of the Viet Nam era. I was intrigued. I am grateful for all our vets of any time era. A zillion times thank you for your sacrifice and service. Enough can never be said, spoken or written to express the thanks we as a nation should give to you all. Thank You.

Anyway, I had never been to a revival meeting and didn't know what it was exactly. I thought it was something that only happened down in our southern states. This was a Tuesday! Church on a Tuesday night? I had never heard of such a thing. At first I declined. I didn't need that stuff, I was okay. After all, I had never killed anybody or anything like that. I was alright. My friend told me the speaker was a former combat marine and liked to go to the shooting range. That raised my eyebrows and piqued my interest. It made for an interesting link. I myself was a firearms instructor and liked to go the shooting range and finding out that a "preacher" liked to go to the shooting range intrigued me. Not knowing any better, I didn't think preachers were supposed to like that sort of thing; you know, fun and all that. So, I went.

My image of preachers was one of robbed figures with clasped hands, funny hats, and a quick, almost singsongy voice. I was in for a wake-up-call. A big one. I pulled into the parking lot and took notice that this church however, had no big steeple, no statues, no fancy expensive stained glass windows, and most interestingly, no collection baskets being passed down the aisles. There was a slotted box up by the pulpit that offerings could be dropped into before and after the service if one felt so led, but no collection plates were passed. Inside the foyer and even inside the sanctuary there was all sorts of noise of folks talking and walking around. There were no statues or paintings of dead people. There was, however, an American flag standing reverently in one corner of the platform. I liked that. Here was a church that had a correct understanding of that so often misused and misquoted phrase, "separation of church and state."

The chatter inside ended when a man got up to the pulpit which was not much higher off the floor than the rows of pews. Just enough for him to see everybody, and vise versa. No higher, making him accessible to the parishioners. He opened with a prayer and it sounded as if he was talking directly to GOD as if He were right there in the room with us! That was different than what I was used to. Everybody sang a song or two and then the Preacher got up to preach. He opened with a brief greeting, he prayed for the meeting to go well and for the salvation of any unsaved persons there. I didn't know what he meant by that, but then he went right into his message. He didn't stand in one place either. He was walking briskly back and forth across the platform talking and giving examples and reading from a black leather covered Bible he was carrying in his hands. Every so often he would stop and bend over and speak to someone in the audience. It wasn't overbearing or odd, but friendly and comfortable. He discussed and then explained verses and passages and put it into perspective for our world today, applying the timeless principles of scripture to what we need in the here-and-now. Shedding light on, and giving understanding to seemingly obscure old testament passages and showing the connection to the New Testament and how we could apply it to our lives today. Clearly The Bible was alive to him, and he made is so for all hearing him.

I had never in my life heard anything like that before; and, I could look at the Bible I had in my hands and see exactly what he was talking about. It wasn't just nonsensical dribble anymore like it had been the usual fare all those previous years. He made the Bible come alive in this way and I finally understood it. No longer was The Bible an out of touch, out of date book to occasionally be dusted off and taken to church a few times a year. I could finally begin to understand it. I began to see the points he was trying to make. I had never heard it put in that way before. In the congregational church I attended off and on over the years, I had heard only soft messages with zero focus on the vileness of MY filthy sin. I had never, not once, ever heard such a plain and clear message of my true fallen nature and my standing before a Holy and Righteous God. I knew that Jesus Christ had come and was born of a virgin, and that He died for everybody. I assumed everybody knew that. But I had never had someone explain it in such a way so I could see, with all clarity, MY need for my personal, one on one need for this Savior. I knew Jesus was the Savior, but I didn't KNOW Him as MY Savior. I knew I needed what that preacher had, and what many others in the room had. A personal relationship with Jesus Christ, God Himself. Jesus Christ IS God.

The message couldn't have been plainer…
1. Realize you are indeed a sinner…
2. Admit and confess such to Christ…
3. Ask Him to forgive you and to save you…

That was it! It seemed so simple, and it was, and IS a simple message. So simple a child can understand and take advantage of it. Perhaps this is why so many adults, and especially "religious" leaders get so offended at the Message of Jesus Christ. All the schooling and learning in the world is really of no value unless Christ is at it's center. It makes us realize that we are unable to DO anything to gain acceptance of God in and of ourselves alone. Our pride doesn't like to hear that kind of message. We are brought up thinking we have to DO something to gain Gods favor. The only thing one need "DO" is make the individual decision to put their trust and faith in Christ and Christ alone. I did exactly that that night and was "Born Again" as the term goes.

Titus 3:5 tells us, Not by works of righteousness which we have done, but according to His mercy He saved us, by the washing and regeneration and renewing of The Holy Ghost.

Jesus and Jesus alone can forgive sins and save souls. Nothing and no one besides Christ the Creator can do it. Sorry if that is "narrow-minded" and "offensive" take up your grievances with Almighty God. It is the truth. Berating the author won't change that.

The evangelist that night certainly had a lot of energy. Moreover he absolutely believed what he was saying. He wasn't just saying things to bolster his ego or fatten his wallet. Not once did he mention money or giving at all. He truly cared for the people he was preaching too.

As I stated above I had gone to church as a lad. On Sunday mornings, my folks, my sibling and I went to a congregational church that had been around almost as long as time itself it seemed. I still went occasionally; a C & E Christian, being Christmas and Easter. That way I could salve my conscience and do what I felt was "my duty" to listen to the unconvicting, soft words from the pulpit. The I'm okay, you're okay messages were the norm I was used to. I incorrectly assumed that I could expect the same from this Church. They were all the same in my book. Imagine a loud alarm clock going off about here.

Nothing could have been further from the truth. In this Church I was actually encouraged to read Gods Word for myself, and I did so beginning with the books of John and Romans and then after being grounded in truth from those two books of scripture, moved onto others. I was encouraged to memorize scripture. I had never thought of trying to memorize any of The Bible. As an unsaved man; why would I? But certain verses. David in psalm 119:11 wrote, "Thy word have a hid in my heart that I might not sin against thee." As well 2 Timothy 3:16, 17 "All scripture is given by inspiration (God breathed) of God and is profitable for reproof for doctrine, (teaching) reproof, (showing) correction, for instruction in righteousness…(17) "That the man of God may be complete, thoroughly furnished unto every good work." There are many others as well. It was clear that memorizing scripture would be a definite benefit to my life. Whenever a situation came up that was questionable for me to partake in. "Bingo" a verse would flash before my mind and help me through whatever it was. No matter what the struggle might be. Greed, lust, anger, language. I had a verse memorized to deal with it.

Part of having Bible knowledge is sharing it with others who do not have it or who might be desperately looking for it without realizing it. This sharing is accomplished through the passing out Gospel Tracts, Through speaking to others when opportunities arose. That is what witnessing is all about. Sadly it is something that the numerous false teaching cults world wide do well in outdistancing many True Christians.

Being confronted with our true nature and being told point blank that we cannot save ourselves and need to have somebody who is willing and able to do the saving for us seems to grate on our nature. In scripture our fallen nature is referred to "the old man", "the flesh" and many other acronyms. Our "Flesh" does not like the message of Salvation and being told it needs a redeemer, or savior. But, such is clearly the truth of scripture.

Simply:

Realizing you need a savior…	That's Conviction…
Admit Christ is the only way you can have any hope of Heaven	That's Confession…
Believing In Christ alone to gain Heavens glory…	That's Commitment, or Faith.

Why that is so difficult for us to do is proof of our fallen nature. We don't want to let go of the sin we enjoy so much, we don't think we need any body or any thing to "help" us. That's prides ugly head rearing up again. My wife came back with me the next night and was heavily "convicted" as the term goes. Soon after she also became a Christian.

My Salvation experience came a good 3 years or so before my cardiac mishap. Even though my wife also had come to a saving knowledge in Christ not long after me, she had some things going on that I did not understand. She had been battling bouts of "depression" Since the birth of our second child. Perhaps the kids being so close in age had a lot to do with it. That along with her family history, were bubbling and festering just below the surface. Like a volcano awaiting eruption. The kids were not what is called Irish twins, a scant 9 or 10 months apart, but they were 14 months apart. Gods timing is perfect, as you shall see.

January and February are usually busy months for my family. My moms birthday is the 23rd, and mine's the 31st of January, and my dads is the same as Lincoln's in February, a scant twelve days beyond mine. Today was Sunday, January 21, 2001 and my family and I arrived home from church to a driveway full of fairly deep snow.

My wife was not having a good day with her mood fluctuations and I, still not knowing what the real issue was, was frustrated. Actually, I was pretty angry, but I didn't voice it or show it. What was the problem? Was it something I'd said? Did I have the wrong color tie on? What was the problem? Not long before I was saved I had a violent and explosive temper. I never hit anyone, but was very good at creative cussing. I also broke quite a few things in my little hissy fits of foolish rage. It is shameful to even talk about it. That me is gone and a new creature exists. (2 corinthians 5:17- "Therefore if any man be in Christ, (a Christian), he is a new creature: old things are passed away; behold, all things are become new."

After I accepted Christ as My Savior that all changed, and it wasn't just me choosing not to do it, but the working of The Holy Spirit that now dwelt inside me. Paul penned under the inspiration of the Holy Sprit of Almighty God to the Galatians. In Galatians 2:20 "I am crucified with Christ: nevertheless I live; yet not I, but Christ liveth in me: and the life which I now live in the flesh I live by the faith of The Son of God, who loved me and gave Himself for me." Compared to what the old man looked like, Isaiah 64:6 "but we all are as an unclean thing, and our iniquities, like the wind have taken us away."

I had been using the incredibly long and tedious drives at work to memorize verses of scripture, and it helped me tremendously. I came across situations where a response was needed and a verse would "come" to mind that would allow me to respond in the proper fashion. I would review these verses continually to keep my frustration and anger in check. Enough on that, back to my driveway.

When we arrived home my wife got out of the van without a word and went inside and lay down in bed. I got the kids unbuckled, we threw a couple of snowballs and then we went inside and I made them some lunch and set them down to eat. One was just out of diapers, and the other, 14 months behind, was not walking yet, not very far anyway. Whilst they were settled into their highchairs chowing down their lunch, I donned my heavy one piece jumpsuit and then headed outside to fire up the snow blower. It is a big orange machine that I had when I was landscaping, and was one of the few pieces of equipment I had kept when I sold my faltering business. It took quite a few pulls to get started and I would always work up a big sweat getting it going. Today was no different, and I indeed worked up a big sweat. While it warmed up I dashed back inside, got the kids cleaned up from lunch, and put them in their respective beds to catch their daily forty winks. I told them I was going out to get the snow off the driveways and to make sure they were sleeping when I got back inside or there'd be a ten hour tickle fest at their expense. My empty threat hung in the air with just a hint of gas and oil from my thick jumpsuit, then I gave them a quick smooch a piece. Business as usual in my book. I'd eat when I got back inside, by then I'd have worked up an appetite, and would enjoy having a few minutes of quiet to sit down and eat and catch up on some reading, or maybe even take an afternoon siesta, myself. Not likely, but who knew! I didn't know, and I sure didn't know what was going to happen within the next hour.

When I got outside my slow blower was all warmed up and waiting for me. I started on my next door neighbor's driveway first. At the time, a dear elderly lady in her late seventies lived there and I liked to keep it clear for her. Either I or the guy across the street would clear the snow, and even take her trash cans out to the curb and back in on trash day. She reminded me of my grandmother in some ways and I'd like to know somebody was looking out for her up in New Hampshire. Besides, it was the right thing to do in my book. I was her neighbor after all.

I brushed off her car, cleared her steps and walkway, did her driveway and made a path to get her trash cans out to the curb. Then took a left 90° and went across in front of her house in the street to start my own drive from the street. I saw her in her front window as I approached my drive and smiled and waved to her, and as I approached my drive I started the snow blowers auger and turned into my yard and started moving snow.

My driveway at that time, was a dirt and stone doublewide driveway that went along the side of the house and into the backyard and then into and also beside the garage. There are no inclines but it is long and as it was unpaved at that point the snow blower tended to pick up and hurl stones and perhaps sticks, and even a matchbox or two that might have been forgotten and left there in the dirt before the snow flew. It usually took me about forty to forty five minutes to do my entire driveway. I was looking forward to lunch and was worrying about how my wife was and hoping my kids were sleeping soundly by now and that the noise of the blower wouldn't wake them. They were both at the far end of our tiny house, so I just prayed they would continue sleeping and plodded forward into the mass of white. I was praying for my wife and our situation also. With all the memory that was lost that day, I distinctly recall praying, "Lord, please help, I don't know what to do. Please do whatever it takes to get her attention." Not a good prayer I admit, perhaps even a tad selfish, but a true one. It was a prayer born from the heart out of complete frustration and utter desperation. I am unable and incapable of doing anything without God's help. That profound and true principle is woven all throughout scripture. I was at the end of my abilities; tapped out and completely empty, something had to change. I don't now how much more there was to that prayer, but that particular phrase I clearly recall. The obvious lesson in that is, We aught to be careful how we pray and what we pray for, because sometimes God grants a hastily issued request. He surely granted this one.

Psalm 50:15. A psalm of Asaph reveals God's heart towards His people. "And call upon me in the day of trouble: I will deliver thee, and thou shalt glorify me." The prayer I uttered doesn't seem like a prayer, I'm sure. But because of my frustration that was how it came out. Trouble comes in all sorts of shapes and sizes. I felt troubled, and I called. Then something happened. I am not saying that God made my heart attack happen. No! I did with my diet and lifestyle. But He knew it was going to happen and He graciously allowed it to happen in a place where I was sure to be seen and not way out back and out of sight. I am not blaming, but rather thanking Him for being kind enough to allow it to happen in a place I'd be seen, as well as being gracious enough to allow someone who just "happened" to have had CPR training in the recent past, be the one who spotted me laying in the snow. My wife had been trained in CPR as well, so I had two additional plusses on my side at that moment.

I don't know how many passes I made before things turned sour. From here on in is where most of the story comes was pieced together from the notes my wife and mom kept. I have no clue as to how far I got before life suddenly changed. For better or worse? Time would tell. I fell straight back and the snow blower stopped dead in it's tracks. When I released my grip the safety handles dropped and the auger and forward momentum stopped, but the engine stayed running.

I fell backwards in the freshly blown snow behind the snowblower. I recall seeing no white lights. I was not floating above my body. I do not recollect any pain thankfully, there was plenty of that to come. I put it like this. I was simply locked in a darkened closet while the room was violently rearranged. If it was not rearranged to my liking, tough cookies, deal with it. The sparrow incident I alluded to down in E.H. happened in here somewhere.

I spent what seemed to me to be eons at a rehab hospital; Hospital for special care in New Britain CT I believe. Because of the anoxic brain injury suffered during the heart attack, these are very sparse.

I was finally home then, and things seemed to be getting back to normal for me anyhow; as well as confusing as well. At that point in time I was both clueless as well as frustrated. Not understanding what Bi-polar disorder was or how it explained many of the mood variations I was seeing, I was at somewhat of a loss to figure out. I did not fully recognize the seriousness of the symptoms my wife had clearly been experiencing, and showing. It was as if a switch had been flipped in her brain that turned her into something and someone she was not. It was night and day at the snap of the fingers. Completely unexplainable to me. I never knew from one moment to the next what to expect or what was going to transpire. Nothing I could do seemed good enough, not to toot my own horn but I was the one who performed the cleaning, meal preparations, laundry, grocery shopping, income provision, bills, diapers, baths and feedings too, at least when I was home. You name it, for the most part I felt as if it were a one man operation. It was not like her, not at all. I couldn't figure our what was going on and it was driving me nuts. As I was not one to air my dirty laundry in public, I didn't say anything to anyone. Except perhaps for my best bud, (The Belch).

Before surfing the web in utter frustration and discovering "Bi-Polar Disorder" one evening, I had no clues as to what was going on. I typed in "mood swings" "menopause", and anything similar I could think of and then found a web-site dealing with Bi-Polar Disorder. That was a WOW moment for me. It must have been God's gentle prodding and direction that led me to it. I never would have thought to look for such if that was not the case. From my perspective all the pieces suddenly fit into place. I thought back to the births of our two kids being so close in age. I couldn't understand it, but surely that threw her system off kilter?

Was this the issue? What else could it be? Where did it come from? Was there any family history of this type of thing in her history? If so, and regardless of such, how do we deal with it? Bi-polar disorder seemed the only answer that made sense. It was something physical after-all that effected hormones and emotions.

From where I stood it seemed that my wife had turned against me in nearly all matters, big or small. I hung in there and kept doing what was right. I did not understand it all and could no longer handle the stress of it. I did not need nor want to endure another stress related heart attack. The stress I endured prior to my first one was unpleasant enough. What was there that I could do? I never liked the idea of being a quitter in anything I did. Such a thing left a distasteful smear as far as I was concerned. Divorce is never God's will, NEVER. He hates divorce because of what it does to his people. He allows for it in cases of adultry, but still prefers reconciliation. It divides and tears asunder what God has joined. What He hath joined let not man tear asunder is how He put it in Mark 10:9. A ruinous divorce was not the answer. There were and are other less destructive means of "helping" than simply quitting and throwing in the towel. One might suggest speaking with friends or pastors who's opinions and council you trust and heed their advice. Marriage is a permanent state. It is not to be entered into flippantly, or on a convenient whim. Marriage in America has become almost a joke. People today it seems change marriages like they change car insurance companies. That should not be so. Marriage is a permanent state between MAN and WOMAN, designed and created by God and thus it is to remain. For LIFE. Not until you get tired of your spouse.

Math 19:4-8 Jesus (God) discusses marriage "and have ye not read, that He which made them at the beginning, made them male and female. (5) and for this cause shall a man leave his mother and father and shall cleave unto his wife: and the twain (two) shall be one flesh? (6) Wherefore they are no more twain, but one flesh. What God hath joined together, let no man put asunder. (7) They then say unto him, why did Moses then command to give a writing of divorcement, and to put her away." (8) He saith unto them, "Moses because of the hardness of your hearts suffered (allowed) you to put away your wives: but from the beginning it was not so. In verse 9 He goes even further and say's that doing so is adultery. The only exception is the death of one spouse or another. So goes the term "until death do us part." That short discourse covers everything we need to know about divorce and even same sex marriage. A quick aside on that particular subject is a short study I wrote a short time ago.

Noah's Ark is mentioned in brevity in this treatise, it is not meant to invoke humor. Rather but to make a very direct and truthful point. Noah's ark, not the cute one depicted on children's books and knapsacks. I mean the real one. The actual barge sized and shaped floating box that God instructed Noah to build. Like it or not, the actual ark that God used to judge sin the first time on this earth is an actual event in human history. It did Happen. A different study covers that subject, this one is on something much more degrading and undermining to human dignity and even man's worship of God (who does not change by the way) After all what kind of God do you wish to serve?

1. An impotent old grandfatherly god who cowtows to your every whim and says you do is fine and dandy and okey-dokey with Him? Sure, he gets "sad" you do bad stuff but will always look the other way. Most people today think who god is thanks to television, music and movies.
2. Or do you want Him to butt out and leave you alone. Except when you want or need something then He'd better hop to it and rush to your side and cough it up.
3. Or do you want to serve a God who lives, who sets standards and rules and expects most prized and dignified creation, "Man." (the only one given an eternal soul) to abide by them, and worship Him as He lays out on His Perfect, Holy and Complete Word. The Bible?

Calling your Creator a liar is dangerous. But it's exactly what you do when you call something "good" that our creator calls SIN. People don't like of the word "sin" today and it is considered taboo in most circles. Now-a-days man just uses the softer more innocuous word "bad" to make the filth God very clearly condemns more palatable for him and easier to swallow. The things God tells us in His Perfect, Unflappable Word, The Bible are an abomination and sin, man turns around and spits in His face and says, "No it's OK, we like it, and we're gonna do it anyway. The Bible doesn't fit us today. We have "evolved," have technology and are smart. We will do as we please."

Unfortunately for those folks, God is still on the throne. He watches and He remembers EVERYTHING! He keeps count as well. Will knowing what God's opinions are on doing and allowing and or supporting such things as gay marriage for starters, and then proving via scripture that doing such things are A FREE WILL CHOICE and "against nature" change your mind? Either you agree with God, or you call Him an unjust liar and move on. Be warned however; the later choice would not be a wise one.

I've only included a few proof verses for space's sake. It aught to be clear enough. The conclusion is obvious. If there's a problem with that, take it up with God. I'm just the messenger.

Excessive drink, drugs, fornication, promiscuity and adultery are bad enough and will be dealt with most harshly unless a turning away and repentance comes first, yet in this brief treatise I am referring specifically to the condemnable practice of "homosexuality." It is not normal! It is a CHOICE! Made of ones own freewill. Thanks to television, movies, music, magazines and books, it is rampant in society. Because of that, such foul practice is considered normal and acceptable today. Such an abominable thing aught not exist yet due to man's sin nature it does. Why do you think such practices are not found in nature? Because it is unnatural! You will never find gay bears, chipmunks, squirrels, possums or any other "gay" animal in nature because they don't exist. Had Noah taken two Woodchucks named Bill and Joe on the Ark there wouldn't be any Woodchucks today. Yes, it really is that simple, physical laws cannot change. As in magnets, like charges repel one another, opposites attract! Clearly, God did not make the homosexual, he made himself by his rebellion to a Holy and all righteous God. It is clearly a choice!

Animals don't have a sin nature, people do because we have an eternal soul, animals do not. Man is a triune being, created in God's image, with a body, an eternal soul and a sprit. Recall in Genesis 2:7 God breathed into man the breath of life and he became a living soul. He did not do this with any other creature. Animals have only body and spirit. Sorry if that offends you, it is truth! Get over it.

There are a plethora of verses both Old and New Testament that prove this fact beyond any shadow of any doubt. They are very clear and specific, there is no doubt what they are talking about. It is Gods opinion on homosexuality:

The God of the Old Testament and The God of the New Testament are one and the same and He does not change. Like it or not, His opinion is still valid. HEBREWS 13:8 "Jesus Christ, the same yesterday today and forever." hmmm.

LEVITICUS 18:22... thou shalt not (don't do it) lie with mankind as with womankind, it is an abomination... (putrefying, disgusting.)

LEVITICUS 20:13... if man lie with man as with a woman, both committed abomination and shall surely be put to death... (sounds like God means business to me)

LEVITICUS 26:16... a burning ague... consume the eyes... (sounds like a horrid disease of some type. Aids? Hmmm Could it be God is serious?)

Oh now that's just mean, Besides that's Old Testament. God is all love, He would never condemn anyone to the literal flames of an eternal Hell for doing those sorts of things today, right? (HEBREWS 13:8!)

OK then, how about the NEW TESTAMENT? oops..., It's even clearer. Guess God's True to His Word after all.

ROMANS 1:27...and likewise also the men, leaving (its a freewill choice) the natural use of the woman (self explanatory) burned in their lust one towards another... men with men woking that which is unseemly (disgusting) and receiving in themselves the error (big mistake) of the recompense (payment) that was due. (deserved) (hmm disease...?)

1 CORINTHIANS 6:9 effeminate / abusers of themselves with mankind.

Hmmm That doesn't sound like something a Holy and Righteous God is pleased with.

Jesus Christ came and judged sin once for all when he suffered horribly on the cross for us. His death burial and resurrection is proof that He was who He claimed to be. God Almighty Himself. His atonement for all sin we have and will ever commit, past present and future, is not a blind blanket that covers us so we can go ahead and live like the devil however we want. No! Yes, it it true that Salvation is freely given. All one need do is ask. It's a personal choice that takes humility and admitting to yourself and or others, and more importantly to God that you are incapable of such of your own accord and asking Him (Jesus Christ) to save you. He'll clean up all the filth afterwards. How can the Christian claim Christianity and also claim that what God calls an abomination is really good and normal? Homosexuality? Abortion? Adultery? What God calls Sin we aught not call righteous and good. What God calls an abomination, we aught not make a law legalizing such as good and normal and trumpet the joys of such lifestyles across the land. Sin is sin however we disguise it and whatever lofty cloak of idea's and words we dress it up with.

Homosexuality is the beginning of the end for a country. History is proof of this. If one were to violate a natural law there will always be a consequence. Always. It has nothing to do with being spiteful or hateful. It is about right and wrong. The Bible is Right in all it shows us. From word one to the very last word. IN THE BEGINNING, and AMEN are those words. The Bible has been given to us to show us and guide us in the paths of righteousness. What The Bible tells us about homosexuality is clear in the above verses.

If you see someone speeding down the road and YOU know the bridge is out and certain death awaits them unless they STOP IMMEDIATELY, it is kind of your duty to warn them. Sure, a part of you wants to say who cares, if they're gonna do something that dumb let them fall to their own folly, but there's a part of you wants to shout a warning and tell them to stop. If they choose to ignore you and continue on in their folly, then you are guiltless. The road to freedom from past guilts starts with repentance. God is willing to forgive any and all, but you have to go to Him on His terms not your own.

It all comes down to one of two choices.

1. Either you believe God
2. You count Him a Liar.

You can't have it both ways. It's either one or the other. Forever is a long time.

Continuing on we can clearly see that scripture gives more clarity on the subject of divorce in MARK 10:9 "Therefore what God hath joined together let not man put asunder." Man and woman, joined together as man and wife for life was Gods intention from the get go. I was not a Christian until well into my marriage, neither of us were. I had warning signs before we were married and I failed to see them clearly, nor heed them. Selfishness and pride blinded me! If I had heeded such warnings, I doubt I would have had a heart attack so early. Eventually for sure because of my poor diet. Let this be a warning to all. Marriage is sacred and the bed undefiled. (Hebrews 13:4) A simple rule to follow is this. Don't touch the girls before you marry em guys (and vice versa) and life can and will be extremely full and joyous. It's the same as cheating. If you won't cheat with her, then you won't cheat on her. The best option is to wait. Unfortunately we were both foolish. We let lusts and passions overwhelm us and were involved in pre-marital-sex (God calls it fornication) before we married and were not in Gods will in so doing. But, how could we have been, we were not even Christians at that point. Having some robed guy shake beads and drip water on your infant forehead does not a Christian make. Its makes an unhappy wet baby is all. It wasn't until after we were married that we found The Lord and were brought to a saving knowledge in Him.

Back then my wife had wanted kids. That I did not until AFTER my salvation experience shows the selfishness of my unregenerate heart. That is man's normal state. Me, me, me. God then changed my heart. We had two children relatively close in age; 14 months. My wife was buried so deep in depression during this time I was at my wits end. I didn't yet understand what was causing it. We had just moved into our house and as it was a bank foreclosure, it needed quite a bit of work here and there, and there and here as well. Many times I would come home from work, usually after an hour or so of driving and find her slumped on the couch staring blankly at the television. My kids running wild, laundry piled up, and no supper in. So I would calm the kids down and play for a few minutes, get supper in and the laundry started and then try and pry out of her any little tidbit I could about her day. My success was next to nonexistent. I equate it to filling the Grand Canyon with a teaspoon. It was an absolutely miserable existence. 98 times out of a 100 I would get the silent treatment, snapped at or talked to like I was a piece of garbage. I did not know what was going on with her, or if it was me or what was up. I prayed continuously for direction, change, guidance, help… During this time I even kept a prayer journal on a daily basis. Everything went in there, frustrations, feelings, hopes, desires. Everything I felt I let fly in those pages. Though there was some self control to an extent. Political history should tell all of us to never say or write anything that might be found by other parties at a later date and sadly, more often than not, mis-interpreted.

I didn't want to, nor enjoy going out at some thankless job 12 or more hours a day. I truly desired to be at home at a good hour after work was complete. My job did not allow for that except on occasion. I was an alarm system installer at a company that went through salesmen like a bottomless bucket goes through water. They would walk in and sell a system, promising customers a world that we installers would then have to make a reality because "That's what they paid for". Oh, it was grand fun, indeed. Thankfully though, there were a few salesmen in the company that were good however who actually understood a little something about construction and were able to design a good workable system. These same salesmen would sometimes even come to the install and help out we installers who, more times than not, were at a site alone.

Now, these "troublesome" jobs that were sold were more times than not an hours plus drive time from the office, and the office was a half hour from home. These selfsame installs were in large homes down along the shoreline. Homes dating back to the 30's and 20's. Sometimes even older than that. The kind of house where the walls were plaster and not sheetrock. The kind of house where mice left presents and nests of chewed up insulation where all my new wires needed to go. The kind of house where space was extremely limited for running and hiding wires and devices such as motion detectors and glass break detectors. Eight times out of ten we installers would discover the devices would not work as the customer had been promised they would work, in the location the customer had been promised. The kind of house where the salesman had told the customer it would be completed at the barest minimum of time letting them get their bonuses while leaving us to explain to a customer and to our installation manager why we were still in the house at 7:00 pm when the salesman told them we'd be out by 4:30. As we had no liberty to come back the next day to finish a job due to the schedule having another install of similar magnitude at the opposite end of the state. Our only alternative was to buck up and get it done. Period! At least we weren't paid by salary. That would really stink.

Don't get me wrong. Hard work was not the problem, or even the real issue. I enjoyed the work and meeting customers and doing all I could to meet their needs. I, for one, did not like having to cut corners or do something that would work, but not be as good if we had the time to do it the right way. Challenges are needed or life would be mundane and boring I suppose. One often needs to push themselves. Needless to say. The boss was not happy because we were putting in overtime. The salesman got upset because his commission suffered when the install actual took the time it SHOULD have taken had he figured it correctly. The main thing was, when I left a job the customers knew how to use their system and were happy with and generally satisfied with it.

One time imparticular I recall was down near the shore, somewhere in Greenwich I believe. I had finished the job about 8:30 pm. Finishing up the day with a satisfied customer and 16 plus hours under my belt. I was beat and looking forward to getting home by about 10:00. I swept up and got all my tools in the van and closed the door and was going to pop back inside to get a signature and double check if my customer was set in the usage of his system or if he had any questions. After getting my signature and heading out the door I reached my van and reached for my keys in my pocket. To my abject horror, they were not there. With a sinking feeling I peered in the window and noticed them on the floor of my "locked" van. I remained calm and checked all the doors, maybe I had not locked one of them. Nope! The van was secure. I called the boss and told him what happened. He was silent for a moment or two while all the ramifications of what that might possibly mean for HIS evening if he had to go to the shop and retrieve the spare van keys we had for all the trucks, and drive an hour to meet me. After a few moments of awkward silence he got back to me and told me to see if the customer had a coat hanger. I even seriously considered smashing a window to get in.

I knocked on the door and after a brief explanation, the customer came out with a coat hanger and we chatted as I started trying to work the coat hanger up through the tightly rolled up window with little to no luck at all. I distinctly recall silently praying something like… Lord, please help, I have to get home. I quoted a verse I had memorized about His being a helper and such. Then I "suddenly remembered" my other key ring; my personal key ring, on which I had a set of 5 "jiggler" keys. Jiggler keys are small, thin metal keys that locksmiths use to move the tumblers inside a lock. I had never used them before, and didn't even know If I knew HOW to use them properly. Regardless of such doubt I got them out and tried. I tried and tried and nothing was happening, then it dawned on me that I hadn't prayed about it. I prayed something to the effect of. "Lord, please let this work, I don't know what else to do, please, you know where the tumblers are I don't. Please make it work." I worked the jiggler keys a little more and all of a sudden. KAKLUNK! And the little knob popped up on the door and I tried the handle and the door opened. I was beyond thrilled. That little seemingly insignificant thing greatly encouraged me. There's no way I could have done that on my own and I don't believe in luck. If God can help in those little insignificant area's. He can certainly take care of the big stuff in our lives. The customer was standing there in disbelief with his jaw hanging open. I looked at him with a smile and he looked back with a bewildered look and said. "How did you do that?!"

I replied the only way I could. "I don't know..., I didn't..., I prayed, tried again, and it's open." I was on a joyous high all the way home. I felt like I could handle anything. All the way I was thanking my Savior. I Nex-teled my boss; who is also a Christian, the one who told me to ask for a coat hanger. I told him the story. It was pretty cool to see that God did indeed work in our ordinary every day lives. When I got home I was still excited about what had happened and wanted to tell my wife.

Arriving at the office in the morning we would receive our days install, extra instructions from the salesman with the occasional. "Oh by the way, I told the customer you'd be happy to do (such and such)" which of course was not on the work order, and thus time for it was not figured into the job, meaning I didn't have the time necessary for it, not and do it right without "cutting corners." But the customer had been "promised" it and we installers had to "make it happen" Without going over on hours on the job. Many times it was doable, it wasn't always fun, but it was doable. The worst ones were the jobs that the house was rather "old" and had an existing alarm system in it. These older systems were normally unsophisticated and had only one or two "zones" for the whole house. The customers understandably wanted them upgraded from the Ben Franklin era to current technology. Because of the way the older systems were wired in one big continuous loop it was not the piece of cake that the salesmen had made it out to be. If there was a loose connection or a break in the wire or an open door or window someplace, the whole system would not work. My meter would show the circuit being "open" when it should be closed. Sometimes these went smooth, but most times things went south rather quickly and not at all smooth and we had to deal with it "on the spot" and make it work to the customer's satisfaction as to what they had been promised. This would normally mean that I would not get home until "late." Sometimes 6:00 pm, but most times 8 or 9:00 Pm. All these different varieties appeared almost daily and thus I never knew when I would get home. I called numerous times each day from the job to see how my wife was doing and if everything was alright. It was a crazy existence. I'm sure the stress was doing wonders for my slowly but surely clogging ticker.

I still did not realize or recognize the symptoms of "depression" that my poor wife was locked in, and was growing increasingly frustrated. Most of the time she was not at home. Whenever I got the word that I had to work late and couldn't be home at a decent time, I dreaded calling her to let her know because I didn't want to have to listen to my wife berate me and then hang up on me. It would have been more tolerable had I recognized the symptoms she had been having. Had I known I could have had more understanding. It wasn't like this ALL the time, but it seemed a good portion of the time. My life really did kind of stink. No, not really kind of, it DID stink, and I hated the drudgery. Adding to the agony was the fact that each guy in the office had to be "on call" 24/7 for one week every four or five weeks. Most of the time the calls were for a dead battery in a transmitter and I would drive an hour and a half down to the shore because the customer had a service contract. These were the calls that usually came in at 11:00 pm Saturday night because the customer couldn't set their system to go to bed and wanted it serviced NOW, ASAP if not sooner. Many times folks were cool about things and we could talk them through a bypass and try to find time to get there come Monday or give it to a guy headed that way. I got so when I did a service call and replaced batteries I would hang onto the old, not quite dead, batteries. These were the little barrel shaped lithium batteries that lasted 3-5 years depending on use. For instance, an entry door would drain faster than a never opened window. If need be we could switch batteries around and make due until a service call could be placed during the week. The problem is, these batteries were expensive and we had to justify using a whole bunch in one fell swoop to our penny pinching corporate overlords. Had service contracts been honored the way they should have been, an ALL AROUND battery change should have been scheduled every 3 years. Regardless of battery life. But in the corporate world the dollar speaks the loudest and that kind of thing was rare. Hmmm, go figure, that company is out of business now...

Normally if one or two went dead in a house within a couple days, they all needed to be changed. When changing them ALL, I didn't toss them but saved the ones that were still viable and I would leave a few of these not quite dead batteries with customers and show them how to open the transmitters and how to change the batteries and reset the system. I kept a small supply of nearly drained batteries in a hidden compartment in my van. A weeks worth of life was better then none at all. Those things were like gold to all us installers and service techs. They could definitely save a trip at midnight to Greenwich. Then I'd be able to come back and do a proper service on the entire system during normal business hours. It was drudgery and misery and with the trials at home? I wanted change. I needed change. I had to have change. Something had to give soon. I didn't care what, but anything, something. Please! That change was on it's way, though not quite what I imagined, or in the quite the way I was thinking. Such is usually the case with hastily breathed prayers.

The stress of the long drives both ways on a daily basis; especially in winter time; like now. As well nine and a half times out of ten times having to grab a quick burger or some other type of fast food drive through deep fried grease bag type of garbage meal on the road was neither cost effective or healthy. But, I was young and not overweight so I arrogantly ignored the warning signs that I can look back on now and clearly recognize meant big trouble a brewing.

The good side of this job was found in the occasional job that was relatively close to home.

There were also those jobs that actually went better than expected and finished earlier than anticipated. These jobs made the boss happy and afforded me the chance to get home at a decent time, even earlier than expected. There I was doing a job that was bringing in the money to make the bills. I had no love for the job but it brought in enough to make the payments, and even a little extra to boot. I still had in my mind to try again with the police exam when it came around again in the spring. I had every intention to continue to train harder and try again. Next time I'd make it for sure.

I hadn't been a Christian all that long and I truly did not understand what The Lord was trying to build, or even how I might be hindering it. I was doing all I knew how to do, and trying even when I didn't know what or how to try. Again, I knew nothing of, or had even considered something like Bi-Polar Disorder. I would not guess/figure out and then confirm that my wife had/has or "suffered" from what is sometimes called Bi-polar disorder? Everything suddenly made perfect and clear sense to me. It came to me as I searched the internet one night for the symptoms of what I had been dealing with. I was amazed at all the similarities I saw and left her a printout on the table I had gotten off the internet. All the buttons seemed to click and I wanted her to know I wasn't blind to it.

It was a vicious cycle. My wife up, and then down. Joyful, and then miserable.

This kind of nonsense continued and continued and continued until one Sunday in January of 2001. We had gone to Church, my wife had been, what seemed to me at the time her usual pillar of joy without a word coming from her. I still didn't completely understand the issues of Bi-polar depression, or even what the real source was. My frustration level was high as usual. I stayed silent, and stuffed, hid, concealed, brushed it aside and buried the feelings like your typical guy and just "dealt" with it. I was used to it all by now and just figured that was the way it was and the way it was, was the way it was. Stress only bothered you if you let it. Still, even if I didn't "let it"; I kinda did, internally anyway.

My wife sat locked in silence during the ride to church, during the Sunday school hour and during the main church service. I said nothing, But I'm certain I was getting a bit irritated. Church ended, I got the kids out of their Sunday school classes and into their car seats. My wife had come right out and was sitting in the van waiting while I got the kids. We came home in silence save for my chatter with the kids. We pulled into a snow covered driveway and my wife got out of the car and went inside without a word to anybody. I got the kids out of their car seats and got them inside and made their lunch and sat them in their respective highchairs. My wife had gone in and lay down in bed. I said nothing to her, but went outside and got the snowblower started and warming up. It had been starting harder each time I used it lately and I probably should have done some preventive maintenance on it the previous fall but hadn't, my own sloth was to blame for that oversight. It took quite a few pulls to get her fired up and going. I'd do a thorough P.M. on the machine in the spring I told myself. I was already irritated and frustrated enough to pull the thing into next week.

I was taking Meds for high blood pressure and this situation wasn't helping it any for sure. I could feel the stress boiling up from my belly like a rising pool of acidic lava preparing to explode into the atmosphere. I finally got the thing started and simply brushed aside the feelings of anger and frustration and pushed ahead. I ran through verses in my mind that I had memorized for times like this and kept moving. As I often say today, yesterday is gone, it is in the past, glean what you can from it and push ahead to tomorrow. You can't get it back and you can't change it by saying "If only", or "what if." Don't worry about the stuff you cannot change like death and taxes, but take what you've been given and run with it, man. Change the things that are within your power to change and press forward. Like I say, I had been working on memorizing scripture verses on the subject of anger to help me in that area. It works. My temper had not been as large an issue as before.

When I felt the old anger churning up inside me I grabbed those verses and brought them to the forefront of my mind. Verses like Colossians 3:8 – Let all wrath and clamor and anger and blasphemy be put away from you, with all malice, and Ephesians 4:26, Proverbs 12:16, Proverbs 14:29, Proverbs 15:1, Proverbs 19:19 and other similar verses concerning anger and about not letting the sun go down on your wrath. That last one simply meaning, don't go to bed mad. If you have a problem with someone, take care of it and sleep peacefully so you don't toss and turn all night and wake up with a raging belly ache, and even madder than you were the night before. The scriptures are literally loaded with verses to help those of us with short fuses learn, with Gods grace, to put off the old man and turn from that way. I write US because no one ever conquers it completely this side of Heaven. It is a daily thing the Christian must do, like Paul wrote of how he "died" daily, not in a physical sense obviously; but that he willingly, with the help of the Holy Spirit put aside any attitudes or thoughts that would hinder him on a daily, even an hour to hour basis. That is how you overcome. Keep the right focus.

Back to the main event I suppose, while the snowblower warmed up I went back inside and changed my clothes and put on my heavy winter coveralls. The kids had finished their lunches so I got them cleaned up and down in their beds for naps so I could go out and snowblow the driveways. I didn't eat. It should only take me an hour to an hour and a half to do two small driveways with walkways and shovel the steps. I did my elderly neighbors car and driveway first and cleared a place for her trash cans and a walkway over to our property and then started on my own driveway. I hadn't eaten much for breakfast either and was looking forward to lunch and maybe a hot cup of tea when I got done. Yeah, that sounded good. I had always liked tea. That was something to look forward to.

My snow blower is a big Ariens 8 horse power model ST-824 that; at this time, had no electric starter on it. No biggie to me, it was a leftover piece of equipment I kept when I sold my landscaping business. It was a good machine and usually; when I kept the upkeep on it current, started in the first few pulls. I cleared our elderly neighbors driveway first. A nice elderly lady we had befriended and helped out occasionally with this or that. Then I started on my own driveway. I recall walking in the street to my own driveway, and waving to her in her window. From this point there is zero memory of the events. What follows is from a notebook my wife started keeping in the hospital. As best as I can gather, I had only made a few passes when IT happened. I do not recall feeling any dizziness or pain; that's fine with me, I don't mind forgetting that kind of stuff. It was simply lights out.

We lived perhaps 1.5 miles from a little community hospital, and from my house to there the ambulance stopped twice so the EMT's could send 200 plus Jules coursing through my limp form to jump start my cantankerous ticker with the paddles in the back of "the wagon".

Nobody would know the extent of the damage until they got a (cathater) in me and sent that glowing dye through the bloodstream that reveal where the blockage, or blockages were. To the surprise of them all from what I hear, they found four completely blocked arteries and at least one that was partially blocked. I needed a quadruple bypass! NOW! This hospital did not have surgeons with the skills needed to save my life, but they obviously kept me going by whatever they did. The next thing that was done was to call on Connecticut's LifeStar Helicopter, one of two in the state at that time, one stationed in Bridgeport and one at Hartford Hospital where I was to be brought. Hartford Hospital has both a helipad and an operating room on the top of the building. They also have some of the best cardiac surgeons in the state if not the country. The doctors with the expertise to repair the physical damage that I had unwittingly caused to my heart with my foul greasy diet and stress; were on hand.

My Mitral valve was completely obliterated and blown apart from the intense pressure it had been under. I had four completely blocked arteries and one that was partially blocked. The heart had all sorts of arterial circulation arteries where it had tried to find ways around the blockages itself over the years I must have been building them up. Random chance could not have created such a brilliant organ by trial and error. The heart was designed and created, it could not possibly have "evolved," over time, for part of a heart is not a heart at all.

I spent a number of weeks at Hartford hospital, but the ride from this hospital to the hospital for special care in New Britain, where the majority of my rehab would take place is my first memory, and that is extremely sketchy. The attendant was very professional and I was kinda disappointed that we went without lights and sirens, but I suppose my condition didn't call for it at this point. That is all I recall, and the bright lights inside the ambulance, and trees zooming by out the window. Other than that it is just vague little snippets of occasional recall. I am extremely thankful though that I am unable to recall Hartford hospital itself though, For I did some stuff there that were both painful and embarrassing. Not to mention dangerous and/or disgusting. One time I was so irritated at all the wires and tubes sticking out of me. I started yanking on tubes and wires and such, including the electrodes temporarily going into my heart! The ones keeping it beating properly. They obviously stopped me in time and strapped my arms down. Restraints while agitated! That was fun! Necessary I suppose, however unpleasant. Another time I thought I was in the middle of a bank robbery and the orderly was one of the crooks and was trying to rob the joint. I was stuffing all the dirty clothes (money) into the hamper to hide it. I had to be held down by 3 or 4 people and strapped to the bed. I'd love to see a video of that one. The only good thing about this is that I was at least a "good guy" and was trying to stop the imaginary heist. Even some of the pictures I've seen of me in there during that time are scary. I don't even recognize myself with those wild eyes. I guess I wasn't a very patient, patient.

The stuff they had me on must have been some heavy duty pain killers. It's amazing that some people drink and take drugs to get that feeling "on purpose." That's crazy. Doing such is beyond foolish in my book. Downright insanity! Somewhere in all this turmoil I got pneumonia and endured fits of violent coughing. I had to do so with pillows clutched tightly to my chest in a death hug because of the intense pain in my chest every time I DID cough. I kept forgetting they had sawed open my chest rather quickly and split my ribcage wide open like a Christmas turkey to get to my dying heart. The place where they rejoined my sternum with wire felt like a hammer blow with every cough, and every cough would produce more coughing, which produced more coughing, which produced more shocks of pain to my sternum and ribcage. Only to flop back on the bed in a cold sweat trembling and tense with agony. It was awful. It felt like I was reopening where the wire had closed the gap in the bone. A horrible, vicious cycle that endured for hours? Days? I don't know, thankfully I cannot recall it. I know this and can write this because of the logs kept by my family. As I sit here and type, bits and pieces of mixed memories are coming to my mind. I thought that agony would never end. But, Thank The Lord, it did. I don't remember it save for the written reports. That's a good thing. Even writing the above paragraph it is in a second person type of setting. That diminutive amount of time of mild discomfort is nothing compared to the agony of an endless eternity without Christ had I died in my driveway not knowing Jesus Christ as my personal Lord and savior. Such an eternity is far more than just "a burning thirst for God" as some have put it. Fortunately, I did know Christ as my Lord and personal savior. Thankfully, that is all it takes to insure a place in His Heaven. Faith in Christ alone and nothing added. Nothing at all. No penance, not amount of monies given. What can you possibly add to the coffers of one who owns the cattle on a thousand hilltops? He owns those selfsame hilltops too. The easy answer is, NOTHING!

One instance I particularly wish never to remember was the day I had to be strapped down to the hospital bed. I don't know what set me off, if I was sick of laying there unable to move, or what it was, but I started pulling on all the wires and tubes going in and out of my chest that were the drains and electrodes going directly into the recovering heart muscle. I imagine I wasn't being very gentle either. Before they got to me I had yanked out my catheter tube while the little balloon inside that holds it in place within the bladder was fully inflated. OUCH, that even hurt to type. That's one memory that I'm extremely grateful to have gone. A bloody mess from what I hear, the worse part is, that catheter had to go back IN. Fortunately that most unpleasant memory is also long gone. Unfortunately I DO remember the one inserted when I had the stroke.

Our kids where both tiny in this parcel of time. Some things had been occurring around home and with my wife that I could not figure out. I touched briefly on this topic above and will add to it here for further clarification. In complete and utter frustration one evening I went web surfing "the web" for sites about menopause, manic-depressive and any of the symptoms I had seen and what, if anything they all had in common. I found a site dealing with Bi-Polar disorder and couldn't believe what I was seeing and reading. I now had something verifiable to go on. Was this it? All the symptoms seemed to fit perfectly what my wife was being dragged through, and bringing the rest of us with her. Could this be the answer? Was Bi-Polar Disorder to blame? Was this the missing piece to the baffling and mind boggling mysterious puzzle that had befuddled us all for so long?

I printed out the site name and information and cautiously showed it to my wife who was rather shocked. She asked me how I knew? That was what her doctor was currently looking into. I could only shrug. I just put the pieces together, and as much as I dislike math, it all seemed to add up. The pieces finally fit together. Well, no matter the difficulty, it could be overcome. What follows is a generic over-all from a website I found on the subject. It's a wide brush but there it is...

Most folks, male or female that seem to be afflicted or suffer from what is called Bipolar disorder have the same goal any one does. To just make it through a day without having any kind of emotional difficulties. There is no 100 percent sure way of stopping these things from happening to you. But, there are countless things you can learn to do to help you to improve your outlook. To get to that point, can start by finding all of the information you can possibly find about this condition so that you can better understand what is happening to you. Bipolar is a condition in which there are extremes in moods and life experiences. You may have heard bipolar called Manic Depression or that a person suffering from it has a manic depressive condition. But, what scientists have come to learn is that manic style behavior is only one extreme of this condition. Another part is it can drag one into many a different depth of depression. Both of these conditions are vitally serious to your well being and even to your life span and must be treated. While doctors do not have a cause for bipolar, they are working on finding one. Along with that, you can be sure that there are many scientists looking for a way to cure the condition. For most people bipolar starts when they are just in their teens. Some believe that it is triggered by puberty. Others will not develop this condition until they are in their early adult years.

If you don't get help for bipolar, your condition is likely to continue to worsen. There is no doubt that depression itself is a killer. Therefore, not getting help is simply not an option. But, the good news is that there are medications, treatments and therapies that can help to reduce the symptoms and help you to cope with your condition. Do You Have Bipolar? The first question that you need to ask is if you have this condition. Learning the signs and symptoms will help you to weigh the need to seek out medical attention. You may have very poor judgment, and you may know this by being told by others that you've made the wrong decision. Your mind is going crazy with thoughts. You may be agitated and feel the need to move your body and your mind. Physical activity may be increased, too. Most cases of what is determined to be Bi-Polar type conditions can be traced back through family gene trees. Much like heart disease, all sorts of factors come into play from genetics to biological. The name makes me think of something some climate-change environmentalist whacko might use when pleading their misguided and fictitious case in an attempt to usurp tax payer funds from congress. In reality, being bi-polar is no picnic. For anyone involved. If you suspect it in someone you care for, get a handle on it before it worsens.

O.K. so we had an answer, now what do we do with it. My frustration level was getting back to the level that it was before I had keeled over due to my cantankerous ticker. Only now it was compounded by my swiss-cheese memory. I also knew I had not been praying as I once had. People would say, "just get a divorce and be done with it and than all your troubles will be over." WRONG, WRONG, and WRONG. Sorry, NO. The opposite is true. That is absolutely horrible, terrible and hideous advice. Marriage is one MAN and one WOMAN for life until death parts them. A divorce was never, and is never part of God's equation. It was allowed for mankind's selfish stupidity, hard heartedness and pride. Thinking that you could not go through something like that again for anybody is a lie and flies in the face of the title I gave this story. With Gods Grace we can accomplish anything that is His Will and Divorce is never, never, never in Gods will. Work through it with patience, love and council if needs be (preferably Biblical council) Jesus speaks to us in Mathew 19:8 Moses because of the hardness (selfish, stubborn, pride) of your hearts suffered (allowed) you to put away your wives: (for convenience) but from the beginning it was not so.

The New testament is pretty clear. Mark 10:9 "What therefore God Hath joined let not man put asunder." Stress is a killer, and it was building again. A divorce is stressful for certain, but not as stressful as living the rest of your life with a person who makes you so miserable you are weary of life itself. With the wrong attitude it can seem as such.

Looking at the situation with improper lenses in my glasses I could not see the big picture. Elsewhere us guys are COMMANDED. "Husbands love your wives, and be not bitter against them." There are no "unless..." "or..." "only if..." hidden in that command. We are just to do it, end of story.

I have seen guys who have "hung in there" for one reason or another. For guilt? For their kids? From all outward appearances they appear completely miserable. Whatever the reason is that would cause a "husband" to cling to such bitterness is a moot point, and we are COMMANDED NOT to do it. End of story. It also appears to be a truth that some people were never meant to be married. God gives the Grace for some people to stay single. I for one like being married, it gives comfort and YES it takes working at. While God hates divorce, he hates the alternative I just mentioned as well. Separate for a time if you have to, but if you are married, "STAY" married. Seek WISE council and work through any "issues" you might have allowed to creep in and "STAY" married. He says that, "whosoever divorces his wife and marries another commits adultery..." that is pretty clear. He also says that whoever "looks" (glance longingly) at a woman TO LUST (emphasis mine) after her has committed adultery with her already in his heart. By that account me and every other normal guy on the planet are already guilty of it and beyond condemned. That's the point! It is all but unavoidable. For BOTH sexes. Even on a dessert island, images come into your mind. It's a done deal, even if it is never acted upon you are guilty. You drive down the road and the billboards are in your face, you go to the grocery store and the magazine rack is right in front of your face at check out. Worse yet, you turn on a television and it is there nearly 24/7. Whether it be commercials, news or "prime time". Sex sells and we live in a sex crazed society. No one can turn on a television for more than five minutes and deny that claim. Is it any wonder divorce is seemingly everywhere in America? It has been made so easy for us to toss out the "old" and embrace the "new." The wise would advise to stay in the battle and don't quit.

Physical contact was a factor in my situation. Sadly, I admit that my wife and I did not wait until marriage before partaking of this cup that is supposed to be for marriage alone. Granted, we were not Christians when we were dating or even when we first were married. Such revelation came later, but it is still no excuse. Ignorance of the law does not make one innocent. There is no excuse. The repercussions and penalties for sin sometimes do not surface until much later in life. Usually when things are going pretty well and you start thinking you got by with something. When those thoughts are present is when your world will fall apart, quite suddenly, and quite messily. A continuous study of scripture will help a person avoid many a pitfall. Seek wise council and heed it. Don't forget, God does not change, HEBREWS 13:8 Jesus Christ the same yesterday, today and forever.

You will obtain a blessing if you listen and obey, a curse if you do not. It is either one or the other, you CANNOT have it both ways. God said as much to the Israelites upon finally getting into the promised land. Guess what they chose? History tells us that story, but Israel is still there. It is the same for US today (Hebrews 13:8) God is unchanging and his principles stand unbending and are eternal. God told the Israelites to go in and take the land because He had already given it to them. The naysayers said "No, we can't." A few like Joshua said, "Yes, we can, let's go guys we can do this easy." But those naysayers and winers ultimately led to Israel's defeat and then they walked around the dessert in circles for 40 years until all such naysayers were dead and their kids got the blessing of obeying God and doing His will. Josh had said "Lets go guys. God said we'll be victorious, C'mon." The majority said "No way, they're too powerful we'll get wiped out." God then said, "Okay, you won't go in, then you WON'T go in." Then they felt guilty at Gods rebuke and tried anyway after God said no and got their hat's handed to them and a foot showed them the door.

Back again to the heart issue, brain injuries come in two basic classifications. Anoxic and traumatic. There are a whole range of dimensions and variations to each type and in each type. Anoxic is when the brain is deprived of oxygen, the longer the deprivation, the worse the injury. If I were to delve into politics with a brain injury of this type I would quite likely fit right in and no one would be the wiser. I would have a perfect excuse as well. When I told someone I didn't recollect something I'd be telling the truth. Traumatic is often far worse. Usually from a blow to the head from an accident, combat, a fall. Many times the damaged portions are permanent. While God has created the brain with the amazing capacity to repair itself. It is very often a painfully slow and maddening process. Things usually occur in spurts, even with compensations. Using things like palm pilots or smart phones with calendars and alarms, or carrying small notepads in your pocket, help. Having your wallets and keys quite literally chained to your belt is good also. Even so, stuff happens. If you're not careful you will inadvertently take something out, be holding it in your hand and place it down to do something else; answer a phone, talk to someone, or worse, walk away for a second. Then say, "Oh Wait", turn back around to get it, and the thing you had is now quite literally "GONE". You are living your life in a constant black hole of twilight zone episodes with no remote control to rewind to find said item, or to even fast forward past the unpalatable parts. It is so, so easy to do. You don't even realize it 'til it is too late. It just "happens." To make matters worse, while in this state, your frustration level will leave you careless and something else you "need" will somehow find itself into the same twilight zone episode. This will frustrate you further. Let me tell you, it IS NOT fun, for ANYBODY involved. You need to distance yourself from the situation and retrace your steps or simply walk away for a while and then come back to whatever task or project you were working on at the time at some later interval. It can be quite maddening. Step back or step away for a while is the best option you have.

For example I have lost my keys on numerous occasions, even though I have them clipped on a loop on my belt. I unhook them to open a door and If I put them on the counter and not back on the loop-chain thingy immediately they simply will "vanish." I do have a spare set on a key-ring holder at home, but that is by no means a guarantee however. At the time of the writing of this segment I had "lost" or rather, somehow conveniently misplaced my Drivers License and other ID's. As soon as I noticed they were gone I called and reported it. I was getting ready to go to a karate class and had opened my wallet to take them both out to put in the side pouch of my workout bag. I placed them on the edge of the bed and turned around and retrieved my work-out bag from the closet. Apparently my turning caused them to "fall" onto the floor, and I picked them up. Or, I thought I had. It was easier to put them in the side pouch of my work out bag than carry my wallet. I didn't want any unscrupulous person finding it and using or selling my identity. Humanities scum will do that sort thing and enjoy it just for kicks. I didn't need that grief on top of everything else I was joggling at the time. I simply could not remember where they had gone. I knew they had to be close, but in times of frustration the memory gets even worse and I wasn't even sure IF I had dropped them in the bedroom or someplace else. Maybe I had even lost them someplace outside the home, the Jeep, a store, the gym, at class? Oh great, that was all I needed. I even telephoned the last store I had been at to see if I had left my ID at the register. It was possible after all, however unlikely. I tried to think of anywhere and everywhere they could possible be. It was maddening. But, they of course weren't there, either. They were just "gone." Inexplicable as it is, but that was the case.

All my attempts to find them failed miserably. I retraced my steps to the point they fell out of my wallet and I had picked them up; from then on it was anybodies guess. I determined they weren't at any store because I had dropped them here at home "after" I had gotten back from said store. They dropped and I had scooped them up quick and hurriedly placed them somewhere else and then "forgotten" the location of said place. NO! They had to be here, in the house. They would turn up. Sure enough, they did. They had fallen from the edge of the bed where I had so absentmindedly placed them, dropping on the floor and landing on a little throw rug so no sound was made on the hardwood floor to alert me. Then somehow they ended up "under" that tiny rug? Probably from my attempt to find them, flipping blankets and pillows in a frenzy I made the situation even worse. Had I just remained calm and looked straight down, I would have seen them.

I absolutely believe in the power of prayer, however I do not believe in prayer being the magic bullet we load every time we are in trouble but rather a continual state between the Creator and Us. It is not "when all else fails," but "before all else fails, pray." Perhaps learning a lesson of some kind is what was needed? Perhaps more dependence on Him for my troubles, no matter how small or minute. He wants to take our troubles anyway, no matter how small we perceive them to be. Why do we so eagerly run ahead with such blind confidence that we can handle anything that comes our way?

Any Christian who is honest with themselves will say Amen to that. That is why James wrote in his epistle, chapter 1 verses 2 and 3 "Count it all joy when you fall into diverse temptations, knowing this, that the trying of your faith worketh patience." Temptations being trials and struggles and grief of all sorts.

People are watching! And we will fall INTO trouble from time to time. Neighbors and coworkers and especially family members are all closely watching The Christian to see how they respond to difficulties. Christians are not immune to troubles and difficulties. Matthew 5:45 tells us, "He maketh His sun to rise on the evil and on the good, and sendeth rain on the just and the unjust." In other words, Just because you become a Christian does not mean all your troubles will disappear. On the contrary they will likely even increase. You will however, have grace and help to get through and overcome whatever trouble you face for certain.

Count it all joy? That is all but impossible in and of ourselves. When every fiber of your being wants to "roar" and exact some sort of vengeance on the nearest inanimate object at hand. Another example is in writing this book, I "misplaced" my Concordance. Anyone who has one or has seen knows the Concordance is not a small book by any means. A concordance is an invaluable tool for Biblical studies! Every single word in The Bible is in there with every verse it is used in. If you can only remember "The Lord said" part of a particular verse, it will give you every location where that particular phrase is used and you can find the verse you are looking for. I had looked high and low without result. I had even looked the same places that turned up nothing moments before just on the off chance I might have overlooked this rather large book. Usually, after I loose something and look for it until I've pulled all my hair out, I will break down and go purchase a replacement. Then, within a day or two; sometimes hours, I will discover the "lost" item.

Then I have a spare. That routine is not the most cost effect way to deal with this type of brain injury, however.

In times such as this I have to step back and say "okay, wait a minute, I give Lord, what do I need to learn? Getting mad at myself is pointless and a complete waste of time. You go bonkers bouncing off the walls for ten minutes and then you wind right back where you were with the same issue. You've accomplished nothing. Better to keep your peace and hold fast than to lose your temper and be a fool. Proverbs 12:16 "A fools wrath is presently known, but a prudent man covereth shame." Proverbs 27:3 "A stone is heavy, and sand weighty, but a fools wrath is heavier than them both." Following the advice in those verses, Pro 10:20,12:18, 18:21, James 1.26, 3.5 3:8.

"How" do things get "lost?" If some of the doctors that I have spoken to are correct, and I often find that questionable, they explained it sort of like this. Imagine your brain is a box with a bunch of different compartments in it that are all connected by little wires. When the oxygen is cut off to the brain those little wires "break" or "get cut" and the connection is gone between the boxes and the information that once flowed easily from box A to box B can't get there. Now box C is screaming at box B because box D is screaming at it because the information it is getting is just a mass of jumbled confusion. In this regard, it is much like how Congress tries to accomplish things. On the flip side, and very much unlike Congress I have been told that the wonderfully created brain works to "rebuild" the connections to get the information "redirected" and flowing freely again. Unfortunately that takes time and until then, the brain and it's owner has to manage as best as possible with whatever tools he or she can use and function with. I fought getting a palm pilot, or PDA, as some call it at first because I had never needed one of "those things" before and sure didn't need one now. Proverbs 16:18 tells us that Pride goeth before a destruction, and a haughty spirit before a fall. Forgetting such verses as the one above I fought it for a brief spell. Now they are called smart phones, and I have to admit I rely on mine constantly. Thankfully, my wavering humility finally lost and I am currently on my sixth palm pilot/smart phone as of this writing, now it is such a part of my "routine" that it would be difficult, though not impossible to get by without one. Palm number five disappeared in the hospital during the stroke rehab. Others simply gave up the ghost and stopped working, or they get wet and stop working, or "dropped" and stop working. After all, they are an electronic device and they do "crash" and need to be serviced from time to time. They also, like certain large books, occasionally get "lost." The one I have currently is both a phone and a palm pilot day planner and even has a camera to boot. This way here I don't have to loose my palm pilot and my phone separately, I can "lose" them both at one time and get the consternation over and done with all in one fell swoop. For additional fun, if I have turned the ringer "off"; for Church or a Movie for example, it makes it harder to find because I can't simply call it and follow the ringing. It's grand fun indeed.

The way the brain re-wires itself is kind of how the heart tries to repair itself. My heart was an amazing mess. From what I have been told it must have been plugged up for quite a while and finally said "enough." The Lateral Circulation was spider-webbed all over my heart. My pump must have been getting clogged up from my teens and even before that to have had as much Lateral Circulation as it did. Had I known about, or more importantly "paid attention" to the warning signs that I clearly had been getting; As well to my own family history a tad more closely, I might very well have avoided this rather unpleasant "lesson" in my life. Had I heeded them, the warning signs were all there in abundant and plentiful supply. The foul hack-wheezing cardiac cough as it is often called, would come on for no apparent reason and linger for a short spell. Shortness of breath in Karate class! Shortness of breath in the State Police exam-run! Shortness of breath in running even short distances. Shortness of breath in daily activities such as up and down stairs with the laundry basket. I had all these signs, but I didn't heed them. I was young after all, I was just out of shape I convinced myself and would push myself even harder in whatever I was doing. That's the stubborn New Englander in me I suppose. Proverbs 8:13 – The fear of The Lord is to hate evil: Pride and arrogance, and the evil way, and the forward mouth, do I hate. Again, Proverbs 16:18- Pride goeth before a destruction, and a haughty spirit before a fall. Prides a killer. Always has been. Such can be traced all the way back to the garden of Eden with Satan wanting Gods job and it not being available and so falling because of his pride. The bite marks are still there long after pride bites you. Usually visibly as scars in our flesh, as well as unpleasant memories.

Brain injuries are sort of like toothaches, they vary in severity from mild to extreme. As I wrote above there are anoxic brain injuries and there are traumatic brain injuries, these also vary in like fashion. Anoxic is when the brain is deprived of oxygen and it starts dying slowly, suffocating, starved for oxygen. Traumatic is just how it sounds, a blow to the head; from a weapon, a fall on the concrete, a car crash. There is obvious visible, physical damage with this type as I understand it. With anoxic brain injuries, the damage is not as obvious or blatant as with many traumatic brain injuries. Some, improve over time as the brain repairs itself and the damaged or severed connections are rebuilt or rerouted. Evolution could never, never, never create such a phenomenally designed computer that repairs itself as the brain is capable of doing.

In joking around I often say, "If you forget to remember, have you? And how would you know if you have anyway?" (or) "is it better to forget to remember, or remember to forget?" Actually, if you remember to forget, you're actually accomplishing something, so it works both ways I suppose. It still is no picnic.

If I were a seaman and were to put having this type of brain injury into nautical terms it would read something like this. My outboard fell overboard. My inboard has a blown head gasket and is also out of gas and seized up. My rigging is knotted and tangled. My sails are ripped and my masts are snapped like dried twigs. One oar is broken and the other is lost. The hull leaks and there are no life jackets aboard. There is no radio and no flare gun. The only bailing pale has no bottom. The waters are shark infested and there is a deep cut on my leg. Things may look pretty bleak. Hopeless to some. All of your options appear to be gone. But you still have to get to where you're going. Find a way. Never, never, never quit the fight, never, never, never give up the ship, even when it is blown from the water beneath you and sinks like a stone. Stay in the fight. Cling to the very last thread, tread water and fight to stay afloat. No matter what, stay in the battle, don't give up, never quit. If you quit and throw in the towel all you will ever know is defeat. It may appear impossible, and alone it is. Never forget that. Philippians 4:13 reminds us "I can do all things through Christ which strengtheneth me." With God's ever-always available help you can do anything that is in His will for you to accomplish.

If you are willing, you can learn a lot while you are floating there in limbo. You will probably not enjoy this time, but, if you remain willing and pliable, you will learn a great deal from the experience. It may well be unpleasant, but God has not promised the Christian a pleasant journey, or even an easy one, only that He would be WITH us ON that journey. Don't forget, He went through far worse than any of us ever will. His suffering was immeasurable, and He was completely innocent. He has promised never to leave us or forsake us. Deuteronomy 31:8 And The Lord, He it is that doth go before thee; He will be with thee, He will not fail thee, neither forsake thee; Fear not, neither be dismayed. That is an awesome promise, and is repeated again in the New Testament in (Hebrews 13:5) God does not forsake His children. He knows better then we do how much each one of "His own" can handle and continually tests and proves us to grow us. If He is not testing you, it might be time to recheck your spiritual condition. God can only use a soldier He has tried, tested, refined, proved, and molded into something valuable. Thank God for your trials and tests and keep on keeping on. Don't quit.

I had begun work again finally with a company that subbed out workers to one of the big box stores taking care of the outdoor plants and such. I had done some landscaping so that was my "in" and I was the one guy the boss kept on the roster when the winter came. It was work and gave me some hours doing "something" and being active. Well, one day around lunchtime I felt terrible. I had the worst headache I had ever had, Advil and Tylenol wasn't touching it. I told the store manager I had to bail out, apologized, logged out and headed for home. It was going to be good to get home and lay down. Aside from the headache I was also exhausted. Odd? I had felt fine earlier. So I headed out for home. On the bridge going over the Connecticut river is when the double vision hit full force. There was no place to pull over so I simply shut the weaker of my two eyes and drove home with the good one open. Without depth perception it was tricky and I just left more room between cars. I was thankful it wasn't rush hour. It was around 2-230, and I wanted home in a bad way. A friends house was right up the street from mine so I went there first but nobody was home, so I just came home. I have never had a headache that severe before. The pressure, the spikes of angry white hot pain knifing through my head was something I don't ever want to experience again. Advil and Tylenol wasn't even touching it. They ran the other direction when I took them. I came in the house and went and lay down. Both kids were home and I told them I felt obscenely horrible and was going to lay down. Such was very uncharacteristic of dad, so I got twenty questions. "What's wrong Dad, what's wrong Dad, you alright?" and the like. "I'm fine, I'm just exhausted and have a bad headache is all." I felt nauseous but nothing came up but dry heaves, I was sweating incredibly profusely. It was Friday and my wife had gone to work, so my daughter called my mom and she came up. I felt for sure it was just some foul bug attacking me and I was resisting their urges to go to the hospital. There's that ugly pride thing again! I finally relented and they took me in and lo and behold I had had what was called a brain stem stroke. Kind of rare from what I was told. The folks at the hospital I went to mentioned to me only one other person they knew of came through it in such fashion as I did. Walking and talking and such.

Through all this, My wife had gone through a bout with thyroid cancer and had the thing removed and thus is on meds for life because of it. Much like I have to be on certain meds for life because of the heart. Quite a pair. What this instance was going to add, I didn't know.

The current technology on defibultors has them lasting about five years between replacements. I'm on my third one at the moment. There was a time I found out that the replacement defribulator that was placed into my chest after the heart attack to regulate the hearts electrical impulses was discovered to be a defective model, and the company paid to have it replaced. As it turned out, the company KNEW it was defective; some had mis-fired and some had battery leaks. They had rolled the dice and crossed their fingers and placed them in patients anyway. How nice and consciencsous of them. They got caught however and paid to have the defib replaced, and as I type this we have learned that the replacement device also has a "known" flaw, though minor. How comforting. The company mailed patients with the questionable devices a machine that is supposed to read the battery level and report to my doctor and the device company if anything is amiss. So far, so good.

Some might turn on their god if he took care of them in such fashion. One health trial after another, what gives here Lord. However doubts and suspicions of Gods motives are uncalled for. He is good. All The Time! If you aren't being tried and tested somehow, it might be time to let your knees hit the floor and check your relationship with The Savior. Trials and tests are a good thing. There is no place for bitterness towards God in our trials. The opposite is true. Thanking and glorifying Him should be the case. We aught to rejoice in every single trail and temptation we face and watch how He delivers us through them. It's awesome that He cares enough to find us unworthy, ungrateful creations of His even worth testing. It is one more proof of His great grace towards us. I look forward to trials; great and small. Not because its fun; but because it means my Savior is working something out either in me or through me. It will probably not be "enjoyable" but it is all working for good. That is as true as it gets because that is exactly what is promised in Romans 8:28 And we know that all things work together for good to them that love God, to them that are the called according to His purpose… Not MOST things, not SOME things, not just the stuff you understand, but ALL things. The Almighty God, Lord Jesus Christ Himself is in complete control. Always. That's awesome. You might well even die for the stand you take. Yet knowing that the stand you take; based on scripture, is accurate and true makes that pill easier to swallow. Knowing too that He cares for you and desires only the best for you, can remove the bitterness and sting of it as well.

Before I was ever born, God knew me and what He was going to do through me and with me. He knew exactly what choices I would choose to make and exactly where those choices would take me. I can look back and clearly see His gentle hand giving warnings and attempting to guide me. Had I been more aware of the subtle spiritual messages He was clearly sending me, I would have avoided much hazard. Not being a Christian at that point, I could neither see nor hear the warnings. Some lessons must be learned the hard way apparently, and well they were. Physical pain is often an excellent teacher. Romans 8:29 For whom He did foreknow, He also did predestinate to be conformed to the image of His Son, that He might be the firstborn among many brethren. God knows the end from the beginning, and He knows who will reject Him and who will turn to Him. That doesn't mean that certain people are predestined for hell, but ALL will have had an opportunity to accept Gods free gift of salvation when all is said and done. He will not and does not force anyone to accept His gracious offer of Salvation. He just gently, patiently and persistently offers it. "Salvation" is not forced as some false world religions offer at the end of a barrel. One cannot blame God if they don't end up in Heaven when it is all said and done. Everyone that has ever set a foot, shoe, sandal, or boot on the face of the ground will have had some type of witness or opportunity to turn to Christ. Even that heathen jungle tribesman will have been given ample opportunity and revelation to come to Christ. Somehow they will "know" the truth and be giving the amount of revelation they need for Salvation. This can be well known because God is Just, ALWAYS. Dueteronomy 32:4. Proves this: He is the Rock, His work is perfect: for all His ways are judgement: a God of truth and without iniquity, just and right is He. God sets up the criteria. It's up to us to respond. That criteria is in His only Son, the second part of the triune Godhead, Jesus Christ. He has clearly made Salvation open to all John 12:32 tells us "and I, if I be lifted up from the earth, will draw all men unto me." He knows most will reject Him and He still offers. He had His beard ripped out, was savagely whipped, punched, beaten, spat upon, mocked and finally nailed to a cross with long hand fashioned nail-spikes driven through His hands and feet.

    The Creator of the universe willingly hung there in absolute agony. Those long spikes pounded through the soft flesh of His hand where the wrist begins. Those rusty hand-fashioned iron nails ripped through tendons and nerves causing continuous shocks of excruciating pain to rocket through His legs, and arms and chest. To catch a breath He had to push up with His feet which were nailed together through the top each feet, spiked together. It hurts when someone accidentally steps on that part or your foot. Imagine having some gruff and hardened centurion gleefully pound nails through them. From what I've read, those guys lived to cause pain. They thoroughly enjoyed their work. Rough wood and long sharp splinters ripped into His already torn flesh from the severe, brutal wiping he endured. His torn flesh screaming in agony with each breath He struggled to take. Don't forget The beating He endured by a blood-fevered crowd left Him a near unrecognizable bloody and raw pulp of a man. They spat on Him, punched Him, and ripped out His beard with their hands.

Abject hatred spewed from many that day. Even more so today, the name Jesus Christ when spoken of righteously, causes strife. It is hard to grasp. Jesus Christ; God Himself; shedding His precious blood for the like's of men who hate and then kill one another with unimaginable brutality, some even claiming it's in His name they do such barbaric things. In Luke 23:47. A Roman centurion who was as hard and disciplined as a man could be; brutal and cold from his years as a soldier, stood below the cross and after a long day of witnessing the mocking and all that had transpired, looked up and remarked "Certainly, this was a righteous man." Meaning he understood Jesus was innocent. In Mark 15 and verse 39. Mark records additionally the words of a soldier who uttered... "Truly this man was the Son of God." Wether it is the same soldier and two different author's points of view, or even two different soldiers is not the main point. The point is that Jesus was innocent, and that is perfectly communicated through these two different first hand accounts. He was innocent! We are not!

Salvation is a bought and paid for gift. Paid in full. All you have to do is accept it. A person who rejects Christ will end up going south for all eternity. It will not be Gods fault! He is not to blame. He has lovingly given us all a free will, and we each individual one of us have the choice to make. Accept Christ as Savior, or reject Christ. In a nutshell, eternity all comes down to that. By accepting Christ one has nothing to lose, and everything to gain. By rejecting Him, one has nothing to gain and everything to lose. Are you going to fear what someone else thinks of you when all eternity is at stake? Who cares what someone else thinks. That brings to mind a brief Bible Study of mine a ways back on the Book of Jonah. It is certainly not exhaustive and much can be added for certain. At the time of it's penning, I simply entitled it Tools!

TOOLS: A brief Jonah study.
God sometimes brings a storm into our lives to get us right with Him, as well as getting those around us (through our example, good or bad) right with Him as well...

God chose Jonah, to serve Him with glee...
Jonah chose not God, but instead rose to flee...

TOOLS:

Even the old, rusty, broken, twisted, bent, and relatively "worthless" tools (people) can be used greatly by a Great GOD, even the ones that have become tarnished or rusty and are lying in the bottom of the box for lack of use, might, and could still be used in a great way by a great God. That's how patient and loving He is. God likes using tools it seems. He is a creative God. He walked Earth as a carpenter after all. Just like a guy who can't let himself throw away that rusty old screwdriver because it can still be used for some job he might have. God doesn't wish to put aside any of His tools either, such seems to be the case with a tool called Jonah.

Here's a guy, that, on the surface seems to be kinda ordinary. We aren't given a whole lot of info on the guy other than he was a prophet, and that he was the son of a guy named Amittai. And all I can see about Amittai in scripture is that his name has seven letters. So it seems that Jonah was simply an ordinary guy, as I. But God wanted to use him, and God prepared a bunch of things in order to prepare Jonah. He easily could have prepared Jonah for the task he was giving him had Jonah simply obeyed from the get go. We aren't told exactly "how" The Word of the Lord came to Jonah... but it very clearly did, and

Jonah apparently, knew exactly what it was, and it certainly was not his imagination, nor to his liking. As Jonah made his preparations to disobey, God was making some preparations of His own...

He prepared a fish... just one...

He prepared a gourd... just one...

He prepared a worm... just one...

God had even prepared the Ninevites, much to Jonah's dismay.

All these preparations to prepare His reluctant prophet...

I don't think it is as important an issue as to HOW Jonah got the message, but that he did indeed GET the message and understood it, clearly and completely. Jonah knew "exactly" what God wanted him to do. As there was no UPS service in those days one might only speculate that perhaps God spoke to his prophet Jonah in a dream? We aren't told, we also aren't told what Jonah "did" before this episode? We don't know so it must not be important or relative. Any guessing on our part is just that, guessing. However, Jonah IS mentioned briefly in the Gospels, by Jesus himself when discussing the events of the crucifixion shortly before He willingly went to the cross and literally "became sin" for us. So, apparently, something a bitter old crab named Jonah has to teach us must be rather significant.

The Bible simply says that the LORD (all caps) indicating God The Father as the speaker, came unto Jonah "saying" so we know it was audible. In verse 2 of chapter 1 God gives Jonah very clear instructions. ARISE! GO! PREACH! 3 explicit commands. God even gives Jonah a reason... "Because their wickedness is come up before Me." That God told him to do it should have been enough, without the reason, God doesn't have to tell us "WHY" all the time. It's not for us to know why, and most of the time it is better that we DON'T know "why", but simply to obey. That is hard to understand, but that's where Faith comes in I suppose. How much do we (I) really trust God? Asking "Why" seems to indicate that we don't trust Him...? I don't know, but even after God gives Jonah the reason, what does he do...? Does he jump on his horse, donkey, camel (if he had one) and gleefully run to do Gods bidding...? Nope.

Ol' Jonah goes the opposite direction as God had commanded him. God said go "this" way and Jonah purposed in his heart to say NO and went "that" way. We can read the whole story and know the ending, but are we any different today concerning our own obedience? Just as we cannot see tomorrow for today, neither could Jonah see the outcome, he only knew what "those Ninevites" were like and went on his assumption of their uselessness without considering Gods view of the lost soul. How closely does our eyesight resemble the Lords?? Or is it closer to Jonah's??

Today The Holy Spirit reveals to us through prayer and the reading of Gods word the direction we should go. But do we (I) heed (listen, follow, obey, his leading.)? Likely, not as we should be doing it. The more you are in The Word of God, reading and studying it, the clearer you will hear God Speaking to you through His Holy Spirit.

I find it interesting how it says that Jonah "rose" up to "flee" to Tarshish "from" the presence of the LORD. Now, I find that wording odd. Jonah is a prophet. He of all people aught to have known that there is no place he could flee to, that was beyond Gods reach. For God is ever, always, everywhere present. You cannot "get away" from God, especially when He has called you and told you to do something important for Him. One way or another, you WILL do it. Jonah is soon to get a quick refresher lesson on just how far Gods grasp is. It appears that Jonah is somewhat far from God at this juncture in his life. We are not told if something had occurred just prior to this event that had soured Jonah's relationship (at least from his standing) with God. Had he been on the shelf for a while? Unused and dormant? Making him kind of bitter? Had he been lazy in his walk with God? Had his prayer life been weak? Whatever his reason for doing so, (disobeying that is) It was unjustified. For God is good. All the time! Any communication problem, was Jonah's. Likewise, with us. The communication problem is ours, not God's. Either we "ask amiss" James 4:3 "Ye ask and receive not, because ye ask amiss, that ye may consume it upon your lusts" or our attitude is wrong. God won't help us if we're carrying hatred around in our hearts, or holding a grudge against somebody. That harms no one but ourselves, so what's the point. Jonah learned this the hard way. It must have been a huge disappointment to him and probably embarrassing too.

Jonah is soon to find out first hand that such blatant disobedience to the creator of the universe has it's costs. The first thing it did was cost him some money. Money in any day and time is hard to come by and likely was for Jonah as well. But he obviously had some money because we are told that he "paid the fair thereof" when he bought his boat ticket to Tarshish. He didn't even barter. In his haste to flee from Almighty God, he just paid whatever they were asking, and climbed aboard. Already his disobedience has wasted his time and his money and he isn't even out to sea yet. He goes down into the "hold," down into the darkness, and lays down. Maybe he thought God wouldn't see him if he put his head under the pillow in a dark corner. Just like a little child when he wants to hide with the cookie he has just swiped before dinnertime, Jonah is cowering from the perfect illumination of God in a dark corner of some cramped, musty, perhaps even questionably seaworthy craft. Not a good move on Jonah's part. He went down into the hold of a tiny ship to "hide" from Almighty God. Twice in verse three alone we read the words "from the presence of the LORD."

That is kind of a scary thought. I don't want to be away from Gods presence, but I know it isn't hard to put myself there. First thing Jonah did was say to himself, "No way, I'm not doing it, I don't like those people, I want God to wipe them out. They're Israel's sworn enemies. What are you thinking God...?" Next thing he did was act on that thought and tried run away.

God however is not going to let Jonah off so easily. We don't know how far he got; just out of port, or miles out to sea but very quickly a rather large, and unexpected storm hits. These sailors were experienced seamen. they were not rubes and would not have set to sea had there been any inclination of bad weather. Before long, the ship is being thrown around most unpleasantly apparently for we read where the sailors were "afraid." These are guys that had certainly been in some storms in their time and knew what they were doing and how to maneuver their vessel. But, they're terrified. This was no ordinary storm! It says that each one of them "cried unto his god" to save them. Apparently nothing happened. They try and lighten the ship by chucking their cargo into the sea. They wouldn't do this lightly because there was certainly a lot of money involved and would cost them. They were truly terrified for their very lives to be willing to do something like this.

Their own personal gods didn't save them…

Their own efforts didn't save them…

Had it been an ordinary storm perhaps doing these "things" might have helped, but we read where the LORD had sent out this great wind and made this storm for a special purpose.

It also says, "But" (during all this) Jonah was "fast asleep." He was completely unaware of anything going on around him. It's probably safe to speculate that it was not too quiet aboard and was not a calm ride at that moment, yet he was sound asleep, oblivious to his surroundings. the sailors were no doubt yelling, the boat being thrown to and fro. It's not easy to sleep on a boat as it is, but one that is being tossed around like a cork in a bathtub doesn't compute good in the human brain. That Jonah could be so "dumb" as to not be aware of his surroundings and his predicament is baffling. But then, how often are "we" (I) in similar Jonah-like circumstances of our own design and in exactly the same place as he…?

The captain comes running down to Jonah and shakes him awake and has what could almost be a comical kind of exchange with him. "Good grief man, what are doing, get up and pray to your own god like everybody else is doing. Maybe that god will do something for us and we won't die." That is an obvious paraphrase of Jonah 1:6.

Apparently, Ol Jonah had put in with a band of heathen in his haste to flee from the one true God. So here he is standing there on a storm tossed ship, rubbing sleep from his eyes only to open them and find a bunch of panicked superstitious sailors staring at him with terrified eyes. They decide to draw straws. Now, games of chance are not exactly a Godly persons past time but God used these guys superstition to nail Ol Jonah. Because we read that "the Lot fell on Jonah." I kinda wonder if he drew first or last and how much tension was in his heart as the lots got tossed or straws picked or however they did it. It must have been somewhat comical in an odd sort of way. Jonah knew better. He likely knew he would be chosen but didn't fess up before hand. Did he somehow think that God was not at work? NO! He knew because he told the other guys as soon as he picked the short straw. He fessed up right quick, "Oh yeah, heh heh, it's me guy's, I'm the one."

Also, now suddenly all these sailors seem to want more info on their passenger, and start asking him twenty questions. Who he was? What he did? Where he came from?, and the like. Apparently his money was the only language they had been concerned with when the ship sailed. I can imagine the look on their faces when he told them he was a Hebrew and served The Lord God who had made the dry land the seas. There's a big "oops" moment huh, yeah.

These guys are at a loss as to what to do. They even asked Jonah. "What are we supposed to do with you so the sea will be calm?" Jonah, seeing his way out, smiles and said. "It's my fault guys, throw me in the ocean and you'll be fine." This is another paraphrase, of Verse 1:12.

I can only imagine Jonah's expression and thoughts as he said that. He might have been thinking that he had won, and pulled one over on God. Ha, what can you do know God, they throw me in and I drown and I don't have to go to Ninevah, OR, the ship sinks and I drown and I don't have to go to Ninevah. Ha. I win.

But the sailors turned away from smug-faced Jonah and tried even harder get the ship turned and manageable but they couldn't do it. The storm got even worse. Then we have these guys moment of truth, and perhaps even salvation? Where apparently they get right with the one True God. They cry out to Him and ask Him not to lay Jonah's death on them because He sent the storm for His own purpose.

Then they pick up Jonah and toss him over the side. Instantly, the storm stopped. It seems the instant Jonah hit the water, the weather abruptly changed. Right here in verse 16 of Chapter 1 we see conversion take place in these guys hearts and minds. Their gods had done nothing for them. We read that, THEY FEARED GOD EXCEEDINGLY! Pretty strong wording, almost indicates a reverential quaking with terror. I wonder if they went back to port scratching their heads as to why this Jonah guy would run away from an all knowing, all powerful God like that.

Then we see Jonah in the water, happily resigned to death and, apparently pleased that he had spoiled God's plans. Then a big fish swallows him whole. There's not much detail other than that God had prepared this fish just for this purpose. He was in that fish for three days and nights.

Jesus pointed to this example in Mathew 16:4 the Pharisees came with their accusations and pompous questions they didn't want answers to. They weren't prepared to listen and especially hear what Jesus had to say. They wanted a sign from heaven for Jesus to "prove" that He was who He claimed to be. Jesus answer shocked an offended them. "A wicked and adulterous generation seeketh after a sign; and there shall no sign be given unto it, but the sign of the prophet Jonah." And He left them, and departed. Jesus spoke of it as if it were common knowledge so by that we can know it is a true tale.

I can only imagine the hideous stink inside of a large fish's belly. It text doesn't specifically say "whale" but likely it was indeed a whale for they are large enough to fit a live man inside, and they breath air. Jonah would need that air for three days. The outside of a fish smells bad enough, but the inside has to be far worse. Not to mention the darkness, the cramped space, the stale air, no food, no fresh water, probably hot and quite humid as well. Not a place for a vacation. Needless to say, it was very likely extremely uncomfortable. It's enough to make a sane man scream for mercy in three minutes let alone three days. Three days being in that kind of environment would do things to a man that could never be undone. What gets me is that Jonah waited three days before finding enough humility to admit to God that he was wrong. Talk about stubborn. It is baffling. But, we are all the same way, if not worse. His attitude change, however temporary it was, can be seen in his prayer in chapter 2 verses 1-9. If it were me I would have lasted about three seconds. God knew Jonah's level of stubborn hardheadedness and exactly what it was going to take to break it, and break it He did.

The three days is important though in reference to the New Testament account of Christ's resurrection on the "third day"! Hence Christ's comment about the "…sign of Jonah…"

Then Jonah is literally "barfed" out of the whale, and it seems that instantaneously, God tells him yet again, and a point is made to say it is the "second" time, to go to Ninevah and preach what I told you to preach. God didn't speak to Jonah in the whale; in fact, He had to wait three whole days before Jonah finally dug down deep and found enough humility to call out to Him. God knows exactly what, and how much it takes to get the attention of His creations.

So, Jonah goes straight to Nineveh. From what is written, it appears he did so without stopping to eat, drink, sleep or bathe, and does Gods bidding. Considering where he'd spent the last three days, he must have been quite a sight. He would have gotten folks attention, that's for sure. We don't know if he preached with a spirit of gratitude to God for being given this opportunity, or an attitude of vengeance towards a hated enemy. However he did it, Jonah preaches Gods message to the Ninevites. And, to his utter shock, the Ninevites repent and plead with God to forgive them, and then receive such forgiveness from Almighty God. These day's many politicians pass laws for "the rest of us" and then sit safely and dominantly above them, and us. But the Ninevites didn't do this. Even the King repented and made a law saying people everywhere in his kingdom were to call on and pray to Jonah's God for mercy and deliverance. He set the example and the people followed suit in repenting. It certainly seems like true repentance from a casual reading of the account. That is what God desires, true repentance and not lip service. Perhaps America should take a lesson from that king; and return our course to the straight path we once trod before it is too late. 2 Chronicles 7:14 reveals such to us. If my people, which are called by my name(the christian, today)shall humble themselves, and pray, and turn from their wicked ways, THEN will I hear them from Heaven and will forgive their sin and will heal their land. The Ninevite's believed the message and proved it repenting from the top down. The judgment of God is still a very real thing. Often times it is our own folly befalling us, but it can also be something far, far worse.

But Ol' Jonah doesn't like the outcome one bit. He goes outside the city gate and has a little pity party. He's mad because the Ninevites sought, and then received mercy from "HIS PEOPLES" God. He's mad because it's hot. He's madder still because God isn't bringing judgment on a people whom he feels are worthless, wicked, and deserving of Gods full blown wrath. Yet because God is ever merciful to His servants He makes a little shade tree grow over Jonah's head to keep him cooler. Then, unbeknownst to Jonah, and to make a point to his bitter servant. The tree gets ate by a worm and dies and Jonah gets all mad again. It's almost as if he is trying to make God look bad by citing many positives about God, such as His loving, caring, forgiving ways. The way he told God that he knew He'd forgive them because He is so merciful is almost like he is trying to butter God up. Then God tells Jonah and gives a number of how many lost souls there were in Nineva before Jonah preached. I would think Jonah would have felt honored and pleased and grateful that he could be used in such a tremendous way by God, but, he isn't? Reading the account in our day, these things are clearer for we can see the beginning and the ending and the results of the players actions.

Our own hearts, how grateful? Do we often flee to our own version of Tarshish to avoid Gods direction and then fight the course change when He brings it along. Do we need the whale to swallow us before we "get it"! Don't we understand that our will, is not going to prevail? Having a new puppy is kind of like that. It is a task to teach him that "my" will is going to prevail and that his will is going to be in submission to me. I don't want him doing it out of fear but because he wants to. It's not easy, but he's starting to get it. It's a similar type of thing with God and His creation, man, I suppose. How much do I/We fight the leash of His will? Do we even hear Him when He says "NO"? What does He have to do to get our attention? I don't want to get "swallowed" by a "whale" for God to get my attention.

Perhaps by replenishing, sharpening, cleaning the tools in my own "toolbox" I can begin to learn how to avoid the whale. Many times it is difficult to see the coastline for the waves and I'm unsure if it is Tarshish or Nineva and whether or not I should keep sailing without knowing for certain my exact heading. I suppose by keeping the toolbox close at hand and the tools cleaned and sharpened the course will take care of itself. Faith.

We don't know if Jonah ever did anything else, or if he ever repented of his actions and his foul attitude. It appears not, for his usage by God seems to end with the dying of that little shade tree. Certainly Jonah had much to think on and consider as he made that long journey home. God loves people! That He knew the exact number of souls in Ninevah is proof of that. Perhaps that number in scripture was only referring to children, and the actual number was far higher. They was scripture talks of them not knowing the left hand from the right is indication of such. Clearly, God would rather forgive than judge His creations. All His creations need do is ask, just like the Ninevites did. 1 John 1:8-10: "If we say we have no sin, we deceive ourselves, and the truth is not in us.(9)If we confess our sins, He is faithful and just to forgive us our sins and to cleanse us from all unrighteousness.(10) If we say that we have not sinned, we make Him a liar, and His word is not in us. It applies equally today.

The only New Testament reference is given by Jesus Himself when being asked for "signs" by the unbelieving Pharisees. Jesus used Jonah in a reference to his 3 days in the Grave VS Jonahs 3 days in the belly of the great fish. Our Lord said, as Matthew recalled. Math 16:4 "A wicked and adulterous generation seeketh after a sign; and there shall no sign be given unto thee but the sign of the Prophet Jonah." Jonah was in the fish's belly for three days, the audience being spoken to by Christ knew exactly what he meant by it. After Christ's resurrection three days after His Cross. Most of them still didn't believe. It's strange how Gods simple plan of salvation can be so hard for people to grasp. It is most especially difficult for those who "should" know to begin with. Mainly, the "religious" leaders in the community. Same goes for today. All the multitudes of learned scholars that write papers and books and give long lectures but still miss the simplicity of the message of The Cross. The story of Jonah is an absolutely true story. It can be nothing else.

You have to believe what God says about you before you will believe His Word.

Like it or not. God made man and He makes the rules. Like it or not, A loving God would indeed have created a place called Hell. He doesn't send people there, people send themselves there. Because of Adam, mankind has a problem called sin that The Law proved he cannot take care of, of his own accord. That's where Jesus fits in.

It is only because of Christ that we can have any hope at all of Heaven. Romans 3:23 For ALL have sinned and come short of the Glory of God. Romans 5:12 Therefore, as through one man (Adam) sin entered the world, and death through sin, and so death passed to all, for all have sinned. Romans 6:23 The wages of sin is death. The whole point of the sometimes confusing conglomeration of words is convince. If we have One birth (physical) we shall have 2 deaths (physical and spiritual) If we have two births (Physical and spiritual) we shall have 1 death (physical)

So, what did the preceding mass of words accomplish? What From my experiences would there be to advice youth? I suppose my advice to all unmarried guys, and girls would simply be this. Don't even touch the other until that veil is lifted. You will save yourself an enormous amount of unnecessary heartache if you wait like you are supposed to. Hormones rage and things happen I know all too well. Keep yourself free of wrong friends and stay away from strong drink, smoke and drugs and it will likely not happen. Be cautious what you view and listen to. Much of that is amoral and has no power unless we give it that power. Unless you are praying and reading Gods word on a daily basis you will be easy game for the vices of the Devil. He hates us humans because our triune makeup of body, soul, spirit reminds of God's triune makeup of father (God) Jesus (son) and Holy Sprit. He ESPECIALLY hates you if you are a Christian and would love nothing more than to destroy you, your testimony, your reputation, and to smear mud on the name of Jesus Christ. The Devils apples look delicious, and very well may even taste delicious, (at first anyway) but in the center there is always a worm eating it from the inside out, don't take up the worm. The worm is death and rot and decay, flee from it. For the laughter you hear as you fall is the devils. In reiteration guys and gals, It is far better to wait until you are married. Simple as that.

Finally, I have included a tract I wrote about the Snow Blower event. The actual tract has a picture of a snow blower on the front as a tease to the reader.

HEART CONDITION

Dear Friend, when your heart beats it's last beat...
And your blood no longer flows...
In an instant you'll stand before your creator, Lord...
It will be too late then to choose your eternal destination...
And you do have a choice...

(*) "This is a salvage operation" The surgeon had said to my family. "we'll do what we can and wait and see."

There was at least four completely blocked arteries and a blown out mitral valve. How was I to know my ticker was so bad? I had no large belly, was athletic, and arrogantly assumed I was "fine". Sure, I took high blood pressure meds and could go all winter in a T-shirt and jeans with just a light wind breaker. I did not put two and two together, then again math was never my strong point.

(*) How long had I been "out" when the pickup truck stopped and the driver got out? Unknown! What I do know is that when I collapsed in the snow that day I could have stood before my Creator-Savior with a clean slate. I could only do so because some years ago, after reading a tract something like this one, I heard a clear presentation of The Gospel, and accepted the free gift of Salvation that Jesus Christ so graciously offers to all men and women. I made a choice and claimed Jesus Christ as my own personal Lord and Savior, and was "Born Again," as the term goes.

(*) My heart stopped beating! Death was reaching for me. I was powerless to do anything to prevent it from laying hold on me.

(*) Do not be deceived, dear reader; on this side of your last heartbeat is the time to make your choice. Let no one tell you different! Where you end up for all of everlasting, and perpetually ceaseless eternity is entirely YOUR choice, nobody else's. It is completely up to YOU, not your parents, not your family, not your friends; nobody but you and you alone are responsible for this decision. You will have no one to blame but yourself for choosing wrongly on this most important of questions.

(*) The text which follows is fundamental for you in determining your final, eternal destination when this extremely short life we have so graciously BEEN GIVEN is over!

(*) Contrary to what you may have been taught, both Heaven and Hell are as real as that seat beneath you, or the ground you are standing on. They are as real as this pamphlet you are right now holding and reading. Which location is in your future...? There are only two choices, so it is either one or the other. We are all born with a sin nature because of Adam and Eve. It is impossible for us to shed this nature alone, and thus need help in so doing. God loves us and yet He created mankind with a free will and will not and does not "force" His Great Gift upon us. He instead gives us a choice to accept or reject it of our own accord. This choice is ours individually to make. No friend or relative can make this choice for us. It is ours alone to make.

Look!

(*) In our world today, machines can breath for us, if necessary, and we live: Between life and death is but one breath... if we don't breath...

WE DIE!

(*) Equally important, machines can even pump our blood throughout our bodies for us, and we live: Albeit without that blood, and more importantly; without that blood FLOWING throughout our bodies...

WE DIE!

(*) Blood is both precious, and absolutely vital for life. For all of man's medical advances and achievements he still cannot reproduce or replace the blood itself that is so essential for human and, even animal life to exist. No synthetic alternative will work, Neither will simply "any" blood do. We must have a specific blood "type" to work in our individual bodies.

(*) The Heart pumps this blood throughout our bodies and the lungs feed that blood with oxygen, giving nutrients to all our organs and extremities. When the heart stops beating, our blood stops flowing and our organs and extremities do not get the oxygen and nutrients it so desperately needs. When the heart ceases to beat, the blood stops flowing and in turn, very quickly...

WE DIE!

(*) Blood is important to our lives in both a physical, and more importantly, a spiritual sense.

Consider the following verses:

Leviticus 17:11 "...the life of the flesh is in the blood."

Hebrews 9:22 "...and without the shedding of blood there is no remission."

(*) Clearly, blood is vital to our well being. There can be no life without it. In Old Testament times, God made it clear that man was born with a problem called "Sin". God graciously allowed an innocent and guiltless replacement to be offered and it's blood spilled "in place of" the person making the offering. This "temporary" system of covered ones sin. With this system offerings were constantly being made. The "innocent" beast died and it's blood was shed to "cover" or "pay" the debt owed by he or she that was making the offering.

The innocent took the place of the guilty, and "paid the price" of the one truly deserving of condemnation.

(*) Hebrews 9:12 reveals God's truth on this to us like this... "Neither by the blood of goats and calves, but by HIS OWN BLOOD, he entered "once" into the Holy Place, having earned eternal redemption for us..."

(*) You see, The Blood of Christ does not simply "cover" our sin for a temporary period of time. it completely washes it away and erases it as if it had never existed! There is no remembrance of such before the eye's of Almighty God.

(*) Revelation 1:5 "Unto Him that loved us, and washed us from our sins IN HIS OWN BLOOD."

(*) How about you...? Scripture tells us for certain in 2 Corinthians 6:2," Behold, NOW is the accepted time: NOW is the day of Salvation."

(*) How many more heartbeats do you have?

You don't know. Only arrogance would say otherwise. It is our own foolish pride that says we have plenty of tomorrows. Death often comes quickly, very suddenly, in the space of a heartbeat it comes with nary the time to say "Ooop's" it comes and you're off into eternity. Then, there is no time to decide.

(*) By waiting, you deny Christ and count Him a liar! By not choosing you have already chosen because you won't have time to choose Christ when your last heartbeat arrives.

(*)NOW IS THE TIME TO CHOOSE...

(*) Death came suddenly for me! By God's grace I am still here. Had God chosen to call me home that Wintry January day, I could have stood before Him unblemished and with a clear conscience... Not by anything I had done, mind you... No...no...no... A thousand times no. Look...

(*) Titus 3:5 reveals this truth to us... "Not by works of righteousness which WE have done, but according to HIS mercy HE saved us, by the washing of regeneration and renewing of The Holy Ghost."

(*) As well Ephesians 2:8-9, "For by Grace are ye saved, and not of yourselves, it is the gift of God,(9)not of works, lest any man should boast.

(*) NOW IS THE TIME TO CHOOSE!

(*) We cannot know our own hearts, But Almighty God, The Lord Jesus Christ Himself, Our Creator, knows them, and His desire for you is to turn from your current path and accept His "FREE GIFT" of Salvation and be "Born Again", that term comes from the mouth of the Savior. It doesn't get any more authoritative than that.

(*) I plead with you! Don't put off this decision!

You aren't promised tomorrow, you aren't even promised the next ten minutes, or even ten seconds. your next heartbeat could be your last heartbeat. That statement is neither alarmist or fear mongering, it is simply the truth. Jeremiah 17:9 tells us this truth: "The heart is deceitful above all things and desperately wicked, who can know it...?"

(*) 1 Timothy 2:4, in speaking of Jesus: Who would have ALL men to be saved, and come into the knowledge of truth...

For instance...

A. You cannot trust your own heart...
B. Your heart condition is fatal...
C. Jesus Christ is your life-line to avoid flat-line... A Raging, Fiery flat-line.

(*) A simple prayer like the following, or something similar in your own words is all it takes... God is not a respecter of persons. He will hear you...

"Lord Jesus, please forgive me, I understand now that I am a sinner and unable to save myself. I claim you now as my personal Lord and Savior. Thank you for taking my place on the cross. Thank you for this free gift of Salvation. In Jesus Name, Amen.

That is all it takes.

Romans 10:9-10 promises (9) That if thou shalt confess wit thy mouth the Lord Jesus, and BELIEVE IN THINE HEART that God hath raised Him from the dead, thou shalt be saved... (thou shalt is a guaranteed promise)(10) for WITH THE HEART man believeth unto righteousness; and with the mouth confession is made unto Salvation.

(*) If you have accepted Christ as your personal Lord and Savior, you have the following promise that you are now indeed a child of God... It is something that can never be lost, or taken away from us.

Acts 2:21 tells us this... AND IT SHALL COME TO PASS THAT WHOSOEVER (that's anybody) CALLETH UPON THE NAME OF THE LORD, SHALL BE SAVED!

(*) That is a promise better than Gold. Only a fool would not accept it. It doesn't matter what you have done, all that matters is what The Lord Jesus Christ has done on The Cross.

Printed in the United States
By Bookmasters